THE CASE OF THE ABANDONED WAREHOUSE

THE MYSTERY HOUSE SERIES, BOOK TWO

Eva Pohler

Eva Pohler Books
20011 Park Ranch
San Antonio, Texas 78259
www.evapohler.com

Publisher's Note: This is a work of fiction. Names, characters, places, and incidents are a product of the author's imagination. Locales and public names are sometimes used for atmospheric purposes. Any resemblance to actual people, living or dead, or to businesses, companies, events, institutions, or locales is completely coincidental.

Book Layout ©2017 BookDesignTemplates.com

Book Cover Design by B Rose Designz

The Case of the Abandoned Warehouse/ Eva Pohler. -- 1st ed.
Paperback ISBN 978-1-958390-25-2

Contents

For the victims of the 1921 Tulsa Massacre and their families.

CHAPTER ONE

La Quinta Tulsa

W hat in the world is that?" Sue asked as she entered Ellen and Tanya's hotel room. Her full figure filled the entryway, where she pointed at the floor.

Ellen thought Sue looked surprisingly perky and refreshed, given what she'd been through the day before.

"Tanya's butterflies," Ellen said.

"Not butterflies." Tanya pushed her blonde hair behind her ears before she picked up the three-foot-by three-foot dome-shaped net that sat on the carpet near the door. About two dozen tiny green cocoons clung to the underside of it. "Chrysalises. I didn't want to leave them behind, just in case they hatched."

"You brought them on the *train*?" Sue's brown hair brushed her shoulders as she bobbed her head in disbelief. "*Dave* couldn't let them out?"

"He's flying to D.C. tomorrow," Tanya said. "I couldn't have them trapped if they hatched while we were gone." Then she added. "And I really didn't want to miss it."

"I think it's pretty cool." Ellen hadn't thought so at first, especially after all the looks she'd had to endure from the other passengers on the train from San Antonio; but, she found herself bonding with the little

3

chrysalises over the past few days, as if they were newborn puppies or kittens. And it had been…surprising.

"Well, then you better not pay too much attention to the windshield on your rental car," Sue said as she sat on the end of one of the double beds. "Tulsa has been swarmed with butterflies lately, and many of them have met an untimely death."

"Oh, stop." Tanya moved the net to the other side of the room, near the sliding glass doors to the balcony, which overlooked their spectacular view of the parking lot.

"Don't be crass, Sue," Ellen whispered.

It seemed to Ellen that Tanya looked thinner than usual and more fragile. It had been just over a year since Tanya's mother passed last September, and Tanya hadn't been able to shake off her depression. Ellen had begun taking antidepressants after her own mother had died last November, and she felt they were helping; but Tanya wanted to avoid medication and was trying things like hatching butterflies and taking vitamins and drinking herbal tea.

In fact, Ellen had been worried Tanya would bail on her at the last minute and not attend Sue's daughter's wedding.

"What made you decide to hatch butterflies anyway, Tanya?" Sue asked.

"I was looking for something new to try, something fun."

"I could have saved you some trouble and taken you to that new Mexican food restaurant near our neighborhood. I hear they serve delicious margaritas," Sue said with a giggle.

Ellen frowned. She doubted Sue could understand the depth of Tanya's despair. Sue didn't belong to the Motherless Club. Sue didn't understand the loneliness that tugged at the heart of a motherless adult child.

"I'm surprised you're here early." Ellen slipped on her shoes and searched around the room for her purse. "Aren't you exhausted after the wedding?"

"Yes, but I'm also starving, and my hunger won out." Then she pointed at Ellen's black capris and emerald-green top. "We could be twins today. We must be on the same wavelength."

"I guess so." Ellen laughed. Tanya was wearing a baby blue top with blue jeans.

"The wedding was beautiful, by the way." Tanya sat in the small chair near the desk to buckle on her sandals. "We didn't get a chance to talk to you much last night, but we enjoyed it."

"Yes. It was nicely done," Ellen said. "Is Tom flying back today?"

Sue shifted on the bed. "Yeah. He offered to fly with my mom so she wouldn't have to travel alone. I'm sure they've landed by now. And Lexi and Stephen are probably landing in Vancouver within the hour. Lexi called from the airport this morning to thank me for all I did."

"That was nice." Ellen found her purse and pulled the strap across her shoulder. "Especially considering how hard it was on you—having the wedding here in the groom's hometown instead of back home in San Antonio."

"Well, like I said before, her college friends are here," Sue said. "And my mother is our only family back in San Antonio. Tom's mother and brother live in Stillwater. It just made sense to have it here." Then Sue added, "It means a lot to me that you girls made the trip to be there."

"We wouldn't have missed it," Ellen said.

"Of course not." Tanya stood up and checked her reflection in the mirror over the desk.

"It's too bad Nolan couldn't make it," Sue said of Ellen's oldest son, in medical school at OSU in Oklahoma City.

"He wanted to, but he's an intern now, and his hours are crazy."

"You must be so proud of him," Sue said.

"And you must be so happy for Lexi," Ellen said.

"Yes, I am. But right now, I'm anxious for lunch. Are y'all ready to go?"

"Ready," Tanya said. "And after we hit the casino, Ellen has something interesting in mind for us."

Sue climbed to her feet. "Oh? What?"

"It's a surprise," Ellen said. "And don't worry. There will be plenty of margaritas to be had where we're going."

CHAPTER TWO

Haunted Pub Crawl

A fter a day of dining and playing the slots at the casino across the street from the La Quinta, Ellen got behind the wheel of the rental car and drove her friends to the Brady Arts District. It was a little past six in the evening, and the sun wouldn't be setting for another couple of hours. Ellen was surprised, however, by how many people were walking the streets and by how few parking places were available. She hadn't expected the arts district of Tulsa to be such a happening place, especially on a Sunday.

When Ellen pulled into the last parking space in front of a sign that read *The Tavern*, Sue said, "So far so good."

"Come on, Ellen," Tanya said from the passenger's seat. "Tell us what you have in mind. The suspense is killing me."

"We're going on a haunted pub crawl," Ellen said with a smile.

Tanya arched a brow. "They have ghosts in Tulsa?"

"Ghosts are everywhere," Sue said.

Tanya shrugged. "I know, but Tulsa doesn't seem like the kind of town that would have *interesting* ghosts. New Orleans, yes. But Tulsa?"

Sue leaned over the front seat from where she sat in the back. "And what exactly do you mean by *crawl?* Are we going to have to do a lot of walking? You know my feet bother me."

"What is wrong with you people?" Ellen said. "I thought you'd be delighted. Isn't this your kind of thing?"

"Walking has never been my kind of thing," Sue said.

"I don't think we'll be going very far." Ellen turned off the car and unbuckled her seatbelt.

Tanya unbuckled as well and opened her door. "Come on, Sue. This should be fun."

They each took a stool at the polished wooden bar inside the art deco establishment with its large mirrors, dramatic drapes, geometric wood furniture, and glass tabletops as they waited for their tour guide and the other attendees to arrive.

The bartender didn't look much younger than they were, though she was quite attractive in her low-cut, cleavage-showing bodice. Her blonde frizzy hair framed a face with beautiful, dark-lined eyes and lashes. The woman wiped her forehead with the back of her wrist before handing over their margaritas and said, "It's too damn hot in here. Will one of you ladies complain to my manager? He won't do anything about it if I tell him."

"It *is* pretty warm," Sue agreed.

"They don't pay me enough to work in these conditions," the bartender complained. "I'm about to strip down to my birthday suit."

"Maybe if you did, you'd get a raise," Ellen offered with a laugh.

"Yeah, but it wouldn't be the kind I'm looking for," the bartender said.

It took Ellen a minute to get why her friends were guffawing. Then she laughed, too, and asked, "Where is he? Your manager?"

"That's him standing back there talking to a patron. Wait 'til he comes back over here behind the bar." The bartender added another shot of tequila to each of their glasses with a wink. "A secret *thank you,* from me to you."

"Mmm," Sue purred. "Delicious."

"Thanks," Tanya said before taking a sip.

Ellen wasn't so sure she could handle *two* shots of tequila, but she took a drink anyway. And as soon as the manager returned to the bar, they all three mentioned how hot it was.

"It might even be cooler outside," Sue added.

The manager shot a look at the bartender before promising to adjust the air conditioner.

Sue was on her second margarita when a woman, maybe five or ten years younger than they with long curly brown hair, stood up from one of the tables. She wore a cute purple dress and matching purple eye shadow. She twisted the bracelet on her thin wrist and said in a loud voice, "If you're here for the haunted pub crawl, please follow me into the back room."

"I need to stop by the ladies' room first," Tanya whispered to Ellen and Sue as they got up from their stools.

"Me, too," Ellen said.

When they discovered that it was a single room with only one toilet, Tanya took Ellen's half-empty margarita glass and insisted that Ellen go first.

Ellen locked the door behind her and was startled by the sudden unrolling of paper towels from the machine beside the mirror over the sink. Then the light overhead blinked on and off several times. For only a moment, Ellen couldn't breathe, and she felt dizzy. Once she took a deep breath, she regained her composure.

Poking her head through the door, she asked Tanya, "Are you messing with me?"

"What? Why?" Tanya stood in the hallway holding each of their glasses—one in each hand. There were no light switches on the walls nearby.

"Never mind. I'll be right out."

After a few minutes, the light stopped blinking, and the machine stopped spitting out paper toweling.

It must be an electrical short, Ellen thought as she washed her hands and left the room to give Tanya her turn.

When Tanya came out, Ellen asked about the lights and the towels, but Tanya wrinkled her brow and said, "It sounds like you're the one messing with me. Nothing like that happened while *I* was in there."

Ellen shrugged it off until they caught up to the group in the private back room where the others were already seated at four small tables, and she overheard their tour guide saying, "As a matter of fact, even the ladies' room in this bar is known to be haunted."

Ellen narrowed her eyes suspiciously at Sue, who only gave her a blank look as she and Tanya sat at the table on either side of her.

Their tour guide, whom Ellen later learned was named Carrie French, was standing in the center of the room as she told some of the history of The Tavern. "This building was once a spectacular hotel, built in 1906, and it was one of the few structures in this area still standing after the race riot of 1921. It eventually became one of the most popular brothels in Tulsa and, later, a flophouse."

"What's a flophouse?" Ellen asked.

Carrie French turned to Ellen and said, "During the oil boom in the early 1900's, a lot of fine hotels were erected, but later, during the Depression, many of them were turned into cheap lodging with lots of small rooms, each containing a bed, sink, and toilet used by transients, prostitutes, and drug addicts. The woman who ran this flophouse in the 1930's is believed to be haunting the place. She's been seen on the vacant floor above by many people over the years, and she also haunts the kitchen and the ladies' room down here in the tavern."

One of the twelve other people gathered in the small private room asked, "Is she a friendly spirit?"

"I wouldn't call her *friendly*," Carrie replied. "She seems to enjoy playing mean tricks on the employees here, especially the dishwashers and cooks, which the bar can't hold onto long enough. They say she resented her landlord and took out her anger on the other tenants. To give you an example of one of her pranks, a few years ago, I went into the ladies' room and was accosted with blinking lights and an out-of-control paper towel dispenser."

Ellen gasped. Had she been set up, or had she just had an encounter with a ghost?

Tanya covered her mouth and looked at Ellen with shock before saying, "That just happened to Ellen!"

Carrie raised her brows. "Really?"

Ellen nodded.

"Congratulations, Ellen," Carrie said. "You now belong to a very exclusive group of three. Only one other person is known to have experienced that, and she quit her job a year ago because it spooked her so bad. But I knew her, and I believe it only happens to those with the gift."

Ellen's face burned as everyone looked at her.

"I knew it," Sue said. "I knew you had the gift, too. I could sense it."

Ellen tried not to roll her eyes at Sue and instead smiled back at the others in the room. This was going to be an interesting night.

CHAPTER THREE

The Hanging Tree

Carrie led the dozen attendees of the haunted pub crawl down Main Street to stand in front of Cain's Ballroom, where she said famous people like Bob Wills and Garth Brooks had often performed. Even tonight loud music poured through the front entrance, and cars lined the sidewalk and filled the adjacent lot. Each of the dozen people on the tour glanced inside the crowded doors before heading to three other chic bars that now stood where old brothels once existed. At each location, everyone on the tour had a drink while Carrie told stories of outlaws, prostitutes, and oil barons and the spirits left behind.

From Main, they walked down Brady Street to see the Brady Theater, where Ellen had an overwhelming feeling that she was suffocating. She thought it might be the tequila affecting her, so she ignored it. But a little later that night, on their way back to The Tavern, they passed the theater again, and, as before, she felt like she couldn't breathe.

"Are you okay?" Tanya asked her.

Ellen nodded. They were at the tail-end of the group walking very slowly for Sue's sake, but if Carrie had been within earshot, Ellen might have asked her if there was anything else she could tell them about the theater. As they approached The Tavern, Carrie gathered everyone around her on the sidewalk beneath the now dark sky and said, "The Brady Arts District is just one of the many haunted areas in Tulsa. If you have an opportunity to visit the Gilcrease Museum or any of the other historic districts, please do. And on your way home tonight, you might drive just a few blocks down Archer to 3 North Lawton Avenue and have a look at The Hanging Tree."

"I've heard of that," someone in their group said. "But I don't recall the story."

Carrie cleared her throat. "From 1870 to 1889, twenty people are known to have been hanged from a now 222-year-old Burr Oak. The old tree has outlived its natural lifespan, and some say the spirits of the Creek Indians and cattle rustlers whose bodies were hanged from it keep it alive because they can't find peace. Many people over the years have gone out to gaze at the tree at night and have sworn to have heard the twisting sound of an old rope on the lowest limb, which hangs twelve feet from the ground."

After the tour, Ellen climbed behind the wheel of the rental car and said, "Why don't we drive by that tree? I'm kind of curious about it."

"You want to?" Tanya asked Sue.

Sue was getting settled in the back seat behind Ellen. "Sure, why not? This has been a fun adventure, hasn't it? Even if I won't be able to walk tomorrow, I really enjoyed tonight. Thank you, Ellen."

"Yeah, thanks, Ellen," Tanya chimed in. "I loved learning all the history."

"Me, too." As Ellen pulled away from The Tavern, she didn't mention how surprised she'd been by the incident in the ladies' room or by the suffocating feeling she'd experienced each time she walked by the Brady Theater. A year ago, Ellen never would have believed that one day she'd be interested in ghosts and the paranormal, but it had become the most fascinating subject to her, probably due to the immense joy and satisfaction she'd felt after bringing closure to the Gold House.

Although most of the activity they'd experienced in the Greek revival hadn't been caused by an actual ghost, Ellen had felt a profound sense of peace and closure when she and her friends helped solve the mystery of the lost gold. Marcia Gold could finally rest. It had been an amazing feeling.

She wanted more of that feeling, almost as badly as an addict wants his next hit.

Tanya turned to Ellen. "What do you think about what Carrie said? About you having the gift?"

Ellen laughed. "I don't know. I've only recently begun to…sense things. And I still wonder if it's all in my head."

"It's because you're just now opening yourself up," Sue said. "The more you practice, the stronger your gift will become. Take it from me."

"What about you, Tanya?" Ellen asked as she turned onto Archer Street. "Do you sense things?"

"Well, I wasn't going to say anything," Tanya began. "But both times we passed that old theater, I felt something heavy in my chest."

"Me, too!" Sue said.

Ellen couldn't believe it. "Are y'all serious? I couldn't breathe. Why didn't either of you say anything?"

"Why didn't *you*?" Sue challenged.

"That is so bizarre," Tanya said.

"Now I'm going to have to Google that theater," Sue said, as they pulled up before the enormous old Burr Oak standing majestically in the light of the half moon. It stood behind a tall fence at what looked like an industrial warehouse. The tree wasn't accessible from the road.

Ellen shuddered at the sight of it. The thought of the hanging victims made her feel nauseous. "Why do people do such cruel things to one another? Can you imagine dying like that, hanging from a tree?"

"Maybe they deserved it," Sue said. "Maybe it was the best way to maintain order."

"I don't believe in capital punishment," Tanya said. "Everyone deserves a chance at redemption and forgiveness."

"I agree," Ellen said. "With maybe very few exceptions."

"If you believe in exceptions, then you are *for* capital punishment," Sue said to Ellen.

"Ellen *always* takes the middle ground," Tanya pointed out.

"Things aren't usually black or white." Ellen turned off the engine and opened her car door. "I want to go look at the tree up close."

Although they were in the first few days of autumn, the evening was still hot and muggy as Ellen and her friends walked across the gravel toward the fence.

"Let's see if we can get a little closer," Ellen said, following the length of fence.

"Haven't we done enough walking?" Sue called from behind.

"Come on, Sue," Ellen said, beckoning to her friends. "There's an alley access back here.

"Great, an alley," Tanya said. "At night, in a strange area we know nothing about."

"I think we passed a Braum's Ice Cream Parlor on the way over," Sue said. "Anyone up for an evening snack?"

Ellen slipped past another fence and managed to get a little closer.

"Look at it," Ellen whispered, mesmerized by the tree.

"It's giving me the creeps," Tanya said. "I vote for the ice cream."

"Fine," Ellen said, "but I want to run an idea by you both first."

"Why can't you run this idea by us at Braum's?" Sue wanted to know.

Ellen reached out a hand and touched the thick trunk of the old tree. "Because I don't want to be overheard."

Tanya and Sue exchanged glances before turning their perplexed looks on Ellen.

"What's going on, Ellen?" Tanya asked.

Ellen tried to think how to word the overwhelming and profound feelings churning inside of her. Tears formed in her eyes as she searched for the right words. She took a deep breath.

"Ellen?" Sue asked. "Your face looks pale. Are you alright?"

"It's just that..." Ellen searched for the words, "what we did with the Gold House was so incredible, you know?"

Her two friends nodded, still waiting for Ellen's explanation.

Ellen continued, "And lately I've been feeling, I don't know, blah again."

"You mean depressed?" Tanya asked. "I thought you were taking medication for that."

"I am, but it's not exactly depression," Ellen said. "It's like I feel a calling, and I've been ignoring it. And ignoring it has been making me feel kind of sick inside."

Tanya covered her cheeks with both hands. "I've actually been feeling the same way, Ellen! This really *is* bizarre! I've been sad and lonely since my mother died, but there's something else, too. It's not quite depression, but a sort of *let down* that began after we finished the Gold House." Tears flooded Tanya's eyes. "To tell you the truth, I'm dreading going back to San Antonio."

"Well, aren't you girls a mess," Sue said, making them laugh.

"Very funny," Tanya said.

"Y'all are definitely going to laugh at what I say next," Ellen warned. Her two friends fixed their eyes on her again. "I want to study the paranormal."

"Oh, my gawd!" Sue practically shouted. "I can't believe it!"

"But I'm not going to assume that every little unexplainable thing is a ghost," she said. "I'm still a skeptic at heart."

"Are you serious? You really want to study this?" Tanya asked.

Ellen nodded. "I think that's what's calling me. After bringing peace to Marcia Gold and her family, I guess I realize there's more work to do."

"Like what?" Tanya asked, batting an insect away.

"I think I want to find other haunted houses and help their ghosts find peace," Ellen said.

As Ellen waited for her friends to reply, she heard something in the tree above them. After a beat, she thought it sounded exactly like the strain of a rope pulling against the lowest branch.

"Oh, my gawd!" Sue whispered.

"Let's get out of here!" Tanya cried.

The three friends scrambled down the alley and around the corner to their rental car.

Once inside, Ellen glanced back at the tree as she turned the ignition. "So y'all heard that too?"

"Like a rope twisting?" Tanya asked.

"Yep," Sue said.

And even Sue, who always had more to say, said nothing else as they peeled away, wondering if what they'd heard had been real.

CHAPTER FOUR

The Ouija Board

While they ate their ice cream in a booth at Braum's, Ellen told Sue and Tanya her secret. For the past three months, she'd been scouring the real estate market in the historic King William District in San Antonio, hoping to find another haunted house to flip.

"But the market has been dead lately," Ellen said. "No pun intended."

"We won't make very good ghost busters if every time we hear a noise we run," Sue said.

"Not busters," Ellen said. "Healers. And we can't expect to become experts right away. We'll get better at it. Are y'all interested?"

"Count me in," Tanya said.

"Why don't we buy a house *here?*" Sue said before taking a bite of her mint chocolate chip.

Tanya licked at her Rocky Road. "That's crazy."

"No, it's not," Sue said. "Tulsa is in the process of revitalizing itself. The market is saturated with historic homes at rock bottom prices, and young urban couples are eating them up." She took a bite and added, "And that pun *was* intended."

"How do you know all this?" Ellen asked, her interest piqued.

"People were talking about it at my table at the wedding," Sue explained. "Tom was thinking about buying a small bed and breakfast here where we could stay whenever we come up to visit Lexi and Stephen. Their apartment is tiny."

Tanya frowned. "I don't want to pay a fortune in hotel bills. It wouldn't be economically feasible."

"Well, that depends on the price of the property versus what we could sell it for after we fix it up," Sue pointed out. "And if Tom and I find a place, the three of us could stay there while we do our renovations."

"I'm only interested if we can find a property known to be haunted," Ellen said. "For me, that's the whole point."

"Carrie French said there are plenty of haunted places in Tulsa," Sue said. "We could look around tomorrow and see if anything suits our fancy."

"Look, I would love to flip another haunted house, but Tulsa is so far away from home," Tanya said. "It took us three months to finish the Gold House."

"You just said you were dreading going back to San Antonio," Sue pointed out to Tanya.

"I know, but…"

"We don't have to be up here during the entire renovation," Ellen said, wiping some of the strawberry ice cream from her chin. "And you liked the train, didn't you?"

"I have an idea!" Sue said a little too loudly.

Tanya and Ellen both *shhhed* her as they looked around at the others in the ice cream parlor staring back at them.

"Sorry." Sue lowered her voice. "Let's go buy an Ouija Board and ask it what we should do."

"What are we, twelve?" Ellen wrinkled her nose.

"Sounds like fun," Tanya said. "But I don't think it will change my mind."

"Well, it should," Sue said. "My mom and I used to ask it questions all the time when I was younger."

"What?" Ellen laughed. "Your mom played the Ouija Board with you?"

"Being an only child wasn't easy," Sue replied. "Don't judge."

"What a good mom," Tanya said.

"Not really," Sue said. "She used to *make* me do it with her, to ask it if she was going to meet a man and fall in love again."

"Oh, gosh," Ellen moaned.

"And?" Tanya asked.

"Sometimes it gave her a name, and she would obsess over it for months, though most of the time it went to *No*," Sue said. "But let me tell you why I believe in it."

Ellen cocked her head to one side. While it was true that she'd had a major change of heart regarding spirits and the paranormal, the Ouija Board was pushing it, in her opinion.

Sue took off her readers and laid them on the table. "I was fourteen years old. I had begun to suspect that my mom was the one moving the plastic thingamajig around on the board. So, one day after school, I took it to my room to ask it questions alone."

"Weren't you scared?" Tanya asked.

"No, I really wasn't. Not at first, anyway. But then, after I asked it my question, it was a long time before I warmed up to it again."

"Why?" Ellen asked. "What was your question?"

"I asked it, 'Who are you?' and it answered, 'Odin.' So, I got out the *World Book Encyclopedia* and looked it up. You can imagine how frightened I was when I discovered that Odin was a *Norse god.*" Sue laughed.

"That's strange," Tanya said with a chuckle. "But it could have been a coincidence."

"I *know* I didn't move that thingamajig," Sue said. "You don't have to believe me, but the whole reason I played it by myself was to make sure my mother hadn't been moving it. It moved on its own. I swear it."

"So did you ever play it again?" Tanya asked.

"Yes, I did. In college. It's how I met Tom. But that's a story for another time." Sue put her readers on and picked up her iPhone. "Just give me one second. Okay. Here we go. There's a Walmart four miles away that has one. I think we should go buy it and take it back to your hotel room."

Less than an hour later, Ellen and her friends sat around the Ouija Board in Ellen and Tanya's hotel room. Sue sat on the edge of her seat in the one armchair. Ellen sat beside her in the smaller desk chair. And Tanya faced them both from where she sat on the end of her bed with her legs crisscrossed, yoga style. The Ouija Board laid across Tanya's lap, and all three ladies had their hands held lightly over the plastic indicator—or planchette—with just their fingertips touching it.

Tanya glanced at each of them with a giddy smile on her face. "What should we ask it first?"

"I know," Sue said. And then more loudly, she said, "Is someone there?"

At first nothing happened, but after a few seconds, the indicator began to move.

Ellen studied the faces of each of her friends. She had a feeling Sue was moving the planchette as it landed on *Yes*.

But Sue looked up with shock and glee and then asked, "What is your name?"

Ellen watched on skeptically as the planchette slowly spelled V-I-V-I-A-N.

Tanya's face paled. "If you're doing that, Sue…"

"I promise you I'm not. I don't even know a Vivian."

"That was Tanya's mother's cousin," Ellen told Sue. "Remember? Tanya's psychic said she saw Vivian beside Tanya at the Gold House."

"You're not moving it, are you, Ellen?" Tanya asked her.

"Cross my heart," Ellen said, still suspicious of Sue. She was also worried about how Tanya would take it if Sue was indeed playing a trick. She gave Sue a warning glance, but Sue furrowed her brows innocently.

Then Tanya surprised her by saying, "Are you my mother's cousin?"

The planchette moved to *Yes*.

Tears flooded Tanya's eyes as she asked, "Is my mother at peace?"

The planchette moved in a circle and returned to *Yes*.

Ellen hoped Sue knew what she was doing, if she was indeed the one controlling the game.

Tanya's fingers trembled beside Ellen's, and tears fell down her cheeks.

"Are you okay, Tanya?" Ellen asked.

Tanya nodded. "I don't know what to ask next. Someone else say something."

"What do you want to tell us?" Sue said to the Ouija Board. "Do you have a message for us, or for Tanya?"

Ellen bit her lower lip as the planchette began to move again. Very slowly, it spelled out H-E-L-P-T-U-L-S-A.

With narrowed eyes, Ellen studied Sue's face. "Swear to God that you didn't do that."

"Ellen, I swear," Sue said. "Why don't you believe me?"

Then Tanya said to Ouija Board, "Can you give us a sign that you're really here, Vivian?"

The three friends sat in silence for what seemed like many minutes, stealing glances at one another, none of them sure how to proceed. Ellen was just about to suggest that they give up when she heard a noise near the balcony.

"What was that?" Sue whispered.

The noise came again. It was like the fluttering of wings.

"It's the chrysalises!" Tanya jumped from the bed.

They all three made their way over to the dome net sitting on the floor by the sliding glass doors to the balcony. The net was shaking from the wings of at least a dozen newly hatched butterflies.

"Oh my gosh," Tanya said, just above a whisper. "They never hatch all at once, and it takes a while before they can fly."

Ellen slid the balcony doors open as Tanya lifted the net and Sue waved her hands to direct the butterflies outside.

"They've never hatched all at once like this!" Tanya said again between tears.

Ellen couldn't tell if Tanya was smiling or frowning as her friend wiped her face with the hem of her blouse.

"This is incredible," Sue muttered with a look of shock on her face.

"Do you think this is Vivian's sign?" Ellen asked. A year ago, Ellen would have insisted it was a coincidence, but now, she wasn't so sure.

"It must be," Tanya said.

Tanya stood between Ellen and Sue on the balcony as they watched the butterflies flutter in circles in the night sky and fly away. Ellen put an arm around Tanya's waist to comfort her and felt Sue's already there. At that moment, Ellen was convinced that something extraordinary had just happened to them. Even if Sue had been controlling the planchette, there was no way she could have orchestrated this.

CHAPTER FIVE

An Abandoned Building

On Monday morning, Ellen and Tanya met Sue downstairs for breakfast. Sue didn't look like her usual cheerful self. She had dark rings beneath her eyes, and her brown hair wasn't curled on the ends.

"Did you sleep okay?" Tanya asked Sue as they joined her with their full plates at a table by the window.

"No, I didn't," Sue admitted. "I guess I was more spooked by Vivian than I realized."

"You should have stayed with us, so you wouldn't have been alone." Ellen took a sip of her coffee.

Sue laughed. "If I couldn't sleep two floors above you, I doubt I would have slept any better in the same room with you and the *ghost*."

"I don't think she stayed." Tanya steeped an herbal tea bag in a mug of hot water, dunking the bag repeatedly before adding honey. "I think she flew away with the butterflies."

"Well, I guess my snoring wouldn't have kept you up after all, since I couldn't sleep," Sue said before taking a bite of her pancakes.

"Tanya and I can share a bed, if you change your mind," Ellen said.

"I think you're just looking for an excuse to sleep with her," Sue said to Ellen with a chuckle. "I see the way you two look at one another."

Ellen and Tanya busted out laughing.

"She's on to us," Tanya said.

Ellen swallowed down a few bites of scrambled egg before saying, "Well, I didn't sleep much either. I stayed up late on my phone searching Tulsa's property listings."

"I did the same thing," Sue said. "Did something in particular catch your eye?"

Ellen shrugged. "The houses I liked were pricier than I'd hoped. If we want something historical, we may have to pay an arm and a leg to get it. I couldn't find the rock bottom prices you mentioned last night."

Sue's face beamed. "Well, I found something, but I need you to keep an open mind."

Ellen drove the rental car while Sue gave her directions from the backseat. Ellen recognized the Brady Arts District, where they had gone on the haunted pub crawl the night before. Sue directed her just past Cain's Ballroom to an abandoned building made of red brick, steel, and glass. To Ellen, it resembled a warehouse with its simplistic industrial design. The many windows along the front of it were the only hint of architectural detail, and they were either broken or covered in grime and dead vines. A six-foot chain-link fence surrounded the three or four acres of dead lawn.

Ellen pulled up to the curb. "You can't be serious."

Sue smirked. "Now you know how I felt when you showed me the Gold House for the first time."

"But this isn't even a house," Tanya said.

"Just hear me out." Sue leaned over the console between the front bucket seats. "This area has been heavily revitalized over the past decade. It reminds me of what happened in San Antonio with the Pearl Brewery and the Quarry area."

"Go on," Ellen prompted.

"In both places in San Antonio," Sue continued, "warehouses were turned into urban loft apartments."

"I've seen that done in other cities on HGTV," Tanya said.

Sue nodded. "I think we could easily do that here and make a killing. And listen to this: the reason this place is still abandoned and now owned by the city of Tulsa and on the market for only *ten thousand dollars* is because it's believed to be haunted."

"Did you say ten thousand dollars?" Tanya asked.

"Yep. The land alone is worth a lot more than that," Sue said. "It's right on the edge of the arts district, so its property value will only go up as the area continues to develop."

"But the highway is right there," Ellen pointed out. "Will people want to live that close to all that noise?"

"Easy access to both downtown and OSU-Tulsa," Sue replied. "Besides, I doubt you'd hear the traffic inside, once the windows are all fixed."

"It *is* conveniently located," Tanya agreed.

Ellen sucked in her lips. For her, it all came down to the story of the place. "Why do people think it's haunted?"

Sue pointed toward the front windshield. "You see that big hole in the fence, to the left of the padlocked gate? According to one website, the city hasn't repaired it yet because there hasn't been a need. The vagrants never stay more than one night before running off. They say they hear voices coming from *inside the walls*."

Ellen turned off the ignition and tucked the key in her purse. "Let's have a look, then."

They stepped out of the car and over the curb, crossing pea gravel until they came to the six-foot chain-link fence. A hole from the top pole to the ground gaped open. As Ellen pulled it back for Tanya and Sue, she wondered what other hands had done this very thing over the years. Whose DNA now mingled with hers on the metal fence?

From the fence to the building spanned at least thirty yards. Dry dirt and tufts of dead grass crunched beneath their feet. The property could use a good rain, Ellen thought, and, fortunately, if the gray clouds overhead were any indication, it just might get one later today.

The entrance to the building was overgrown with dead vines, weeds, and five large Texas Sage bushes that appeared to be thriving with their colorful purple blooms. Once the three friends made their way through the brush, they found three concrete steps leading up to a small concrete porch. No overhang covered it, and the enormous entry was boarded shut. Graffiti warning people to keep out or die was painted on the weathered boards, along with "Simol was here 6-5-77."

"Now what?" Tanya asked.

"Let's see if there's another way to get in," Ellen suggested.

She led her friends around the east side of the building, dodging more half-dead brush along the way. The sight of a face peering at her from the weeds halted her in her tracks. She screamed and clutched her chest.

Tanya and Sue grabbed her from behind.

"What?' Sue cried.

When the face didn't move, Ellen studied it. Then she let out a sigh of relief.

"There, in the weeds." She pointed to the face. "I thought that was a real person, but it's some kind of statue. What is that?"

"Is that the head of a clown?" Tanya asked, moving closer.

Ellen reached through the weeds and tapped it with her fingers before pulling at it.

"A creepy clown bust," Ellen said, turning it over.

It was made of hollow plaster. The inside was full of dead bugs and cobwebs, and the outside had the painted face of a clown. The paint was chipped and dull, which was why it hadn't registered as a clown at first to Ellen—though, if it had, it might have been even creepier, she thought.

"I wonder what it's doing here?" Tanya said.

"Let's keep going," Sue prompted them.

Ellen carried the clown bust as they continued around the side of the building.

"Maybe we should contact a realtor to let us in," Tanya said. "What if we get caught snooping around?"

"Let's just see if it's worth our time first," Ellen said. "Oh, look!"

Around the corner on the east side of the building was what could only be described as a hobo camp. The double wooden doors on the side swung open, and through them Ellen could see old mattresses, one cot, cardboard boxes, discarded clothing, and a bunch of trash.

"What a dump," Sue said.

"I'm going to be sick." Tanya covered her mouth and nose from the stench.

"Wait here, then." Ellen walked through the open doors. "I'm going to have a look around."

"What if someone's in there?" Sue called from behind. "I can't let you go alone. At least I have a gun."

"I don't want to be left out here by myself," Tanya cried, as she followed.

"Hello?" Ellen said. "Anyone here? We're friends, not foes."

"That's so lame," Sue whispered. "Why would anyone say that? And who would believe that a foe would *say* he's a foe?"

Tanya giggled. "This is crazy, guys. What are we doing?"

"Come on," Ellen said again as she stepped from the room into a hallway.

"Oh, lord, the smell's getting worse," Sue complained.

Ellen pushed the heavy door on the right until it opened. Four commodes without stalls lined the back wall. A broken sink was mounted to another. She closed the door because the stench was overwhelming.

Sue pushed the heavy door on the left to reveal more commodes with moldy pink curtains hanging over the front windows.

"Let's keep going," Ellen said as she led them further down the hall.

The ten-foot hallway ended with a wooden door that was slightly ajar. When Ellen pulled on it, it creaked in the otherwise silent building, causing her heart to pick up speed. When she bravely stepped through, she was surprised to find an enormous room with high ceilings, at least thirty feet high, with glass skylights overhead. The skylights, along with the high windows at the front of the building, let in a tremendous amount of natural light, even on a cloudy day. It streaked throughout the room, illuminating risers along the perimeter, as if for a choir or for stadium-style seating. A few blankets lay curled up on the risers where transients must have once slept. The wooden floorboards beneath them were heavily scratched and worn, but they didn't look rotten. Ellen was already imagining them sanded down and stained to perfection.

Behind them, from the smaller rooms they had just entered, were stairs leading to two other floors and catwalks on each level spanning the depth of the building. Some of the doors above them contained more graffiti. Trash lay everywhere, but the stench in here wasn't as strong. Fresh air came in through the broken windows and made the room less stifling.

But as Ellen looked around at the room, she began to feel the same suffocating feeling she'd experienced when she had walked by the Brady Theater. Was it all in her head? Was she coming down with something? Or were the two experiences somehow related?

"I need to get out of here," Tanya said. "My chest feels tight."

"Mine, too," Sue said. "Like last night."

"At the theater," Ellen said.

Sue nodded. "Exactly."

"This is too bizarre," Tanya whispered.

"Let's see if there's a way out on the other side." Ellen crossed the twenty or so yards to an arched doorway that led into another large room with the same dimensions as the last. This room also had risers, only the floor was littered with dry hay, and there were wooden stalls and the remnants of wooden fencing, for keeping animals.

"Was this a barn?" Sue asked.

"It smells like one," Tanya said, covering her mouth and nose with her hand.

More trash littered the floor along one side of the room, and at the end of it were stairs leading up to the second and third floors with a catwalk across each level from the front to the back of the building. The building was symmetrical: three floors on either side of two enormous rooms in the middle.

"Should we go upstairs and look around?" Ellen asked.

"Maybe we should wait for the realtor," Tanya said. "I don't want to die here."

"I think Tanya's right," Sue said. "But I would definitely be in favor of coming back later tonight for a séance."

"No way," Tanya said. "That's probably when the hobos come back."

"But the website said they don't stay," Sue said.

"And everything online is the gospel truth," Tanya challenged.

Ellen sighed. "Let's contact a realtor and go from there."

She led them through the west end of the building. It had a similar hallway as the east wing, leading to similar bathrooms, but the furthest room, though shaped like the first one they had entered, looked like it had once been a bowling alley. Old, grimy bowling pins were scattered in the far corners, and there were four wooden lanes with gutters on each side.

"What a strange building," Sue said. "I'm anxious to learn more about its history."

As Ellen pushed, to no avail, on the big wooden doors, she thought Sue whispered something.

"What?" Ellen asked.

"I didn't say anything," Sue said.

"I heard something, too," Tanya said. "Let's get out of here."

But the wooden doors wouldn't budge.

"We're going to have to go back the way we came in," Ellen said.

As they crossed the room, the sound of whispering came again. This time, it was clear to Ellen, and she dropped the clown bust in mortal fear. It broke into pieces at her feet.

Don't ignore us.

Tanya must have heard it, too, because she took off running through the rooms to the east exit.

Ellen froze and met Sue's frightened eyes. They stood there, still as statues. Was someone else in the building with them? And if so, was that someone alive or dead?

Then Sue surprised Ellen by saying, "We don't want to ignore you. Tell us who you are."

Ellen could barely hear over the hammering of her heart against her ribs and in her head, but she held her breath and waited with Sue in silence. Sue took out her cell phone—why, Ellen wasn't sure—but then she whispered, "That's weird. My phone's dead."

Ellen pulled hers from her pocket and handed it to Sue. "Use mine. Are you going to try to make a recording, or what?"

"I wanted to, but your phone is dead, too."

"That can't be. Give it here."

Sue was right. Ellen's battery was dead.

After a few minutes, they heard Tanya calling out to them, so they floundered through the building until they were outside of it again, where Tanya was waiting for them in the rain.

CHAPTER SIX

An Official Tour

Tuesday afternoon, Ellen drove her friends back to the strange abandoned building, which was now surrounded by a large field of mud left behind by the rain. The building looked sad today, and Ellen felt as though it was calling out to her for help.

HELP TULSA.

Another vehicle was already parked along the curb.

Tanya unbuckled her seatbelt. "Do you think that's the realtor?"

"Who else would it be?" Sue asked.

"What was her name again?" Ellen turned off the ignition and tucked the key in her purse.

"Gayle something or other," Tanya said.

"Gayle Boring," Sue said. "Hopefully she doesn't live up to her name."

The woman standing outside of the vehicle wore a blue pantsuit and a silver barrette in her red hair. She was thin and short, even shorter than Sue, with freckles on her pale, severe face. Ellen thought she was probably in her late twenties.

"It's a blessing to meet you," Gayle Boring said to each of them as she shook their hands.

"Likewise," Sue said.

"What can you tell us about this place?" Tanya asked. "And do you know if anyone was ever murdered here?"

"Someone *was* murdered here," Gayle said.

Tanya's face paled. "Then that's a deal breaker for me."

"Oh, come on Tanya," Ellen said. "Let's at least give it a chance."

"I don't know." Tanya picked at the cuff of her sleeve.

"Well, since we're here, why don't I tell you what I know about this place?" Gayle suggested.

"That's a good idea," Ellen said, not wanting to give up on the property just yet.

"It was built in 1915," Gayle said. "It was originally a social club with a roller rink, a ballroom, a bowling alley, and a dinner club, but in 1921, the owner sold it to a man who turned it into an illegal gambling hall and a speakeasy."

Ellen frowned. She'd been hoping for a more honorable history than this.

The realtor continued. "Then in the thirties, the building was sold to the St. Vincent de Paul Society and turned into a rehabilitation home for alcoholic men."

"A rehabilitation center?" Tanya asked.

"We seem to be drawn to them," Sue mumbled.

"That's when the murder took place," Gayle said.

"What happened?" Sue asked.

"A nurse murdered a patient in his sleep," Gayle replied. "Then the nurse killed himself. No one was ever able to find out why."

Ellen, Sue, and Tanya exchanged worried glances. Ellen knew that Tanya would not be comfortable moving forward with a building with that kind of history, but Ellen felt a connection to it in the same way she had felt one with the Gold House.

"Don't assume he was evil," Ellen said to Tanya. "Maybe they were lovers who would rather die than live a life together that most people didn't approve of back then."

Tanya continued to pick at her sleeve but said nothing.

"And even if he was evil," Sue said, "we can do a sage smudge stick ceremony to get rid of him."

The realtor lifted her brows. "Are you ladies ghost busters or something?"

Ellen laughed. "No, not at all."

"Not busters," Sue said. "Healers. We're ghost healers, but we don't want to work with anyone evil."

"I bet my mother's psychic would be willing to help you," Gayle offered.

"That's good to know," Sue said. "Thank you. We'll let you know if we're interested."

"What happened to the St. Vincent de Paul's home for men?" Ellen asked. "How long did it operate, and why did it close down?"

"In 1945, after the murder and the scandal surrounding it, the St. Vincent de Paul Society sold the building to a circus," Gayle said. "The circus operated in the building and the grounds from 1945 to the late 1960's, when it went out of business. That's when the city of Tulsa took possession of it."

"A circus?" Sue smiled. "How fun."

"Why didn't the city ever do anything with it?" Ellen asked.

"Asbestos," Gayle explained. "The city was planning to turn it into a storage facility, but when it was found to contain asbestos, they abandoned the project."

"But why? Why not remove the asbestos?" Tanya asked.

"For a building this large, it would cost at least fifty thousand dollars, and the city doesn't want to invest that kind of money in it," Gayle said. "In fact, funds are being raised for demolition. Because of the asbestos, it has to be done a certain way. So, if it doesn't sell before the funds are raised, this historical building will be lost to us forever."

The idea of such an interesting historical building being wiped from the face of the earth was disturbing to Ellen. It made her want to save the building and to solve the mystery of the ghosts even that much more.

"Can we take a look inside?" Sue asked.

Gayle smiled. "Of course. Follow me."

She led them to a set of double doors made of chain-linked fencing and unlocked the padlock before swinging them open.

When they reached the entrance to the hobo camp, the red-headed realtor frowned. "These doors aren't secure. I'm so sorry about that. I'll let the city know."

Ellen and her friends pretended to be viewing the building for the first time as they followed Gayle inside.

"This was originally the dining hall," Gayle said. "It was last used as a room of curiosities by the circus. The two-headed woman, the man with no body, and other freakish things were hidden behind curtains in here and shown to each customer for a nickel."

"How creepy," Sue said as they followed Gayle from the room to the narrow hallway.

"Restroom facilities here and there," Gayle pushed one of the doors open.

Ellen glanced inside and nodded before continuing to the first of the two large rooms.

"This was the ballroom, originally," Gayle explained. "Then it became the gambling hall, and later a bunkroom for the men's home. The circus brought in the risers and used the room for shows." She pointed to the ceiling. "That chain up there is the last of a trapeze that once hung there." She pointed to the north-facing wall. "And in that back wall is a dumbwaiter that lifts up to each of those two other floors. Would you like to see those rooms?"

"Yes, please," Tanya said.

They followed Gayle up the first flight of rickety wooden steps as Gayle said, "They were originally VIP rooms for special out-of-town guests. Historians speculate that the rooms were used for prostitution when the place was a gambling hall. When the St. Vincent de Paul Society took over, the employees who ran the home lived in them. Later, some of the circus people lived in them."

The first landing led to two doors, and behind each of them were identical rooms with a bed, table, and closet. The rooms were bathed with light from the windows, showing every scrap of garbage left behind by transients.

"Could people still be using this place?" Ellen asked.

"It's possible," Gayle said. "I'll be sure and notify the city that the building needs to be secured, and that should help keep the vagrants out."

Gayle showed them the third floor, where there were two more rooms, identical to the ones on the second floor. Then they went downstairs and into the second large room.

"This was originally a roller-skating rink," Gayle said. "The wooden floors are supposed to be of the highest quality—in the old ballroom, too. You may be able to salvage them."

"It looks more like a barn," Sue said, pinching her nose.

"Yes, the circus used this for their animal attractions, and I believe they kept the larger animals in those stables over there," Gayle said. "They had elephants, lions, monkeys, and dogs, I believe. And when it was the men's home, this was the sick side. So they kept the well men in the other room and the sick ones in here."

As Gayle told more about the circus, Ellen went behind the risers to the north-facing brick wall. As in the ballroom, the skating rink had a dumbwaiter too. It was a stainless-steel box about four feet high, three feet wide, and two feet deep. It was full of dirt and old cobwebs. There was a steel handle at the top, and when she pulled on it, a sliding door came down, but not easily and not quietly.

"What are you doing?" Sue asked.

"Just checking out this dumbwaiter. It's pretty creepy."

She pulled the handle back up and was startled by a spider leaping out at her. She flinched, but didn't scream, as she batted it away and regained her composure. Laughing at herself, she finished lifting the sliding door. There was a control panel to the right, built into the brick wall but without electricity, it was useless. As she turned to leave, she heard whispers: *Don't ignore us. We are here.*

Ellen froze. Her first thought was that someone alive must be playing a trick on her. The voice had been too clear to have been made by a spectral. But as she re-examined the dumbwaiter, the control panel, and the brick wall, she couldn't imagine how any living person could have gotten close enough to her to whisper. Maybe someone was speaking through the elevator shaft from one of the upper levels? No, she thought. This must be a ghost—had to be. Her skepticism and her desire to believe were at odds with one another.

In any case, she wanted to be brave and to ask the voice some questions—like Who are you?—but she chickened out and hurried back to the others.

"The upstairs rooms are constructed in the same fashion as the rooms on the other side," Gayle was saying, "but I'd be happy to take you up there, if you'd like."

"I don't need to see them," Sue said.

"Me either," Tanya said. "Not if they're identical to the others."

"What about you, Ellen?" Sue asked her. Then she added, "Are you okay? You look flustered."

"I'm fine," she said. "And yes, I'd like to see the upstairs on this side, too."

She followed Gayle up the rickety steps, and Tanya decided to come, too. Sue waited below.

The two rooms on the second floor were identical to the ones on the west end, except the one in back, against the north-facing wall, had at least a dozen dreamcatchers strewn about and hanging on the walls. There were also crucifixes on the bedside table and one glass candle holder with the image of the Virgin Mary on it. A quilt covered the one bed.

"It looks like someone lives here," Ellen said. She studied the north-facing wall at the end of the catwalk, where the dumbwaiter elevator was, and wondered if whoever lived here could have been the one whispering a few moments before.

Ellen kept her eye out for signs of a person hiding in the building as they took the stairs to the third floor and looked around. Of the eight rooms in the building—four on the west end and four on the east end—only the one with the dreamcatchers appeared to have been recently used. The other beds contained bare mattresses and discarded junk on the floors, whereas the one with the dreamcatchers and crucifixes had a blanket and appeared tidy in comparison.

Downstairs, Gayle told them about the nine-pin bowling alley that was once operated in the most western room. "This is one area that stayed the same through all four owners. Even the illegal gambling club used the bowling alley. The home for men used it, and the circus, did, too, though they added a few carnival games over there." She pointed to the south-facing wall.

"How interesting," Sue said.

"Why don't we step out into the fresh air, and I'll answer any questions you might have," Gayle said as she slipped her key into the side door.

"What do y'all think?" Sue asked Ellen and Tanya once they were outside waiting for Gayle to lock up.

"I don't know," Tanya said. "It sounds like the asbestos removal would be too costly. Would we really be able to make any money?"

Gayle turned from the door. "The city is anxious to unload this property and to see it developed. They're asking $10,000, but I bet you could get them to come down in price."

"How far down are you thinking?" Ellen asked.

"If it were me," Gayle said, "I'd offer half and see what they say. They just might take it."

The corners of Ellen's mouth twitched into a smile. "We should think about it, ladies. Even with the asbestos removal, $55,000 for a property this big in this location could be a lucrative deal for us."

Tanya folded her arms in front of her and asked the realtor, "Can we have the name and number of that psychic you mentioned earlier?"

"Of course," Gayle said.

The two ladies took out their cell phones.

"Oh, I'll have to text it to you later," Gayle said. "My phone just died."

"Mine, too," Tanya said. "That's so bizarre. It was fully charged."

Ellen and Sue checked their phones as well.

Dead.

CHAPTER SEVEN

The Local Psychic

When Gayle's psychic still hadn't returned Sue's phone call or texts by dinner time, Ellen suggested that they look for someone else. "We only have a few more days here."

"I have a feeling there aren't many psychics in Tulsa," Tanya said from where she lay propped on pillows against the headboard of her hotel bed.

After their tour of the abandoned building, they'd gone to the Philbrook and Gilcrease museums and were now resting in Ellen and Tanya's room until dinner.

Sue sat in the armchair with her iPhone. "Google shows two. Should I call the other one?"

"Might as well," Ellen said from the desk chair, where she sipped at a water bottle. "Maybe we could schedule a reading and feel her out."

"*Him*," Sue corrected. "His name is Eduardo Mankiller."

"Mankiller? You're kidding," Tanya said. "That's not creepy."

"Okay. Here goes." Sue put her phone on speaker, and they waited for someone to answer.

When they were greeted by a voicemail message, Sue glanced at Ellen and Tanya and mouthed, "Should I leave a message?"

Ellen nodded.

"Um, hello, this is Sue Graham. Could you please call me back? I'd like to schedule a session at your earliest convenience for me and my two friends, while we're in town." Sue recited her phone number and then ended the call.

"Now what?" Tanya asked.

"Let's go eat," Sue suggested.

Not wanting to go far, they drove across the street to the Hard Rock Café and Casino to eat and to play a few slot machines before heading back to the hotel just before dark. They hadn't yet made it to the La Quinta when Sue received a text from Eduardo Mankiller.

"He wants to know if we can come now," Sue said.

"How far away is he?" Tanya asked.

Sue texted him for an address and then searched it on Google Maps. "Fifteen minutes down I-244 West. But…"

"What?" Ellen asked.

"Well, he doesn't live in the best part of town." Sue shrugged. "But hopefully he's not a serial killer or someone who just plans to kill us for our car."

Ellen rolled her eyes. "Thanks a lot, Sue. Now we'll never get Tanya to go."

"I'll go in the *morning*," Tanya offered.

"Let me text him." Sue pushed on her phone and, in the next moment, read, "'Won't be available tomorrow. What about Friday afternoon?' That won't work. We'll be gone by then. What should I say?"

"Say we're coming tonight," Ellen said. "We'll be extra careful. Okay, Tanya?"

"I don't know about this," Tanya said. "It sounds like a dumb idea to me."

"Too late," Sue said. "I told him we'll be there in fifteen."

Ellen was surprised to find herself back near the Brady Arts District, in the residential area known as Greenwood. The buildings on the street where Eduardo Mankiller resided looked like they were falling apart.

The lawns were all dead and, in many cases, served as additional parking. The street wasn't far from the Oklahoma State University-Tulsa campus, so she told herself again and again that the area was probably safe and full of poor college students and *not* thieves and killers.

By the time they pulled up to the white wooden duplex, night had fallen, and the house was in darkness except for the light cast by their headlights.

"Call him and make sure this is the right place," Ellen said.

Sue tapped in the psychic's number. Then she said, "Hello, Mr. Mankiller?"

Tanya crossed her arms and whispered, "This is stupid, guys."

Sue continued. "Yes, of course, Eduardo. We think we've reached your house, but there aren't any lights on."

At that moment, a porch light came on.

Ellen and Tanya exchanged worried looks.

Sue laughed. "We just want to make sure you aren't planning to kill us, given your name."

"Sue!" Ellen cried.

"That's true," Sue said into her phone. "We're *women*, not men. So we should be safe then? Hahaha. Yes, I bet you *do* get that a lot. Sorry."

Then Sue whispered, "He's going to meet us on the porch." Into the phone, she said, "Okay, Eduardo. Oh, yes. I see you now."

Once she had ended the call, Sue added, "I don't think we have anything to worry about. He sounded gay."

"How does someone *sound gay*?" Tanya, whose oldest son had just come out, said in an exasperated voice.

"Well, you know how I have a gift for detecting ghosts?" Sue asked. "I have a gift for detecting gays, too."

"Oh, Sue," Ellen said, still worried about what they we're getting themselves into. "Stop teasing."

"What has being gay got to do with anything, anyway?" Tanya asked defensively.

"It means we're not in danger of being raped," Sue said calmly. "Now let's go."

Ellen busted out laughing. Fear and a kind of delirium had taken over. If she was to be killed tonight, at least it was while trying to do something good.

As she followed Sue up the steps to the front porch, she was relieved to see that Eduardo did not look like a hoodlum. Given his run-down house, she was impressed by how impeccably he was dressed, in a black, long-sleeved shirt and black trousers. He had short black hair, black eyes, and a short black beard, and his face was very attractive, especially when he smiled down at them. His body looked strong and lean, and he appeared to be in his late twenties or early thirties. All of this didn't mean he wasn't a killer, though, Ellen thought.

"Hello, dears. It's a pleasure to meet you." He shook each of their hands as they introduced themselves. "Why don't you have a seat here on the porch? I can do the reading out here. Or, if you would rather go inside…"

"Out here is fine," Tanya said.

"You've brought someone with you," Eduardo said to Tanya. "Someone from the other side."

Tanya clasped her hands together. "Who?"

"She's not yet ready to talk to me, but I'll let you know if she opens up," he said. "She's an older woman. Perhaps a relative?"

Tanya said nothing, and although Ellen wanted to ask if it was Vivian, she kept her mouth shut. She was glad that Sue did the same. This man could be a fake.

Ellen and Tanya sat on a bench while Sue took a wicker chair. Eduardo pulled up a stool and sat so that he was within arm's reach of each of them.

"Who would like to go first?" he asked enthusiastically.

"I'll go," Sue said.

Eduardo reached into his back trouser pocket and pulled out a—
Ellen held her breath, hoping it wasn't a gun—deck of cards. She sighed
with relief. The cards were small and worn, as though they'd been used
for years. As he shuffled and cut them, Ellen realized they were regular
playing cards—not what she'd expected.

"I'm asking the universe to speak to me through these," he explained. "If the universe has a message for Sue, may it please reveal it in
the cards."

Eduardo asked Sue to pull out three cards from the deck.

He took the first card—a three of clubs—and said, "In the past, you
were an important part of someone's healing."

Ellen widened her eyes, thinking of Marcia Gold, but then she realized what Eduardo was saying was broad and could be applied to anything.

"I get the sense that the person you healed had already died," Eduardo said. "And this spirit continues to dwell close to you—no, not to
you, to your mother. The person you healed now watches over your
mother. Oh, that's so incredible. Could this be right?"

Not so broad anymore, Ellen thought.

Sue nodded at Eduardo as he took the eight of hearts from her.

"This card is telling me, warning me, that you need to do something
fun and interesting at this time in your life. You've been working hard
recently, and your energy needs to be revitalized."

"My daughter was just married," Sue said. "And I did work hard."

"Oh, you poor thing. Now would be a good time to go on a trip or
to begin a new adventure," Eduardo said.

Sue raised her brows at Ellen and Tanya as Eduardo took her final
card.

"The ace of spades is telling me that in the future, you will make a
profound sacrifice for a higher good," he said.

"What kind of sacrifice?" Sue asked.

"One that could harm you, if you aren't careful," Eduardo said. "Just be sure not to put your own health and spiritual wellbeing on the back burner, okay Sue? Take time to meditate and exercise so you can build the strength and endurance required of this noble sacrifice."

"I'm not sure I like the sound of that," Sue said.

"Oh, you will be magnificent," he said. "Just be careful."

Then he turned to Ellen. "Ready for your turn, dear?"

Ellen nodded as he returned the cards to the deck, shuffled, and cut. Then she chose three and handed over the first.

"The two of hearts tells me that you have a gift for picking up signals from the universe," Eduardo said. "Are you also psychic?"

Ellen shook her head. "I don't think so."

"Oh, this card suggests that you are, and that, in the past, you used this gift to help others. You can improve your talent through practice and through meditation or by keeping a journal. I can also recommend some books, if you're interested in developing your gift further."

Ellen didn't have to look at Sue to know she was green with envy. Ellen simply nodded at the psychic and handed over her second card.

"The ace of hearts," he said and then frowned.

"Is that bad?" Ellen asked.

"Well, this card is telling me that you are currently struggling in your love relationship. You feel estranged from the one you love, and you long for a deeper connection, but something is in the way."

"What's in the way?" Ellen asked, stunned by the accuracy of the card.

"You," he said.

Blood rushed to Ellen's face. How was she in the way of her own happiness with Paul?

Eduardo took her third card. "The ten of diamonds. Harmony."

"Harmony?" Ellen thought this sounded like a good thing.

"You must restore it," he said. "Oh, I'm sorry, dear, but this card is saying that you are in need of harmony, that you need to pay attention to your feelings. The card is also telling me that once you restore harmony to yourself, you will then be able to restore harmony to the world around you. The card suggests that this is a goal of yours. You want to bring balance and peace to others. This is good but futile if you remain imbalanced in your personal life."

Ellen frowned. This wasn't what she'd wanted to hear.

Eduardo turned to Tanya. "Ready?"

Tanya nodded as Eduardo shuffled and cut. Then Tanya pulled her cards.

"The queen of diamonds wishes to remind you of both your outer and inner beauty," Eduardo said.

"Yeah, right." Tanya laughed.

"Oh, I'm serious, dear," he said. "You have a tendency toward self-deprecation, even though it is completely unwarranted. The card whispers the reminder that you are beautiful. Don't get caught up in the superficial notions of beauty of our time, because your beauty is timeless."

Ellen was surprised to see tears forming in Tanya's eyes. They were visible beneath the porchlight.

Then Eduardo said, "So you're finally ready to speak?"

"What?" Tanya looked confused.

"Your cousin," he said. "She says your mother was the same way."

"My cousin?" Tanya asked. "Where is she? Which cousin?"

"She's standing right behind you, dear." Eduardo pointed. "She hasn't told me her name, but she says she's your cousin and guardian angel. She promised your mother—oh, she's your mother's cousin. She promised your mother she'd stay and watch over you for a while."

Tanya covered her face with her hands and sobbed. The other two cards Tanya had pulled fell in her lap.

Eduardo picked them up, so they wouldn't slide to the floor. Then he said, "Intuition. The seven of hearts is telling me that you don't trust your own intuition. Your instinct is to run away in fear of everything, but your intuition knows when you need to be brave. This card goes well with the first: You don't give yourself enough credit, dear. Trust yourself. Trust your gut. It will not fail you, as long as you don't blind yourself to its message and allow your flight instinct to take over."

Tanya wiped her eyes and nodded.

Eduardo held up the king of clubs. "The father."

"My father?" Tanya asked with bent brows.

Eduardo shook his head. "It's a symbol. This card is saying that you need to step into the world and own your power. Take ownership of it. Stop holding back. You are creating your own limitations, your own obstacles. Release them, take risks, and jump into your power."

Tanya blinked.

"He's saying we should buy that building," Sue said.

Tanya grinned. "Oh, Sue."

"She's nodding," Eduardo said, looking past Tanya. "Your guardian angel wants you to buy the building."

"But why?" Tanya asked.

"She says her name is Vivian," Eduardo said.

Ellen's mouth dropped open, mirroring the look on her two friends' faces. What were the chances of him getting that right? Unless? He must not be a fake, Ellen decided.

"They need your help," Eduardo said. "Who needs their help, Vivian? She's shaking her head. I can't get a clear answer."

"Please come to the building," Ellen said, her heart racing. "We're thinking of buying it, but our train leaves from Oklahoma City on Friday morning."

"I'm tied up all week," he said.

"It's not far," Sue said. "Would you be willing to go tonight?"

CHAPTER EIGHT

Fire

As Ellen pulled up to the curb in front of the abandoned building, she wanted to pinch herself. She couldn't believe Eduardo had agreed to come—and he wasn't even charging them anything. He had said he was curious, after seeing how urgently Vivian had insisted he come.

Ellen studied him beside her in the passenger seat. Then she glanced in the rearview mirror at the reflections of Tanya and Sue.

"Are we really going to do this?" she asked them.

"Is Vivian still with us?" Sue asked.

"Not in the car," Eduardo replied. "But she's close, I think."

"She wouldn't lead us into danger," Tanya said. "My gut is saying we'll be okay."

"Well, far be it for us to argue with your gut," Sue said. "But I'll take my gun, just in case."

The moon was a waning crescent, barely visible among the stars in the otherwise clear night, as they each used the light from their phones to climb through the hole in the fence and trod toward the east side of the building. The music from Cain's Ballroom echoed down the paved streets where cars were parked along the curb and in the adjacent lot. There were no signs of people other than the music and the cars.

Ellen led the way, her heart pounding hard. Eduardo was close behind her. She was trying not to think, trying to ignore the warnings in her mind, along with the doubt that she had a gift of any kind. What had she been thinking when she'd decided to study the paranormal, to help heal the ghosts that haunted houses? What kind of person with as little knowledge as she jumps into something like this, feet first?

When she rounded the corner, she held her breath as she shined her light on the east entrance to the building. The doors that had been open were now shut.

Ellen glanced back at her friends.

"See if they're locked," Sue urged her.

Sue's hand disappeared inside her large purse, and Ellen didn't need to see it to know that Sue was holding her gun.

Ellen turned the knob and pulled the door open.

She and Eduardo shined their lights all around the hobo camp and found no signs of people. Ellen swallowed hard and stepped inside. Eduardo and her friends followed.

When she came to the hallway, Ellen pushed open the doors to each of the bathrooms and shined her light to be sure no one was hiding inside. With trembling hands, she continued down the hall into the first of the large rooms.

She hadn't stepped in more than a few feet when something rubbed against the back of her leg. She jumped and shined her light all around and saw nothing. Maybe it was her imagination, she thought.

Then Eduardo, who caught up to her, suddenly flinched.

"What's wrong?" Tanya asked from behind him.

"Oh, I sense an incredible amount of negative energy in this space," he whispered. "Anger, hate, bitterness. It's overwhelming. And it's not coming from one person, but many. This building is filled with angry spirits. Oh, I can barely breathe."

"We felt that too," Ellen said, not mentioning the thing she had just felt at the back of her leg. "Though not as fully as you. Can you see anyone? Can you tell why they're so angry?"

"I think we should get out of here," Tanya whispered. "I don't want to be around negative energy. I just can't."

"Do you think we're in danger?" Sue asked Eduardo.

"I don't know," he said. "I've never sensed anything like this before. Ever."

"What if you try to communicate with someone?" Sue suggested.

Tanya looked around, edging back toward the way they had come. "Is Vivian with us?"

"I don't see her. I don't know," Eduardo said, also looking around. "Maybe if we had a candle, we could attract them with a flame."

"I have a lighter in my purse," Sue said. She brought it out. "Should I light it?"

"No!"

The four of them jumped at the sound of someone else in the room with them. The voice had sounded old and female. They moved closer to one another, putting their backs together as they shined their lights all around the room, revealing no one.

Ellen was trembling so badly that she felt faint. Her knees were weak, and she couldn't even feel her feet. Her heart pounded erratically, and it was fast and loud. She wondered if the others could hear it.

Finally, Ellen said, "Who's there?"

No one answered.

"Make a flame," Eduardo said. "See what happens."

Sue lifted her lighter with a trembling hand and flicked up a flame.

A scream came from close by. Ellen dropped her phone. She bent over the floor, feeling around in the garbage at her feet. In the next moment, someone was there with them. The person blew out the flame. Sue's gun went off, and one of the windows above them shattered and fell with a crash across the room. Ellen screamed and fell to the floor.

"Is everyone okay?" Tanya asked, shining her light all around them.

Her phone light fell on a face—small and wrinkled. Tanya jumped back, her phone unsteady in her quivering hand. Then her light went out.

"Who are you?" Eduardo asked, shining his light on the face.

Ellen recovered her phone and began to dial 9-1-1, but her phone died, even though it had just been fully charged. She looked up at the face in the light of Eduardo's phone. It belonged to an old Native American woman. Her skin had been badly scarred from chicken pox. Her hair and eyebrows were white. The terrible body odor coming from the rags she wore meant she was alive and not a ghost.

"Who are you?" Eduardo asked again.

Ellen climbed to her feet, panting with fear.

"Don't light the flame," the woman said in her gravelly, Native American voice. "The spirits don't like it."

"What spirits?" Sue asked.

"The ones who stay here," the woman said.

"Do you know anything about them?" Eduardo asked.

"They do *not* like fire," she said.

"How do you know that?" Ellen asked. "Does something happen when you make a fire?"

The woman nodded. "The spirits scream."

Ellen glanced at her friends. "What else can you tell us about the spirits?"

The woman glared at Ellen. "They do *not* like white people. They will kill you if you stay."

"I think we should leave," Tanya said.

"Why are they here?" Ellen asked the woman. "Why don't they move on?"

"They're trapped," she said. "That's what I think. Now go. You're in danger."

"Come on, guys!" Tanya cried as she headed toward the door.

Ellen glanced at Sue and Eduardo, and then turned to the old woman. Ellen felt something holding here there in the room. It was almost a whisper—*Don't ignore us.* "You live here, don't you? Is that why you want us to leave? The spirits don't really want to kill us, do they? *You* want us to go, not them." Ellen suspected the woman lived in the upstairs bedroom with the dreamcatchers and crucifixes.

"Light your flame and see if I lie," the woman challenged.

Sue glanced at both Ellen and Eduardo. Tanya was standing in the hallway, waiting for them to follow her.

"Try it," Eduardo said.

Sue's hand was shaking so badly that it took her a few tries before she produced a flame. As soon as it appeared, it was extinguished. Sue tried again. Once again, the flame went out.

"It's brand new," Sue said. "I bought it for my eyeliner. I don't know why it won't stay lit."

"It's Vivian," Eduardo said. "I can't see her, but I sense her. I think she's blowing it out."

At that moment, the old woman lifted her bony arm in the air and produced her own flame with her lighter. She held it high above her head. The room began to hiss.

"What is that?" Tanya asked.

"Go!" the old woman said, still holding the flame. "Go before they kill you!"

The hissing grew in volume—like the sound of an approaching train. Tanya cried out for Ellen and Sue to follow her as the room became filled with the moans of agony.

"Now!" the old woman shouted.

Sue and Ellen followed Eduardo to the east wing, where, in the room with the hobo camp, Tanya was pulling on a door that wouldn't open.

"Turn the knob!" Ellen shouted as she moved to try it. "What?" It wouldn't turn.

Eduardo tried, too, pushing against the double doors with his shoulder. They wouldn't budge.

"Let us out!" Sue cried—to whom, Ellen wasn't sure.

A scream came from the large ballroom, followed by "No!"

Eduardo rushed toward the voice, following the small glow of his phone. Ellen followed, too.

Her hands rushed to her cheeks at the sight of flames leaping from the floor where the old woman had been standing. Was the woman on fire?

Eduardo pulled his shirt over his head and bat at the flames.

His shirt caught fire, and he dropped it onto the floor, stomping on it with his shoes. But the fire caught onto more of the garbage and began to spread.

Sue cried out, "Spirits who dwell here! Please help us! Please help us, and we will not ignore you!"

Suddenly a violent wind whipped in through the broken windows. Ellen's hair was blown against her face, and an audible *whoosh* sound floated around her as the wind extinguished the fire. Ellen's mouth fell open with disbelief. The skeptical side of her considered the possibility of a storm causing it. A cold front might have come in. But another side of her was trying to accept the idea that spirits exist and that they impact the world of the living.

The sound of the Indian woman running away toward the west wing brought them all to attention.

"Wait!" Ellen shouted. Then to the others, she asked, "Should we follow her? Maybe she knows a way out."

"Let's go," Eduardo said, grabbing his charred shirt.

Ellen covered her mouth and nose with one hand, trying to block the lingering smoke from the fire, as she followed the small light of Eduardo's phone in front of her. She glanced back at Tanya and Sue just behind her.

When she turned back to follow Eduardo, she tripped on something and stumbled to her knees. She used her hand to get to her feet but felt something hard, smooth, and round beneath her palm.

Sue bent over her with her light. "You okay?"

Ellen cried out, a kind of choked scream. Partially wrapped in an old blanket was what appeared to be the skull and bones of a human child. Ellen's hand had landed on the bones of the arm, splayed out from the blanket, as if reaching out to her for help.

Ellen gasped. "Oh, my God. Look. Someone call the police."

The others crouched around her.

"What is that?" Tanya asked.

"A child," Eduardo said.

"Can you sense him or her?" Sue asked him.

"I sense too many souls in here to single anyone out," he said.

"Call 9-1-1," Ellen said.

"No," Sue said. "We'll get in trouble for trespassing. And they might even think we started the fire and killed whoever that was. Think about it. *I shot my gun.* If we're suspects, they won't let us leave the state."

"It's obvious this child didn't die tonight," Ellen countered.

"Don't call the police," Eduardo agreed.

Tanya paced around them. "Then what do we do? We can't just ignore this."

"We'll call Gayle in the morning," Sue said. "We'll ask to see the building again. We'll call the police tomorrow and pretend we're seeing the bones for the first time."

"But I touched them," Ellen said, her throat tight, her head dizzy. She could hardly breathe. "When I fell. My DNA, my fingerprints."

"Take the ones you touched," Eduardo said. "And let's get out of here."

Sue shined her shaky light on the remains as Ellen found the arm bones where her hand had landed. She shivered as she reached her fingers around them and pulled them from the socket at the shoulder joint. At first, they wouldn't budge. Then Eduardo stepped his boot onto the clavicle, and she pulled again, breaking the small skeleton arm free. Cringing at the sound of the crack of bone, she held it up in the light of

Sue and Eduardo's phones, not sure where to put it and hoping whatever spirit once inhabited the body would forgive her for breaking it.

Sue leaned over with her big open purse. "Stuff it in here and come on."

As Ellen drove Eduardo back to his home, she wondered what in the world she was going to do with the little skeleton arm in Sue's purse. Should they take it on the train back to San Antonio? What if it was discovered in their luggage? She couldn't just dump it somewhere with her fingerprints all over it.

Then a new idea hit her: Maybe she should send it to that online lab that had helped her find Cynthia Piers.

"That was weird that the doors wouldn't open," Eduardo, the first to break the silence since they'd been in the car, said. "I don't understand it."

"Me, either," Sue agreed. "They were unlocked when we went in."

"If the old woman wanted us to leave," Tanya said, "she wouldn't have locked us inside."

"You would think that would be the case," Sue said as Ellen pulled up to the psychic's duplex.

"Maybe the spirits wanted to keep us there," Tanya said.

"And I can't believe my phone died again," Ellen said.

"Mine too," Tanya said. "It's so bizarre."

"Spirits are known to siphon electricity," Eduardo explained. "It gives them the energy they need to communicate with us."

They thanked Eduardo again and again for helping them, saying they might call him the next time they were in town. They begged him not to say a word to anyone about what had happened. He gave them his word and wished them luck as he hurried from the car to his house.

Tanya climbed into the passenger seat. "I think we scared him more than the Indian woman or even the ghosts."

"I'm sorry I shot my gun," Sue said. "I shouldn't have done that."

Ellen turned toward the highway. "I'm glad you had your gun. It may have saved our lives from that crazy woman. You never know."

"Where should we dump these bones?" Sue asked.

"We should bury them," Tanya said. "Near that building, so the spirit can find peace."

"I want to send them to that online lab," Ellen admitted. "We can come back and bury them after the lab returns them to me."

"Why don't you let the police handle it?" Tanya suggested.

Ellen didn't know the answer to that question. She felt compelled to solve the mystery of the abandoned building in the same way she had felt with the Gold House. "Are y'all wanting to forget about this place? Is it too much?"

"Not me," Sue said. "What about you, Tanya? What does your gut tell you?"

"Well, my gut wasn't so accurate last time. Vivian nearly had us killed."

"But we *weren't* killed," Sue said. "We have to be brave if we're going to do this thing."

When Tanya didn't reply, Ellen said, "I don't know. Maybe it *is* too much. Maybe this one is out of our league."

Ellen slept very little in the hotel room that night with the skeleton arm wrapped in the hotel dry-cleaning bag and packed in her suitcase. When she did find sleep, she was plagued with nightmares in which she and a room full of people were being engulfed by flames.

The next day, Sue arranged to meet Gayle for a second viewing at the old, abandoned building across from Cain's Ballroom. Cain's looked different during the day without all the cars and the music. It was dead, adding to the overall creepiness of the abandoned building across from it.

Ellen went directly to the first large room.

The bones and the blanket from the night before had disappeared.

Ellen ran though the skating rink and up the stairs of the western wing, toward the room with the dreamcatchers and the crucifixes.

"Is everything okay?" Gayle asked her from below.

Ellen tried to play it cool. "Yes. Yes, I just want to check something up here..."

"Did you sense a spirit?" Sue helped her out.

"I think so." The room looked the same as it had the previous day, though the blanket on the bed was folded down. Otherwise, there was no sign of the Native American woman or the child's bones she'd left behind.

Ellen returned downstairs, confused as ever.

As they were about to leave the old skating rink to check out the last room (the old bowling alley), Ellen asked Gayle, "Do you know if a fire ever killed a large group of people in this building?"

"There's no record of it that I'm aware of," Gayle replied. "Why?"

"Just curious," Ellen said.

"We're picking up on paranormal activity here," Sue explained. "And we're all having dreams of dying in a fire."

Ellen hadn't shared her dreams with her friends. She bent her brows. Had Sue been having the same dreams as she?

As they reached the bowling alley, Gayle said, "The only fire I've heard of in this area supposedly occurred in 1921, but we don't talk about it much around here."

"What fire?" Tanya asked.

"It supposedly happened during a race riot," Gayle said. "But no one likes to talk about it—not the Whites or the Blacks. Makes people...uncomfortable."

"Can you tell us what you know?" Ellen asked.

"Not much," Gayle said. "My parents don't even believe it ever happened. But you can visit the Greenwood Cultural Center a few blocks that way and find information there. Take it all with a grain of salt, though."

"Were any other buildings affected?" Tanya asked.

Gayle shrugged. "They say around thirty or so square blocks were burned to the ground."

Ellen shuddered. The image from her dreams of being suffocated in the black smoke as hot flames surrounded her took her breath away.

"Are you okay?" Sue asked her.

Ellen nodded. "Would that include the Brady Theater?"

"That building was one of the few that supposedly wasn't affected," Gayle said. "This one, too. The fire was all around them, but these two buildings supposedly weren't touched, along with a few others in the Brady Arts District."

Ellen frowned. If the buildings weren't affected by the fire, then why did they make her feel like she was suffocating?

"They say the Brady Theater was used as a detention center for the black men," Gayle continued.

"Detention center?" Sue echoed. "Why?"

Gayle shrugged again. "I really don't know the whole story. My parents discouraged me from buying into it. They think it was a conspiracy created by the Blacks to get money out of the Whites."

As they stepped from the building into the open air, Ellen was sure she heard something coming from the building. It was low and guttural, like a growl. No one else seemed to hear it.

She pulled her phone from her pocket. Sure enough, the battery was dead.

"So, are you ladies thinking about putting in an offer?" Gayle asked as she locked the doors to the west entrance.

"Thinking about it," Sue said. "We'll be in touch."

<u>CHAPTER NINE</u>

The Greenwood Cultural Center

The original plan was to drive back to Oklahoma City on Wednesday and spend Thursday there before catching the train Friday morning back to San Antonio. Ellen had even hoped to meet her son Nolan for dinner one night while they were there; but, as they drove away from the abandoned building, the ladies decided to stay in Tulsa for as long as possible to do more research. After a quick lunch at a salad and sandwich shop, they headed to the Greenwood Cultural Center to find out what they could about the race riot of 1921, which Gayle had said may or may not have happened.

On the way, Tanya, who'd been fixated on the missing bones all during lunch, finally said, "If the old woman didn't hide the skeleton, then it had to have been a coyote. They couldn't have just disappeared."

"Agreed," Sue said as Ellen pulled into the parking lot.

An old man with a long black face and smiling eyes greeted them in the lobby.

"We were hoping to learn about the riot," Ellen said.

The old man pointed to a wall to their left. "Start there. And if you have any questions, Miss Frances will help you out."

Ellen thanked him and turned in the direction he'd shown her to find an entire wall covered with framed newspaper articles and old photographs. The first showed pictures of what was called Black Wall Street.

According to the article, the Greenwood District was considered the most prominent African American community in America in the early 1900's. Even though it was separated from White Tulsa, it, was, at one time, just as grand with its hotels, theaters, ballrooms, and prosperous businesses and stately homes. Ellen asked Sue to take a photo of it with her phone.

"Oh, my gawd," Sue whispered. "I never knew about all this."

"I wonder why it isn't taught in school," Tanya said.

"The worst race riot in American history?" Ellen read. "Over twelve hundred homes destroyed by fire? Thirty-six square blocks of the black district, including churches, stores, hotels, businesses, two newspapers, a school, a hospital, and a library—all burned to the ground.'"

They continued to read in silence for many minutes, until Ellen said, "All because a black teenager named Dick Rowland needed to use the bathroom? It says he had to go to the Drexler Building because of segregation. It was the only bathroom for Blacks in the area where he worked as a shoe shiner."

"It says he may have assaulted an elevator girl," Sue pointed out. "Someone heard her shout."

"But it also speculates that they must have known one another and may have been secretly involved," Tanya said. "Maybe they were having a lover's quarrel."

"The girl never pressed charges," Ellen said. "But that doesn't mean he didn't try to hurt her."

Tanya moved down the wall to the next article. "Even so, this newspaper article printed on May 31st, 1921 used the headline 'Nab a Negro.' The boy was already in police custody by the time it was written. That doesn't make any sense."

"They wanted to lynch him," Ellen said. "They didn't believe in mixing the races, so even if he was innocent…"

"This is making my stomach hurt," Tanya, whose husband, Dave, was Hispanic, said. "Look here. It says over 1500 Whites crowded around the courthouse, where the boy was held prisoner. You think they wanted to take matters into their own hands?"

"He was only nineteen," Ellen muttered. "Alison is only a year older than that."

"This article is saying that a truckload of black war veterans arrived with guns," Sue said. "That probably scared the Whites, don't you think?"

Ellen nodded. "I suppose. But it says they were offering the sheriff help in protecting the prisoner from the mob. They were worried their boy was going to be lynched."

"The sheriff turned the black men away—twice," Sue said. "So, what started the riot?"

"Over here," Tanya said, pointing to another article. "It says a white man asked a black man what he was going to do with his gun, and the Black said he would use it if necessary. Then the White tried to disarm him, and the gun went off. Then all hell broke loose."

"There was so much fear and tension between the races," Ellen said. "They didn't trust one another."

"That's still true in some places," Tanya said.

"But how did the *fire* start?" Sue asked. "How did gunshots translate into thirty-six square blocks getting burned to the ground?"

Tanya beckoned them to another article on the wall. "It says here that the Whites feared a Negro uprising, so they used fire to put black people in their place. How awful."

"They had to call in the National Guard," Sue said from where she stood further away, reading another article. "The guards led dozens of black men to two detention centers—the convention hall and the fair grounds. The convention hall is now called the Brady Theater."

"Seriously? What about *our* building?" Ellen asked.

"No mention of it yet," Sue said. "But get this: the black men were told it was for their protection, yet they were disarmed and detained like prisoners while their homes burned to the ground."

Ellen felt tears prick her eyes. How could people be so cruel to one another?

"This has got to be it," Tanya said pointing to the same article. "This is what Vivian meant when she told us to help Tulsa."

"What do you mean?" Sue asked.

"It says here that while the official death count was 36, the Red Cross and other experts estimate that at least 300 black people were killed in the shooting and fires, and most of those bodies were buried in unmarked mass graves."

"Where?" Ellen asked.

"That's just it," Tanya said. "No one knows."

Ellen looked at the date on the article. "1996. You would think that since then, the city would have made some effort to locate them."

"Why don't we ask Miss Frances?" Sue suggested.

Miss Frances turned out to be the office manager, and, upon hearing the ladies' interest in the riot, she pointed them to the office of their Director of Program Development.

A young black woman with stunning golden eyes welcomed them into her tidy office with its sunny windows and view of the pond out front. She stood leaning against the front of her desk in a chic red leather blazer and black fitted skirt and, after introducing herself as Michelle, invited them to have a seat.

"What can I do for you ladies?" she asked.

"We just finished looking over the photos and articles about Black Wall Street and the 1921 Race Riot," Sue began. "But we're still not clear on how the story ends. Were mass graves ever found? Was anything ever done for the victims?"

"Unfortunately, no mass graves were ever found," the director said. "There were efforts made to find them, but nothing ever came of them. And, as far as the victims, well they've all passed, but some of them lived to see the Black Wall Street Memorial that was erected in 1996.

There were also discussions of reparations, but, as with the graves, nothing ever came of those efforts, either."

Ellen shook her head. "We can't believe we've never heard of this."

"I can," Michelle said. "The atrocities were kept under wraps for decades. Black people didn't want their children to know about them, because they didn't want them growing up believing they were inferior to white people, and they also didn't want to instill anger and hatred in them. And white people didn't talk about it either. Many of them felt Blacks had it coming to them, and once it was done, and the Blacks were put in their place, there was nothing left to say about it."

"This is making me feel nauseated," Tanya said. "I think I'm going to be sick."

"Can I get you some water?" the young woman offered.

"No, thank you," Tanya said.

Ellen raised her chin. "Is there any way we can learn more about the past searches for the mass graves?"

"I can recommend a book that covers that information." The director took a pen and scribbled the title and author on a post-it note. As she handed it over to Ellen she asked, "Do you mind if I ask about the reason for your interest in this matter?"

The three friends exchanged looks that showed that none was sure how to reply.

Finally, Sue said, "We're thinking about buying an abandoned building near Cain's Ballroom on the outskirts of the Brady Arts District, to convert into apartments, but we had a paranormal experience there that we think might be related to the victims of the riot."

The young woman frowned. "I see. Are you ladies from around here? Have relatives in Tulsa?"

"We live in San Antonio," Ellen said.

"My daughter was married this past weekend to a boy from here," Sue said. "I guess that means I do have relatives here now."

The director nodded. "I see. Let me just warn you ladies about talking to too many people about the mass graves. Most Tulsans have put that idea behind them. We're moving forward, onward, looking to the future. Looking for the dead will only cause more conflict in a town that is still healing after all these years."

"But wouldn't the recovery of the dead bring peace, not only to the dead, but to their families?" Ellen asked.

"Yes, it would," the young woman said. "It would be a miracle. But I'm fairly certain that any efforts you made toward that endeavor would be put to rest by those with influence in this city. Don't quote me on this, but there are powerful forces in Tulsa who'll make sure that the only digging going on in these parts is that done with an oil rig."

THE CASE OF THE ABANDONED WAREHOUSE | 65

CHAPTER TEN

The Other Psychic of Tulsa

On their way to the hotel from the Greenwood Cultural Center, Sue received a call from Gayle's psychic. The three friends made plans to meet with Miss Margaret Myrtle an hour before dinner.

Miss Myrtle lived in the poorest part of the Greenwood District, two blocks away from Eduardo Mankiller; but, in the light of day, the neighborhood wasn't nearly as daunting. Ellen pulled up to a shabby but quaint bungalow with a pretty little garden bordering its dilapidated front porch.

The three ladies climbed out of the rental car and met Miss Myrtle at the torn screen door.

"Come on in, friends," she said, holding open her screen door. "Come into my parlor and have a seat, why don't you?"

Ellen followed Sue and Tanya into the small, cozy front room, where they all squeezed together on the one white sofa. Miss Myrtle, a black woman in her late seventies with a short afro and a colorful scarf, reminded Ellen of her late grandmother. The woman was sharply dressed, her face made up, and even her nails were polished.

"Are you all comfortable sitting together like that? I can go get another chair."

"We're fine," Tanya, who was the one most squeezed in the middle, said.

Miss Myrtle turned to Sue. "You wear that weight nicely. Those are the prettiest chubby cheeks I ever did see. It's a good thing most of your weight goes to your hips. That's what the men prefer." Then she pointed to Ellen. "You, on the other hand, are all chin. You probably wish you could give some of that over to this one here, don't you?" She pointed to Tanya. "You a skinny thing, aren't you? You might want to get out more often."

Ellen tried not to show any offense to Miss Myrtle's direct way of speaking as she forced a smile and said, "Thank you for meeting with us."

"It's always a pleasure to make a little bit of money doing something good for other folks. Do any of you have a particular question you want to ask, or are you interested in receiving a general reading from me?"

"We have particular questions," Sue said.

Miss Myrtle took the seat across from them. "Alrighty, then. Ask away."

Sue gave Ellen a nod. Ellen hadn't realized she was the one expected to speak, but she swallowed, cleared her throat, and began.

"We're thinking about making a major purchase together."

Before Ellen could continue, Miss Myrtle nodded and said, "I sense a very strong energy around you ladies. You feel called to a higher purpose. It is better to die for a cause you believe in than to live comfortably but passively. You ladies are entering a phase of your life where you are being called to be warriors for something. So why do you want to make this purchase? What is calling you to it?"

"Ghosts," Sue said.

Miss Myrtle's eyes widened. "You have the gift?"

"Yes," Sue said. "All three of us sensed and heard something while we were there. The purchase we want to make is of a building here in Tulsa."

"We're having dreams of being suffocated by fire," Tanya added. "And we think my mother's cousin Vivian, who has passed away, is trying to tell us something about that building."

"Oh, you do, do you? What makes you think that? Has she made contact with you?"

They all three nodded.

"How glorious," she said. "I do love it when they speak to us from the other side. Would you like to try to make contact with her again today? I can help with that."

"Sure," Ellen said.

The woman opened a drawer to an old wooden table near her chair and pulled out a candelabra holding three small candles. As she struck a match and lighted them, she asked, "Where exactly is this building?"

"Over by Cain's Ballroom in the Brady Arts District," Ellen said.

Miss Myrtle looked up at her sharply. "Why all you white folks want to buy up old Greenwood?"

Ellen was taken aback, not sure what to say.

Sue said, "Miss Myrtle, that building has been sitting there abandoned for decades. It's not like we're cheating any black buyers out of a deal. No one else wants it."

Miss Myrtle sucked in her lips as she continued to light the candles.

Then Tanya asked, "Do you know anything about unmarked mass graves that may have resulted from the 1921 race riot?"

"No, I don't. Why?"

Tanya clasped her hands together. "We think there might be a connection between that building and the ghosts of some of the riot victims."

"We could be way off," Ellen interrupted when she saw Miss Myrtle frown. "The spirits we sensed could be American Indians who were burned in a fire way before the riot ever happened. We don't know."

"Vivian seems to be urging us forward," Sue said. "And we were hoping you could tell us why."

"I don't want to be a part of anything pertaining to the riot," Miss Myrtle said. "How 'bout I read your cards or your palms instead?"

Ellen blanched. "Why not? If you don't mind my asking."

"I *do* mind." Miss Myrtle blew out the candles she had only just lit.

"Fine," Sue said, holding out her palm. "Tell me what you see."

Miss Myrtle took Sue's hand in hers and leaned over it. "We'll, I'll be."

She reached out for Tanya's and inspected it as well.

"Show me yours, too," she said to Ellen.

Ellen sat on the edge of the sofa, stretched out her arm, and held up her palm.

"Well, aren't you some lucky ladies. You three are about to come into some big money. I hope you'll remember me when you do!"

Ellen hid her disappointment as she reached into her purse and brought out a twenty-dollar bill. Tanya and Sue did the same—the fee they'd agreed on over the phone.

"Thanks for your time," Sue said as she climbed to her feet.

"Let me show you out," Miss Myrtle held open her screen door, and the three friends left.

As they climbed into the car, Tanya muttered, "What a rip-off."

"Let's go try that barbecue place we saw on the way over," Sue said. "That should cheer us up."

While they ate, Tanya had the idea of contacting Carrie French, their haunted pub crawl guide. "Maybe she can help us."

Sue used her phone to find Carrie's website and phone number. Ellen called but was taken to voicemail, so she left a message.

Discouraged, she finished her last bite and said, "Now what?" But her friends only shrugged. They were out of ideas, too.

On the way back to the hotel, Ellen stopped at a UPS Store for a shipping box. Then she returned to the hotel and began the disturbing process of packing the little skeleton arm with a letter to the online lab.

They had already changed trains in Fort Worth and were halfway to San Antonio, when Ellen, who'd been reading the book the Director of Programming at the Greenwood Cultural Center had recommended, arrived at the place that discussed the search for unmarked mass graves. The book, *Riot and Remembrance: America's Worst Race Riot and Its Legacy*, by James S. Hirsch, told how a black journalist and politician named Don Ross was outraged when the 1995 bombing of Oklahoma City received worldwide attention as the worst urban tragedy in America, while the riot of 1921 seemed to have all but disappeared from human memory. He had already made it his personal mission to fight for old Greenwood, and after the Oklahoma City bombing, he spearheaded the passing of a bill that created the Tulsa Race Riot Commission. Eleven members were appointed to identify survivors, establish an official account of what had happened, and make recommendations for reparations.

A white historian named Scott Ellsworth, who'd already published a book about the riot, was hired by the commission to help. Ellsworth convinced the commission, the historical society, and independent scholars to help him search for bodies, insisting that they could reveal information about the victims' identities and how they were killed, which would provide a clearer picture of what happened. Additionally, the exhumed bodies could be given the proper burial they deserved.

"Listen to this," she told Tanya, who sat beside her, and Sue, who sat across the aisle from her facing the same direction, toward the front of the train. "Ellsworth got the director of the Oklahoma Archaeological Survey at the University of Oklahoma to lead a team through Newblock Park, Rolling Oaks Memorial Park, and Oaklawn Cemetery with ground-penetrating radar to look for the graves. They even dug with loud hydraulic machines and manually operated rods, but never found the bodies. Eventually, the commission reversed its decision to continue the search."

"That's too bad," Sue said. "Sounds like they could have looked around a bit more before giving up."

"How do we know the spirits in that building have anything to do with the missing bodies?" Tanya asked. "What if they're unrelated?"

"We have to go back," Sue said. "We have to go back and have a séance."

Ellen sat up and leaned forward, "I agree, but this time, we need to be better prepared. I've been doing some research about paranormal investigations. I even ordered a ghost hunting starter kit, but it hasn't come in yet."

"Seriously?" Sue laughed.

"I'm very serious," Ellen said. "And I found a team of investigators in San Antonio. I think we should contact them and ask if we can observe how they operate."

"I'm up for that," Tanya said.

"Sue?" Ellen raised her eyebrows.

"Count me in."

"Great. As soon as we get wi-fi again, I'll email the team."

CHAPTER ELEVEN

The San Antonio Ghost Busters

W here are you going?" Paul asked when he entered the master bathroom, where Ellen was getting dressed.

"Sue and Tanya and I are going to observe a paranormal investigation tonight. Doesn't that sound interesting?"

"You haven't even been home one day, and you're already leaving again," Paul complained.

Ellen was caught off guard by his remark. They rarely made plans together anymore, and he always seemed content sitting in his recliner watching the history channel, or the gold digger show, or the Alaskan crabbing show. "Was there something else you wanted to do?"

Paul shrugged and left the room.

After she finished dressing, she went into the den, where he'd made himself comfortable in his chair.

"I'm planning on eating with the girls, but I could whip something up for you real quick if you're tired of doing your own cooking."

"I'll find something," he said. "You go on."

She hesitated, wishing she could read his mind. He used to tell her that she needed to be more independent, back in the days when she used to complain about all the golfing and fishing and hunting he did. Now that she was being more independent, he still seemed unhappy with her.

"Okay, then," she finally said. "I'll see you later."

She went to the front room, to her own chair, with her new ghost hunting kit, and waited for Sue, who arrived within a few minutes. Together they picked up Tanya and headed to the new Mexican food restaurant Sue wanted to try, and, from there, to the east side of town to meet the paranormal team at a local residence.

"That margarita was a disappointment," Sue said from behind the wheel.

"Are you sure you're okay to drive?" Tanya asked from the backseat.

"One margarita doesn't affect me like it does you, skinny bones," Sue assured her.

"Oh, hush," Tanya said. "I've actually put on weight since my mother passed. I can barely fit into these pants anymore."

Sue and Ellen exchanged eye rolling.

"You poor thing," Ellen said. "It must be so hard being you."

When they were only a few minutes away from their destination, Sue said, "This neighborhood is as shady as Greenwood."

"This was my grandmother's neighborhood." Ellen's grandmother had passed eleven years before at the ripe old age of ninety-two. "It brings back so many memories."

"Well, your grandmother lived in a shady neighborhood," Sue repeated with a laugh.

"It's just old and run down," Ellen said.

"Isn't that the definition of shady?" Sue challenged as she followed the directions on the GPS.

"Just because it's poor doesn't mean it's shady," Ellen said.

They pulled up to a worn down, one-story cottage in dire need of new siding. It sat on a corner lot with a huge oak tree infringing upon the short, narrow driveway leading to what was once the garage but was now part of the house. A corner lot, it sloped precariously toward the side street where a thorny bush and a hill of weeds met the curb. The windows of the house were barred, as was the front door.

Sue parked behind the red van already sitting beside the curb. "We're here," she said in a tone that sounded unsure that they should be.

"Should I take in my ghost hunting kit?" Ellen said. "Or do you think they'd be offended?"

"I'd leave it in the car," Tanya said. "Maybe you can use it next time."

They stepped from Sue's SUV and climbed the short hill to the front door, navigating over the massive roots of the oak tree that took up most of the front lawn. When they reached the front door, Ellen took a deep breath and knocked.

"Yeah?" a man asked suspiciously at the door. He was young—probably mid-twenties—and Hispanic with a thin mustache and very short hair. He wore an open plaid shirt over a white muscle shirt and a pair of very baggy jeans. A tattoo stretched up from his neckline to the right side of his face.

"We're here for the paranormal investigation," Ellen said.

The man frowned. "Ah man, Philip! You didn't tell me no one was comin'!"

Ellen's mouth dropped open and blood rushed to her cheeks. "I'm sorry. Is this a bad time?"

Another man, about the same age, but white with blond hair and a five o'clock shadow, came to the door abruptly and said, "Not at all. Don't mind Ernest. He didn't mean to sound so rude. Come inside, please. I'm Philip."

After introducing themselves, Ellen followed Sue and Tanya into the small living room. Not only was it small, but it was filled with every knickknack imaginable. Shadowboxes full of figurines covered the walls, and three bookcases with a handful of books and at least a dozen dolls, teacups, Christmas globes (even though Christmas was still three months away), and crocheted figures crammed every square inch of the scratched oak veneer finish.

The sofa on the left side of the room was covered with boxes, and the table, at the back of the room, held an array of equipment. On the one armchair sat a young woman, also in her late twenties, with her brown hair pulled back in a ponytail and a little boy, maybe six years of age, held protectively on her lap. She had tears in her eyes, as she bounced her boy on a shaky thigh.

"Amanda, I hope you don't mind if a few interested observers join us tonight," Philip said to the woman.

Another young woman stood with a camcorder on her shoulder, her blonde curly hair pulled back with a headband. "This probably wasn't the right job for them to come on."

Ellen frowned again, getting the impression that Philip was the only one among them that wanted them there. "Should we leave?"

The woman with camera said, "Just stay close to us. Don't wander off. And be prepared to leave if things get bad."

Philip clasped his hands together and said, "We said we wanted more exposure in the community, Brenda. Well, this is an opportunity for that, okay?" Then to Ellen and her friends, he said, "Just stand there, and I'll answer your questions when we've finished. We were in the process of interviewing the client just before you arrived."

Ellen nodded and stood by the crowded front window beside the woman with the camcorder. Sue and Tanya squeezed beside her.

Philip picked up a laptop from the table in back and sat it on a rickety kitchen chair beside Amanda and her son, pointing what Ellen recognized as an Xbox Kinect device in the mother's direction. Ellen noticed a colorful screen with skeleton-like lines on the images of Amanda and her son. Ernest hovered near him with another device in his hand.

"Can you show us the marks?" Brenda asked Amanda.

Amanda lifted her son's Spiderman t-shirt to reveal dark bruising around his ribs.

Ellen covered her mouth.

"And you think this happened at night in his room while he was sleeping?" Brenda asked from behind the camera.

Amanda nodded. "More than once."

"And you and your son are the only living humans in the house?" Brenda asked.

"That's right," Amanda said.

"Has the boy ever come home from school with new marks on him?" Brenda asked.

Amanda shook her head.

"And do you often receive visitors? Or does the boy ever stay with friends or relatives?" Brenda asked.

"I don't got time for visitors. He sees his father every other weekend, but John would never harm his own son," Amanda insisted.

"What makes you suspect there's a demon in Timmy's room, other than the markings?" Brenda asked.

"At night, I hear footsteps," she said. "And when I go in and check, Timmy is sound asleep."

"How often does this occur?" Philip asked.

"At least twice a week, sometimes more often," Amanda said. "And Timmy sees something." She kissed the top of the little boy's head. "Tell them what you see, Timmy."

He shook his head and pressed his face against his mother's neck.

"He told me it's a dark shadow standing at the foot of his bed," Amanda said. "He says it comes from his closet."

Brenda turned to Philip. "Are you getting anything?"

"Nothing yet," he said, looking at the laptop screen. "It's just the two of them."

"I think we need to go to Timmy's bedroom. For now, you and Timmy stay here," she said to Amanda.

"What about us?" Sue asked.

Ernest rolled his eyes, but Philip said, "They can stand in the hallway and look on, can't they?"

Brenda nodded. "Follow me but stay back."

Philip led the way, carrying his laptop, with Ernest behind him. Brenda took up the rear of her team, and then Ellen and her friends made their way behind her through the cluttered room to the hallway. They passed a tiny kitchen at the back of the house that smelled strongly of onion and garlic. The first room on the right was Timmy's. Through the doorway from where she stood behind Sue, Ellen could see toys on the floor and the twin bed that was pushed against the corner of the room. Dusty blinds covered the front window, which had a dresser in front of it, covered with more knickknacks. A closet opened to the left wall, but Ellen couldn't see inside of it, as Ernest stood in front of it with his device.

"She said Timmy sees it come from the closet," Brenda said, pointing her camera in that direction. "I'm going to begin. Ready Philip?"

Philip had his laptop on his lap where he sat on the edge of Timmy's bed, pointing the Xbox Kinect device at the closet. Ernest stood with his back against the wall near the closet door. He had a handheld device that was currently blinking.

"Ready," Philip said.

Ernest nodded. He turned off the bedroom light. The only light remaining in the room was a kind of black light coming from Brenda's camera, turning everything an eerie pale purple.

"If there's a demon in this room," Brenda said. "This is your chance to prove it. Show yourself to us now."

Ellen was surprised with the brazen way the young woman was challenging a supposed demon, but she watched on. Unlike the feelings of suffocation that she had felt in the abandoned building in Tulsa, she sensed nothing in this house.

"Why are you hurting Timmy?" Brenda asked. "Speak to us. Tell us what you want. Prove to us that you exist."

Ernest put his hand to his head and bowed forward.

"Are you alright, man?" Philip asked him.

"That was frickin weird, man," he whispered. "My hand feels like ice, and I feel sick as a dog. Are you getting anything?"

"No, not yet," Philip said. "Play back the recorder, and let's have a listen."

"I'm feeling sick, too," Brenda said. "Something evil is definitely in here with us."

Ellen glanced at her friends with a questioning look, but they shook their heads and shrugged. None of them were feeling it.

Ernest pushed a button on his device, which played back Brenda's speech. In between her speeches were some unintelligible moments of static, which seemed to make both Philip and Ernest very excited.

"Whoa, man!" Ernest said. "Did you hear that? Let me play it back."

"Is that laughter?" Philip asked. "The demon's frickin' laughing at us."

To Ellen, it sounded like empty static.

"I'm feeling sick," Brenda said. "I'm not sure how much longer I can take this. Are you picking up on anything, Philip?"

"Not on the screen, but I definitely feel it, too. Cut the black light for a minute."

Timmy's room became bathed in darkness.

Then more loudly Philip said, "If you're here, demon, show us a sign. Touch me. Grab me. Do anything you want. Prove to me that you're here."

Ernest flinched and said, "What the hell was that?"

Brenda asked, "What? Are you okay?"

"Something hit me, right here on my back. Lift my shirt. Can you see anything?"

Philip turned on the bedroom light and lifted Ernest's shirt. "I see something. It's very light, but something got you. Let me take a shot of that with my phone."

Ellen squinted but could see nothing on Ernest's back.

"You ladies stay back," Brenda warned. "There's something evil in here. We need to expunge it."

Brenda pulled something out of the front pocket of her blue jeans and handed it to Philip. "Use the holy water."

Philip sprinkled some of the water from the plastic bottle into the closet and around the room, especially over the bed. As he did so, he said, "We rebuke you in the name of Jesus Christ. Be gone, evil demon!"

Then he turned off the bedroom light and returned to the bed to his laptop.

"Anything?" Brenda asked him.

"No, but I can definitely feel a difference. Can you?" he asked her.

"It's much less oppressive, that's for sure," Brenda agreed. She turned on her black light, bringing the pale purple back into the room.

"What do you think, Ernest?" Philip asked. "Do you think it's gone?"

"Man, what a change. I feel like I could run around the block ten times. I would say that's a success! I can't wait to look over the video and see if Brenda caught any anomalies."

"I'm sure I did," Brenda said. "That presence was overwhelming. It must have left behind something for us."

When it was all over and Ellen and her friends were climbing back into Sue's SUV, Ellen felt disappointed. "Either I don't have the gift like I thought, or those people were delusional."

"I think it's the latter," Sue said. "And we need to call Child Protective Services for that poor boy."

"I agree about CPS," Tanya said.

"Do you think we're imagining things, Tanya?" Ellen asked.

"No, way. Don't compare us to them."

"But how do we know we're any different?" Ellen said, staring at her ghost hunting kit with disdain. "What if everything we've experienced has all been a shared delusion?"

CHAPTER TWELVE

Back to Tulsa

A week after Ellen had returned to San Antonio from Tulsa, she received an email from Carrie French, in reply to Ellen's query about a paranormal investigation at the abandoned building next to Cain's Ballroom. Carrie wrote:

Hi Ellen,

I am very interested in investigating the old circus grounds. I will first have to see if I can get permission from the city. It would be easier to get permission if you put in an offer to buy the property. Although this would require some earnest money, you would still have time to pull out of the sale until three days after closing. Please let me know if you want to go this route. Otherwise, it may take months to get permission.

If you do decide to put in an offer, we should schedule the investigation around the next new moon, which is Sunday, October 30th. Our readings tend to be more reliable as we move closer to the new moon, as an abundance of moonlight can create false images easily mistaken as orbs or spiritual manifestations not truly present.

This would also give me time to conduct research on the property. I know it was once a circus, but I'd like to find out its complete history. I will also have a geological survey done on the grounds to see if there are any anomalies and contact the EPA to see if any known neurotoxins or other contaminants have ever been reported in the area. And I can make note of the proximity of power lines, etc., to the building. I like to create a map on graph paper of all the known variables we can find before we begin the investigation on the property.

In addition to this research, I will need to interview you and your friends separately about what you experienced while you were in the building that provoked you to want an investigation. Please do not discuss your experiences with each other (it's okay if you already have but try not to any further from here on out). But please do write down—each of you separately—as much as you can recall so that when I interview you, you can use those notes to refresh your memories.

Please let me know as soon as possible if you decide to move forward with an offer on the property. If you decide not to do so, I'll do my best to pull whatever strings I have in this city.

Yours Truly,

Carrie French

Ellen forwarded the email to Sue and Tanya and then called Sue. When she didn't answer, she called Tanya and told her to read the email.

"What do you think?" Ellen asked her. "Should we put in an offer?"

"I suppose we could offer five thousand, like the realtor suggested," Tanya said. "Between the three of us, that's not a lot of money, anyway."

Ellen's heart began to pump faster. She'd been feeling down over the past week, especially after the experience they'd had with the San Antonio Ghost Busters. She'd even been questioning all that had happened at the Gold House, wondering if there was ever real proof that Marcia's ghost had haunted it.

Don't ignore us.

Couldn't that have been the wind? she'd thought. Or that old Native American woman playing games with them?

And even though she'd continue to have the suffocating nightmares of being engulfed by flames, she'd attributed that to the book she'd been reading about the riot and her preoccupation with the devastation that occurred in its wake.

But this email sparked a new feeling in Ellen: a renewed hope. Carrie's interest and the thorough preparation she was willing to undergo made Ellen consider that maybe she hadn't imagined all that had happened in Tulsa. The butterflies hatching all at once after Tanya had asked for a sign, Eduardo Mankiller identifying Vivian by name, and the sudden extinguishing of the fire after Sue called out to the spirits for help—that couldn't have been without significance.

Sue phoned while Ellen was still talking to Tanya, so she put Tanya on hold to answer the call.

"I just read your email," Sue said. "Let's do it!"

Paul wasn't thrilled to learn that Ellen would be returning to Tulsa at the end of the month, so she did her best over the next few weeks to cook meals he loved, to keep the house in pristine condition, and to watch some of his shows with him in the den. She didn't hate *Storage Wars* or *Shark Tank*, but she didn't love them either. She'd rather be in her comfy chair in the front room reading a book or out in her backyard studio painting. She spent this time with him so he would be less resistant about her trip.

One night, after *Storage Wars*, Paul got up, said he was hitting the sack, and asked if she was going to stay up late.

It was the most direct he ever got at asking for intimacy. It was awkward for Ellen, since she usually went straight to her son's old room.

"I think I'll hit the sack, too," she said, turning off the TV.

She followed him into their master bedroom, where she changed into her nightgown, since she'd never completely moved out of the room. The whole time she wondered how to transition into the bed with him. Should she just be direct?

"Want to exchange backrubs?" she finally asked.

"Sounds good to me," he said.

They were talking in code. Why should two people who'd been married for over thirty years need to take such measures to be with one another?

She climbed into her old spot—her side of the bed, realizing she'd missed the plush mattress top that her son's bed lacked. She pulled the thick comforter over her and scooted against her husband's side. The warmth of his body radiated onto her, calming her. He lay on his back, skipping the pretense of a back rub, so she stroked his chest and sighed.

It felt good to be in his arms. Why was it so difficult for her to get there? And why was it such a rare event?

She recalled what Eduardo Mankiller had said while reading her cards: *she* was the thing getting in the way of her relationship. It was *her* fault.

"This feels nice," Paul said.

"Yes, it does."

"I wish you weren't leaving next weekend," he said.

She was at first moved, until he added, "It's a lot of expense, traveling back and forth. And I would have liked to see the building before you went and bought it."

"I didn't buy it yet. We don't close until the second week of November."

"You know what I mean. And you said yourself that it's believed to have asbestos. It's going to be nothing but a money pit."

What possessed him to bring this all up now, while on the brink of intimacy, was beyond Ellen's comprehension. The romantic mood she'd been in when she'd first crawled in beside him vanished.

"I'm sorry you feel that way," she said. "I'm not dipping into our savings, though, I promise. I'm using interest I've made on the gold money."

"Isn't that ours, too? Or do you consider that money your own to do with as you please?"

Ellen sat up. "You didn't seem this strongly against the idea when I first told you about it."

"What was the point? You and your friends had already made the decision."

"Then why bring it up now?"

"So maybe next time, you'll include me in these kinds of decisions, so you know I'm not happy with how you went about this."

"Okay. Got it. I'm truly sorry I didn't discuss this with you, but I was planning to before making the decision to buy. We just wanted to get an offer in so we could conduct the research. We still haven't decided whether we're going to move forward." She was beginning to feel angry that he'd brought this up just when she thought they were going to be together. She'd forgotten how much she'd missed being close to him. "And, you know what? It's exactly $1670. That's almost as much as you spend on hunting and fishing trips in a year, wouldn't you say?"

"What about the asbestos removal? A hundred grand?"

She climbed from the bed.

"Where are you going?" he asked.

"To bed. Good night."

CHAPTER THIRTEEN

A Paranormal Investigation

T he train ride to Oklahoma City seemed longer to Ellen the second time, but she kept herself busy reading an ebook about paranormal investigations. She was rewarded in Oklahoma City, where the stars aligned, and Nolan was free to meet them for dinner. Seeing her son renewed her strength and energy, giving her the boost she needed to face the ghosts in Tulsa.

Sue offered to drive the rental car from Oklahoma City to Tulsa to the little inn on Main Street, only two blocks down from the abandoned building. Tanya and Ellen had talked Sue into staying with them in a two-room studio, where Ellen and Tanya would share a king bed in one room, and Sue would sleep on the sofa sleeper in another. There was a door between them to block out Sue's snoring, which was important to her because she was self-conscious about it. Plus, she had said she didn't want to know about any possible lesbian activities going on in the other room.

"You're a hoot," Tanya had said in reply.

They planned to stay for a week, and the little studio room was cheap. Sue had considered staying with Lexi and Stephen but had said their one-bedroom apartment wasn't much bigger than the hotel room. Sue also thought it might be too soon after the wedding for Stephen to have his mother-in-law as an overnight guest for a week.

Tanya and Ellen also convinced Sue to walk, rather than drive, the two blocks down Main Street Sunday night to meet Carrie French and her team for the investigation.

It was already dark as they made their way down the street on foot. Ellen was once again surprised by how many people and cars were in the area at bars, restaurants, and art galleries. The lights around Cain's Ballroom, where country music could be heard pouring from its doors, lit up the end of the block. But even the light from Cain's and from the lampposts along the sidewalk couldn't compete with the twinkling stars overhead. Without the light of the moon reflecting the sun across the sky, more than the brightest could be seen overhead.

Tanya pulled her jacket tightly around her. "It's getting cold out here."

"You just don't have enough insulation," Sue teased. "This is nothing."

When they reached the building, Carrie and her team were already there, waiting outside the gate. Ellen unlocked the double-wide gate with the key she'd borrowed from Gayle and pulled it open so Carrie could pull the van closer to the building to unload their equipment.

Ellen was shocked to discover that both Eduardo Mankiller and Miss Margaret Myrtle were members of Carrie's team. There was a fourth member as well—a young man in his early twenties. Carrie introduced him as her son, Justin.

After the introductions and after all the equipment had been unloaded, Carrie turned to her team. "Eduardo, I need you to record the temperature and EMF readings in each room downstairs, including the bathrooms. Make note of any odors you notice as well. Okay?"

"How fun," Eduardo said, already using a handheld device and notebook in the hobo room.

"Justin," Carrie said to her son. "Will you please set up the passive infrared motion detectors?"

"Which rooms?" Justin asked.

"This one, the two big rooms, and the bowling alley." Then Carrie added, "Then set up the full-spec cameras from three angles in the two larger rooms for now."

"Got it," Justin said.

"What about me?" Miss Myrtle asked.

"Justin already set up a card table and chairs in the first big room, Margaret. Why don't you use that area to create some initial sketches as a baseline, and we'll go from there?"

"Sure thing, sweetie," Miss Myrtle said.

"I thought you didn't want to be involved in anything that might be related to the riot?" Ellen asked her.

"Who says this place has anything to with that?" Miss Myrtle asked. "Besides, my team can count on me, no matter what."

Ellen's confidence in Carrie French was severely diminished, but she couldn't very well call off the investigation. She may as well see how it all turned out. She'd left her own ghost hunting equipment back at the hotel, unsure if it would be welcome here.

When the others had left the room, Carrie said, "I'd like to ask each of you a few questions, privately, while the others are setting up. Who'd like to go first?"

Ellen volunteered. Carrie asked Tanya and Sue to wait with Miss Myrtle until she was ready for them.

"I'm going to video record our session," Carrie said, pointing the camera on her shoulder at Ellen. It reminded Ellen of the one used by Brenda from the San Antonio Ghost Busters. "Are you ready?"

Ellen nodded, wishing she had a chair to sit in as she stood there awkwardly with her hands in her trouser pockets. Although there were no chairs, two lamps had been set up and plugged into a generator, illuminating the room. There was also a light on Carrie's video camera.

Carrie asked Ellen to report in detail what she had experienced in the building. Ellen told her about the whispers she'd heard—first with her friends, and later alone by the dumbwaiter.

"Did you feel a change in temperature or in mood?" Carrie asked.

Ellen shook her head. "Oh, but our phones died."

"Eduardo told me what happened that night you came back here with him," Carrie said. "Don't worry. I'm not going to share that with anyone. Can you tell me what you remember about that night?"

Ellen didn't like the idea of admitting all that had happened on camera, but once she started recounting the evening, she told Carrie everything—including the details about the child skeleton and the arm she sent to the online lab. She also mentioned the disappearance of the rest of the skeleton when they'd returned with the realtor the following day.

"The wind that put out the fire," Carrie began. "It came right after Sue asked the spirits for help?"

Ellen nodded.

"Okay, that's good for now. Could you go sit with Margaret and send one of your friends over to talk to me?"

It felt good to sit down after the walking and standing. Sue left and took her turn with Carrie as Tanya and Ellen quietly watched Miss Myrtle sketch. There were two floor lamps set up in this room as well, along with the lights on the camcorders that were placed on tripods in three corners of the room.

"I'm sensing a great deal of pain and sorrow in this building," Miss Myrtle said. "And anger. A whole lot of pent-up anger."

Ellen's mouth fell open as the image on Miss Myrtle's sketch pad came to life: it was a crowd of angry black men surrounded by flames.

Once the interviews had been conducted and the equipment had been set up, the team convened in the old ballroom. Carrie gave Ellen and her friends a handheld recorder and asked them to tie back their hair with some rubber bands she'd brought along.

"We need each person here to keep their audio recorders on at all times so we can get accurate data," Carrie said. Then to Justin, she said,

"Put the EMF recorder on the floor. I'm afraid it's going to move around on that chair."

Justin did as his mother had asked.

"Okay, then," Carrie said. "Everyone ready?"

Everyone else in the room nodded. Ellen stood beside her friends towards the front of the room near the card table, where Miss Myrtle was continually sketching, as if in a trance. One of the three cameras was behind them. Justin stood opposite them near another camera and the machine he'd just placed on the floor by the back risers. Eduardo stood on the west side of the room near the archway to the old skating rink. The third camera was to his left, and to his right were the charred floorboards and broken glass from the night they'd encountered the old woman.

"Let me do the talking," Carrie said from where she stood in the middle of the room. The three cameras on tripods pointed at her from the different angles. "Go ahead and turn off the lamps."

Justin and Eduardo killed the lights that were near them. Only the pale purple glow of the cameras barely illuminated the room.

Then more loudly, Carrie said, "Spirits who may be here among us, we mean you no harm. We come in goodwill out of a desire to help, not hurt."

Carrie paused for a moment before continuing. "We have brought equipment with us today that we hope might help us to communicate with you. We'd like to hear your voice and see your image. We've brought an electromagnetic pump along to feed you the energy you may need to make contact with us. Please feel free to use that energy."

After another moment of silence, Carrie said, "Is there anyone here who would like to talk to us?"

Ellen glanced at Sue, whose eyes were wide open, as though she could see something above Carrie's head, but Ellen dared not talk. She didn't want to ruin the investigation.

"If there is someone here," Carrie continued. "Can you tell us your name?"

Ellen felt the room get colder. She thought it was all in her mind until Carrie asked them, "Do you feel that? Eduardo? Are you seeing a change in temp?"

Eduardo nodded. "From sixty-four degrees to sixty."

Aloud, Carrie said, "Is there only one spirit here? Or are there more of you? How many are here with us?"

The light on Eduardo's device began blinking rapidly. Ellen wondered what that meant as the feeling of being suffocated began to make her uncomfortable. She wanted to go outside and get air, but she didn't dare move from her spot.

"Why do you remain here?" Carrie continued. "Is there something keeping you here, in this place?"

From the corner of her eye, Ellen noticed Miss Myrtle's frantic writing over and over of one word: *Fire*.

Carrie noticed this, too. "Eduardo? Tell me what you're feeling right now."

"I'm getting a reading of fifty-seven degrees, but I feel much hotter. I find it hard to breathe, like the room's filled with smoke."

Ellen nodded, wanting to add that she sensed the same thing, but she was afraid to interfere.

"Are you feeling it, too, Ellen?" Carrie asked when she noticed her nodding.

"Yes," Ellen said. "It's suffocating."

Sue nodded. "Tanya and I sense it, too."

Aloud, Carrie said, "Do you have a message for us?" After a moment of silence, she asked, "Were you alive during the Indian Removal Act in the late 1800's? Were you part of the Trail of Tears?"

After another moment, she asked, "Were you alive on June 1st, 1921, during the Tulsa Race Riot?"

The lights on the cameras suddenly went out, and the room was nearly pitch dark.

"Everyone stay where you are," Carrie whispered. "Tell me, though, if you sense anything else unusual."

Ellen blinked several times, trying to adjust her eyes to the darkness. Her heart had picked up its pace and her knees felt weak. She hoped to God she wasn't going to pass out.

The room became very cold.

"It's fifty-two degrees," Eduardo said softly.

"Can you sense anyone with us, Eduardo?" Carrie asked.

"Too many to isolate."

"Any idea how many?" Carrie asked.

"At least a hundred," he said.

Aloud, Carrie asked, "Were you alive when this was the St. Vincent de Paul Society's home for men?"

Ellen held her breath, wondering if the spirit of the murderer could also be here.

Then, Carrie asked, "Were you alive when this was a circus?"

For a moment, the stifling air cleared.

Then Carrie asked, "Where are your bodies? Can you show us where your bodies are?"

As they waited in silence, Ellen thought she heard a growl. She'd forgotten that she'd heard it once before.

Hesitantly, she asked the others, "Did you hear that?"

"What did you hear?" Carrie asked her.

"It sounded like a growl," she said.

"I heard it, too," Tanya said.

"Me, too," Sue said.

"What about you, Margaret?" Carrie asked. "Did you hear it?"

Margaret didn't answer.

"Margaret?" Carrie repeated. "Miss Myrtle, are you okay?"

A flashlight suddenly flickered to life and was shined in the direction of Miss Myrtle.

Carrie neared her with the light. "Miss Myrtle?"

Eduardo joined her with his flashlight as well.

Miss Myrtle was in a trance, as before. She kept writing the same line on her paper over and over: *We are here. We are here. We are here.*

CHAPTER FOURTEEN

Reviewing the Evidence

The next day, Ellen and her friends received a call after breakfast from Carrie. She wanted them to come to her home on the other side of Tulsa to go over some of the data she'd compiled from the previous night.

As they passed the La Quinta, Sue, who was driving, said, "I wish we'd stayed there again. I could have used my points and gotten my own room. I didn't get much sleep with the two of you getting up every few minutes."

"That must have been Tanya," Ellen said from the backseat. "I slept like a rock. I had nightmares, but I never woke up from them."

"I got up *one time* to use the bathroom," Tanya said.

"You got up more than once," Sue said. "Every time you opened and closed the bathroom door, it woke me up."

"I swear it wasn't more than one time," Tanya said from the passenger seat. "You must have been hearing things."

"I know what I heard," Sue said. "Maybe you were sleep walking."

Tanya sighed. "I wasn't going to mention this before because I thought it was my imagination. And maybe it was. But, when I went to the bathroom, I thought I saw a man in there."

"What are you talking about?" Ellen asked.

"I'm not sure," Tanya replied. "It was more like a dark silhouette of a man—totally black, like a shadow. When I opened the door, he was standing in front of the commode. I almost screamed, but, instead, I turned on the light. When I did, he vanished. But after I'd used the restroom and was walking back to my bed, it felt like he was following me. It took me a while to fall back asleep."

"Great," Sue said. "I doubt I'll sleep tonight, either."

Carrie French lived in a quaint little townhouse in a quiet cul-de-sac. The van from the night before was parked in her driveway next to a white Prius. Jack-o-lanterns lined the short sidewalk to the front of the house. Sue parked behind the van, and the three of them went up to the door where they were greeted by a Halloween wreath adorned with a raven and a skull.

Before Sue had knocked, the door swung open, and Carrie said, "You've got to see this."

They followed her into a small living area where the sofa and two chairs had been pushed all the way back against the walls to make space for an eight-foot plastic and metal folding table in the middle of the room. The table was covered with equipment. Justin sat at one end of the table with a laptop. Eduardo was looking at the screen over Justin's shoulder.

Ellen and her friends squeezed together behind Justin next to Eduardo while Carrie said, "We compiled audio from the EVP recorders with video from our full spectrum cameras using some special software. You won't believe what we captured last night. Have a look."

"Ready?" Justin asked his mother.

She nodded. He struck a key on the laptop as everyone watched the screen.

They were looking at Carrie from the point of view of the back of the room, where Justin had been standing. In fact, part of Justin's arm was visible in the shot. Carrie stood in the center of the room, and you could see Sue and Tanya on the far left of the screen. You could also see the back of Miss Myrtle's head and Ellen's arm beside Sue. Eduardo was standing at very back of the screen.

On screen, they watched Carrie begin. "Spirits who may be here among us, we mean you no harm. We come in goodwill out of a desire to help, not hurt."

So far, nothing looked out of the ordinary. They watched as Carrie continued. "We have brought equipment with us today that we hope might help us to communicate with you. We'd like to hear your voice and see your image. We've brought an electromagnetic pump along to feed you the energy you may need to make contact with us. Please feel free to use that energy."

Both lamps flickered.

"Did you see that?" Carrie pointed as Justin paused the screen.

"Yes!" Ellen said. "I didn't notice it last night."

"Me either," Sue said.

"None of us did," Eduardo pointed out. "It wasn't visible to the naked eye. Justin slowed the video down so we could see it."

"Could it have been the generator malfunctioning?" Tanya asked.

"Our cameras were running on the same generator," Carrie said. "We try not to rely on batteries, because they often get drained. Go ahead, Justin."

Justin unpaused the recording.

On screen, Carrie said, "Is there anyone here who would like to talk to us?"

A dark orb flickered over Carrie's head and then disappeared.

"Oh my gosh!" Sue said. "I thought I saw something above you last night, but it was so fleeting, I wasn't sure. You captured exactly what I saw!"

"Did anyone else notice it?" Carrie asked.

Ellen and the others shook their heads.

"Go ahead, Justin," Carrie said. "Roll it."

"If there is someone here," Carrie said on screen. "Can you tell us your name?"

The dark orb flickered beside Tanya, and in the next moment, the silhouette of a man became visible. Justin paused the screen.

"See it?" Carrie said.

"It's just like the shadow I saw last night," Tanya said. "Exactly."

"He must have followed you home," Eduardo said. "For some reason, you seem to have an affinity for spirits—Vivian the other day, and then yesterday, this one. It stays with you through the duration of the video."

"Are you serious?" Tanya asked, with a frightened face. "Do you think he's with me now?"

"I don't sense him," Eduardo said.

"Neither do I," Carrie said. "But watch the rest of our coverage. Notice how he flickers in and out between you and Margaret."

Justin unpaused the recording.

On screen, Carrie asked, "Do you feel that? Eduardo? Are you seeing a change in temp?"

At the back of the screen, Eduardo said, "From sixty-four degrees to sixty."

Aloud, Carrie said, "Is there only one spirit here? Or are there more of you? How many are here with us?"

The dark silhouette beside Tanya lifted its arms in the air and opened and closed its jaws. Justin paused the screen.

"You can barely hear this, so I'm going to turn up the volume all the way and slow down the play speed," Justin said.

In a low, guttural sound, Ellen heard one word play over the laptop: *Many.*

Justin paused the screen. "Hear that?"

"Many!" Sue said. "It sounded like the ghost said many!"

"Exactly," Carrie said. "Play it again, Justin."

Justin took it back and replayed the audio. Again, very clearly, they heard: *Many.*

Ellen still wondered if it was at all possible that the old Native American woman was responsible for the EVP.

"I listened to all of your handheld recorders and confirmed that none of us whispered the word, and the sound seemed to come from the silhouette near Tanya." Carrie pointed to the screen. "Now watch the screen very carefully for what appears next."

"Why do you remain here?" the Carrie on the screen continued. "Is there something keeping you here, in this place?"

In three different spots on the screen, gray little smudges appeared and disappeared.

"See them?" Justin pointed to them.

"What are they?" Tanya asked.

Justin shrugged as the Carrie on the screen said, "Eduardo? Tell me what you're feeling right now."

"I'm getting a reading of fifty-seven degrees, but I feel much hotter. I can barely breathe, as if the room were filled with smoke."

"Is it smoke?" Ellen asked, squinting at the laptop screen.

"Maybe some kind of imprinted memory of smoke," Carrie said.

On screen, Carrie said, "Are you feeling it, too, Ellen?"

"Yes," Ellen said on screen. "It's suffocating."

"Tanya and I sense it, too," the Sue on the screen said.

Then Carrie said, "Do you have a message for us?" After a moment of silence, she asked, "Were you alive during the Indian Removal Act in the late 1800's? Were you part of the Trail of Tears?"

After another moment, she asked, "Were you alive on June 1st, 1921, during the Tulsa Race Riot?"

The black lights on the camera turned off, and now the screen was a spectrum of colors, because the camera had filmed the images using infrared light.

"Everyone stay where you are," the Carrie on the screen said. Ellen could see the outline of her body and the colorful heat it produced. She could also see the outlines of the others. Beside Tanya was a very subtle white orb where the dark silhouette had been. It began to move up and down beside Tanya. "Tell me, though, if you sense anything else unusual," the Carrie on the screen said.

"What is that?" Tanya asked, pointing to the orb beside her.

Justin paused the screen. "It's the shadow man getting excited."

"We think it could be an indication that he's one of the riot victims," Carrie said. "Now, watch the back of the screen near where Eduardo is standing."

Justin played the video.

On screen, Eduardo said, "It's fifty-two degrees."

"Can you sense anyone with us, Eduardo?" Carrie asked in the video.

"Too many to isolate," he replied just as a white orb flickered above his head.

Justin paused the video and pointed at the screen. "We captured this one, and one other over by me. Watch the right side of the screen now." He pressed play.

"Any idea how many?" Carrie asked on the screen.

"At least a hundred," Eduardo said.

In the video, Carrie asked, "Were you alive when this was the St. Vincent de Paul Society's home for men?" And then, after another moment, she asked, "Were you alive when this was a circus?"

The figure beside Tanya disappeared.

"Where are your bodies? Can you show us where your bodies are?" Carrie's voice came over the laptop.

On the right side of the screen beside Justin's arm, another white orb danced for a few seconds before flickering out. The one next to Eduardo had also disappeared, but the one beside Tanya reappeared and began to jump up and down.

"Now check this out," Justin said. "I'm going to slow down the speed again and turn up the volume all the way." He pressed play and clicked the mouse on the volume to crank it up.

Ellen listened carefully as a low and drawn-out moan played throughout the room.

"Oh, gosh!" Sue said. "It sounded more like a growl last night. But is it a moan?"

"I'm not sure," Carrie said.

"It could be both," Eduardo pointed out. "A sound of desperation in between a growl and a moan."

"Keep listening," Justin said, resuming the video.

"Did you hear that?" the Ellen on the video asked.

"What did you hear?" Carrie asked her.

"It sounded like a growl," she said.

"I heard it, too," Tanya said.

"Me, too," Sue said.

"What about you, Margaret?" Carrie asked. "Did you hear it?"

"Margaret?" Carrie repeated. "Miss Myrtle, are you okay?"

"I edited in the point of view of the other camera here," Justin said. "Check out Miss Myrtle."

From this new angle, Eduardo was no longer in the shot, as the camera was somewhere beside him looking at Miss Myrtle's profile. The back of Tanya was in the shot, and the dark silhouette was still beside her. The image was no longer in the colorful infrared designs but in the white light of the flashlights pointed at Miss Myrtle. Her eyes were rolled back, revealing their whites. Her lips were moving, though no sound came from them. And she was suddenly surrounded by at least a dozen dark orbs bouncing over and around her head as she fiercely pressed her pencil to the paper.

We are here, she wrote, again and again.

Justin stopped the video.

"Where's Miss Myrtle now?" Sue asked.

"She's not feeling well today," Eduardo said.

"And I need her rested up for tonight," Carrie said.

"Do y'all have Halloween plans together?" Ellen asked.

"We're going back to the property," Carrie said. "I want to try to capture more evidence in some of the other rooms. Want to come?"

CHAPTER FIFTEEN

Miss Myrtle's Past

Before Ellen and her friends left the home of Carrie French, Carrie invited them to join her later at one of her favorite Greek restaurants for lunch. It was directly across from The Tavern, where they had met weeks before, for the haunted pub crawl.

After they had ordered their food, Carrie said, "I wanted to meet with you away from the rest of my team, because I need you to understand something about Miss Myrtle."

Sue arched a brow. "We're listening."

"There's a good reason why she doesn't like to talk about the riot," Carrie said before taking a sip of her water. "Her ancestors were victims, and when she was a young woman, she worked with black politicians to get justice, but people around here put a stop to that."

"Who? And how?" Tanya asked.

"The Klan," Carrie said. "And to this day, she's still afraid if it."

"Wouldn't the members of the Klan be dead by now?" Ellen asked.

"Oh, no," Carrie lowered her voice. "The KKK is alive and well in America *and* here in Tulsa. So please be careful of what you say and who you talk to about finding the bodies of riot victims."

"Seriously?" Tanya asked. "I didn't know that."

"Wasn't the Klan responsible for that church shooting in South Carolina a couple of years back?" Sue asked.

"I think that was a lone white supremacist," Tanya said.

"Well, the Klan is still active," Carrie said. "You have nothing to fear from me and my team, but there are others in this town who aren't so sympathetic, and Margaret has had firsthand experiences with them."

Their food arrived. Once the waitress had left and they had begun to dig in, Carrie said, "Margaret's grandfather, Clayton Myrtle, was seventeen when the riot happened. He'd gone to his high school prom, on his very first date, with a girl his mama didn't approve of, when, after the dance let out, he and his classmates were rounded up by the National Guard and led to the Fair Grounds in a detainment camp. The boys were put in one area and the girls in another. Miss Myrtle sometimes laughs when she recalls what her grandfather used to say when he told the story: 'It seemed my mama, the city of Tulsa, and the whole damned nation was set against me having my first kiss.'"

"That's actually pretty sad and not funny at all," Sue said.

"Margaret is a joyful soul, as was her grandfather, and they tried to find humor anywhere they could," Carrie said. "They had to."

"I guess so," Ellen said.

Carrie finished a bite of her salad and said, "Clayton was a shoe shiner for a lot of uppity white men, so he was able to get himself released from the detainment camp as one of the 'good' Negroes—a label he hated like the devil. The Whites back then believed that there were two kinds of Blacks—the cooperative ones who knew their place and the rebellious ones who thought too highly of themselves. Clayton resented these labels as much as his peers, but he took advantage of the situation so he could run home and check on his mama and his younger brother, Jeffrey. Their daddy had been killed in a car accident a few years earlier, so Clayton had become the man of the house."

"And did he find them okay?" Sue asked.

"All of their belongings had been thrown into the middle of the street, including the birthday presents his little brother Jeffrey had received two days earlier."

"How senseless!" Ellen said, losing her appetite. She'd read about other riot survivors, such as George Monroe, who, at age five, had hid under the bed with his siblings as four white men carrying torches entered his house and set fire to the curtains, one of them unwittingly stepping on little George's hand in the process. Reading about it had outraged her, but knowing a woman whose family had suffered made it feel more personal to her.

"And all the homes across from them had burned to the ground," Carrie said.

"But their house wasn't burned?" Tanya asked.

"Clayton's mama told the men who came to her door that if they wanted to be guilty of murder, they could go ahead and burn her house down, but she wasn't going to leave it," Carrie said. "And since the houses were so close together, they didn't burn that one row of homes. It was one of the few that remained standing in the wake of the riot."

"Miss Myrtle's great-grandmother must have been a strong woman," Ellen said.

"Clayton used to say she was just lucky," Carrie said. "There were a lot of other strong women in Greenwood who lost everything."

"It's so hard to believe something like that could happen," Tanya said.

"Miss Myrtle was born in 1943," Carrie continued. "Her father died fighting in World War II, so her mother moved in with Clayton and his wife Sonia so they could help raise Margaret. Clayton was more like a father to her, you see. And when Margaret was nine years old, she watched her grandparents scrape together every dime they had to help rebuild Mount Zion Baptist Church."

"Isn't that one of the churches destroyed in the riot?" Ellen asked.

"It had just been built and had had its first service in April 1921," Carrie said. "And then was burned to the ground on May 31, 1921. The parish was devastated. Can you imagine? Only a month old and burned to the ground. They had a $50,000 loan to pay back, which they finally did years later. They then had to save to rebuild. Thirty-one years after the riot, they finally did. It was a huge accomplishment for a community that had been ravished and then virtually ignored."

"Yes, that is an accomplishment," Ellen said.

"How unfair," Tanya said. "Shouldn't the city have been responsible for it?"

"Miss Myrtle tried to fight that battle when she was a young woman. She went to college and majored in criminal justice. But when she started the conversation on the political scene in 1975, she received numerous threats."

"What kind of threats?" Sue asked.

"They started as phone calls," Carrie said. "Someone would call and say she should leave Tulsa, if she knew what was good for her. Once they even asked how her grandmother was doing."

"Oh, my gawd," Sue said. "They threatened her grandmother?"

"That's not the worst of it," Carrie said. "They started throwing rocks through her grandparents' front windows and car windshields. The rocks sometimes had papers tied to them with messages that said: 'The Ku Klux Klan is watching you.'"

"So that's how she knew it was the Klan," Ellen said.

"Exactly," Carrie said. "They took full responsibility, though they never mentioned their names individually. They hid behind their organization in their white hoods."

"Wow," Tanya said. "No wonder she gave up the fight."

"She kept at it for another few years, even after all those threats," Carrie said. "It wasn't until her grandmother was murdered in 1981 that she finally gave in to the terrorists."

"Murdered?" Sue asked.

"By the Klan?" Ellen asked.

Carrie shrugged. "It was never proven that the Klan was responsible. It was ruled a suicide. Sonia was found with a shotgun in her hand, her head blown to bits. But Margaret knew her grandmother. She knew there was no way that woman could have committed suicide—and especially not that way. She was a proud woman who always kept up her appearance—hair and makeup always pristine. Blowing her head off was definitely not her style."

"No wonder Miss Myrtle refused to talk about the riot with us last month, when we first met her," Tanya said.

"That explains why she blew us off with the thing about coming into money," Sue added.

"She's only doing this investigation because I asked for her help," Carrie said. "And I wanted you to be aware of how sensitive this topic is for her and for all of us."

"Do you think the danger of the Klan is as bad today as it was in 1981?" Ellen asked.

"I'm sure of it," Carrie said, without hesitation.

CHAPTER SIXTEEN

Halloween Night

Monday evening after an early dinner with Lexi and Stephen at a restaurant across town, Ellen and her friends walked the two blocks from their hotel to meet Carrie and the paranormal investigation team at the property on the other side of Cain's at five o'clock. Carrie and her team hoped to take advantage of the diminishing daylight as they set up their equipment in nearly every room of the building. Unlike Ellen and her friends, they were prepared to spend the entire night on site—even the seventy-three-year-old Miss Myrtle. They'd brought cots and sleeping bags and snacks, along with even more equipment than the previous night.

Ellen and her friends had agreed to stay as long as they could, and, although they weren't excited about the possibility of the shadow man following Tanya to their hotel room again, they were less excited about sleeping in the abandoned building.

Once the equipment was in place, Carrie asked the team to convene in the old skating rink, where they were set up in the same formation as they'd been the previous night in the pale purple glow of the black lights emanating from the full spectrum cameras. All the other light sources had been turned off, including the flashlights each of them held, courtesy of Carrie. Miss Myrtle sat at the card table drawing while Carrie asked the spirits questions. Most of them were a repeat from the night before, but she spent a little more time asking about the fire and the riot. During those questions, Ellen tried not to stare at Miss Myrtle and think about what was going through that poor woman's mind.

Tonight, Carrie also had a set of dowsing rods made of copper. She handed the portable camera over to Justin and then held a rod in each hand, pointing straight out from her body, parallel to one another and about shoulder width apart. Justin trained his camera on her as she told the spirits about the rods.

"With your help, these can guide me to your bodies," she said. "As I move in the right direction toward your position, cross the rods together like this." She overlapped the ends of the rods. "As I move away from your position, push the rods further apart, like this." She pushed the ends of the rods open to form a wide V, with her body at the apex.

She returned the rods to their original position, parallel to one another, shoulder width apart. "Spirits, if you understand, please tell us if you will help us. You can cross the rod tips together now to indicate *Yes* and spread them apart to indicate *No*."

Everyone watched on in silence as Carrie waited, standing in the center of the room. Just when Ellen thought nothing was going to happen, the ends of the rod tips crossed.

Carrie said, "Please note that the rods have crossed on their own, indicating that the spirits are willing to guide me."

Carrie moved the tips parallel to one another and crossed the room toward the old bowling alley. "Spirits, please tell me if I'm moving toward your bodies by crossing the rod tips. Indicate that I'm moving away from your bodies by spreading the rod tips apart.

As Carrie continued down the hall, with Justin following, Ellen lost sight of her.

Eduardo, meanwhile, had moved near Tanya with his handheld EMF and temperature reader. "I sense someone with you again. It's not Vivian. It may be the same spirit that attached to you last night. Can you sense anything?"

"I'm really cold," Tanya said. "And very tired. But otherwise, I don't feel any different."

"Close your eyes, dear, and try to connect with the spirit," Eduardo said. "Maybe you could talk to him. Ask him to touch your hand and see if you can feel anything."

While Eduardo worked with Tanya, Sue and Ellen watched Miss Myrtle sketch. This time, she drew a truck pulling a flatbed trailer containing a mound of human bodies. Ellen covered her mouth and glanced at Sue. The book Ellen had been reading mentioned that eyewitnesses spoke of such a truck hauling dead bodies away from Greenwood.

But maybe Miss Myrtle was recalling stories about the riot and wasn't necessarily communicating with spirits.

Carrie returned to the room and walked in the direction of the hobo camp. "Please cross the rods as I move close to your bodies and spread them apart as I move away from you." The rods remained parallel.

Sue turned sharply toward Tanya. "I saw him. From the corner of my eye, I saw the shadow man. He was standing right next to you, Tanya."

"I saw him, too. I can still see him," Eduardo said. "Tanya, ask him to point to his body. Ask him where his body is."

After giving Ellen and Sue a look that meant she was unsure of herself, Tanya did as Eduardo asked.

"He's pointing north," Eduardo said.

Hearing this, Carrie pointed her rods north. The tips moved closer together.

Ellen's heart picked up its pace at the prospect of finding the body of this spirit and possibly a mass grave, but she tried not to get her hopes up. Could Eduardo truly see a spirit pointing north? Why was it so hard for her to believe? Nevertheless, she followed Carrie and Justin across the room to the back wall, where the dumbwaiter was. The tips continued to move closer together.

"Let's take this outside," Carrie said.

Ellen and Sue followed Carrie and Justin through the old ballroom and then down the hallway to the hobo camp and out the east entrance toward the north side of the building, toward the highway. At first, the rods went slack, back to parallel, but as Carrie continued north toward the highway, the tips moved toward one another again. Then about thirty yards from the building, the rod tips crossed and pointed down to the ground.

"Oh, my goodness!" Carrie shouted into the dark night. "I feel a strong force right over this spot."

Justin trained the camera at her. "Do you think this may be where the bodies from the riot are buried?"

"Only one way to find out," Carrie said.

"Dig?" Sue asked.

"We won't be able to do that until you close on the property," Carrie said.

Ellen recalled the methods used by the anthropologist, which she'd read about in the book on the riot. She told them about the ground-penetrating radar technology and the probes the university professor once used in the local cemeteries.

"Do you think that professor is still alive?" Carrie asked her.

"Only one way to find out," Ellen said with a smile.

As Justin hammered a stick into the ground to mark the spot, they were startled by a sudden *swish* immediately behind him, and the air around them moved.

"Did you hear that?" Carrie asked.

"Something flew up from the ground," Ellen said, shaken.

Had Justin released a spirit when he'd penetrated the ground?

CHAPTER SEVENTEEN:

The Shadow Man

That night, Ellen and her friends had a hard time going to sleep. Now that they knew a shadow man had attached himself to Tanya the previous night, they were afraid he might be in the room with them again. Ellen reminded them that he hadn't done them any harm, but even she was spooked.

Sue had just changed into her nightgown and had washed her face when she came into Tanya and Ellen's room and said, "How would y'all feel about making a circle of protection?"

"What's that?" Ellen asked, realizing she still had a lot to learn.

"It's a circle that you can draw out of salt or some other mineral," Sue explained. "It's even more helpful if you can mark the cardinal points with candles or water or some kind of natural element. Then you cast a protection spell forbidding any spirits from entering the circle."

Ellen bit her lip. How could they possibly manage such a circle? And, if they could, would it work? Even though she'd accepted the existence of ghosts, she wasn't sure she believed that a circle of salt could keep out the spirits.

"It might help us get a little sleep tonight," Sue added. "Should we try it?"

"How?" Tanya asked. "What can we use?"

Ellen searched through her ghost hunter kit but didn't find anything in it for protection.

"I have a few salt packets from that doggie bag I brought back yesterday from the burger joint," Sue said.

"That won't be enough, will it?" Ellen asked. It seemed to her that if salt was really going to prevent a spirit from crossing, it would take more than a few packets.

"It doesn't take much," Sue said. "And then we can light that scented candle I bought for my mom at that gift shop down the street, and we can use cups of water for the other cardinal points."

"Where would we make the circle?" Tanya asked.

"Well, around your bed," Sue said.

Ellen bent her brows. "But then you won't be protected."

"Unless Tanya scoots over," Sue said. "I know I'm a big girl, but I don't need much room. I like to hug the edge of the bed. And we can turn on the TV to drown out my snoring."

"I don't know if I can sleep with the TV on," Ellen said. Then when she saw Sue frown, she added, "But I'm so tired tonight, I just might be able to."

Sue took out the new candle she'd bought and used her lighter to produce a flame. "Let's see. I have a compass phone app. Let me find north. Here it is. I'll put the candle on this nightstand."

Then she opened each salt packet and sprinkled the salt on the floor around the bed and along the top of the headboard. Ellen could only imagine what the cleaning lady would think in the morning.

After Sue laid three plastic cups of water on the floor along the circle, she said, "Now we just need the words."

"What happens if we get up and use the restroom?" Ellen asked, still not sure she was going to buy into this whole thing. "Will that break the circle?"

"I'm glad you asked, because you have to open and close it," Sue said. "I haven't closed it yet, so you're okay. But once I do, you'll need to turn counter-clockwise two times to open it and then two times clockwise to close it again."

"What if the shadow man gets in while one of us is in the restroom?" Tanya asked.

"Dang, I should have tried to incorporate the bathroom," Sue said. "Now we're going to have to say the words out loud every time we close it."

"What are the words?" Ellen asked.

Sue picked up her phone and read the words out loud as she waved one hand in the air and turned clockwise by the bed twice:

Guardians of the North, South, East, and West,
Elements of Earth, Air, Fire, and Water,
Bless this circle and protect those within,
Whether father, mother, son, or daughter.
No unwanted entities shall enter,
And safety shall prevail in the center.
This circle is cast.
Grant it shall last.

"That's a lot to remember every time we go to the restroom," Tanya pointed out.

"I'll write it down for you," Sue said. "Unless you have any better ideas."

"I'm fine with it," Ellen said, realizing that Sue truly was frightened. If the circle brought her comfort and security, so be it.

Tanya shrugged. "It's better than all of us just lying here listening for noises in the dark."

"Well, I still may do that," Sue said.

Once they were all three settled with Ellen and Sue each hugging their respective sides of the bed so as not to crowd Tanya, Sue turned on the television to HGTV, and they all tried their best to fall asleep.

At some point in the middle of the night, Ellen couldn't take it any-more. Between Sue's snoring and the infomercial blasting from the tele-vision, along with the fear that any time she'd move she'd awaken the others, Ellen was too anxious to sleep. Deciding to take her chances with the shadow man, she picked up her pillow and went to the couch. As she settled into the cushions, without bothering to open the sleeper sofa, she began to worry that she should have closed the circle of pro-tection. What if her friends were attacked all because of her?

Just because you don't believe it doesn't mean it isn't true.

She returned to the other room and found her copy of the words on the night table by her side of the bed. Could she close the circle while remaining on the outside? She wasn't sure. Was she being selfish in breaking it after all the trouble Sue had gone to in protecting them?

Tears pricked her eyes. All she wanted was some damn sleep.

She decided to stand on the outside of the circle and use her finger like a wand to close the circle as she whispered the words:

Guardians of the North, South, East, and West,
Elements of Earth, Air, Fire, and Water,
Bless this circle and protect those within,
Whether father, mother, son, or daughter.
No unwanted entities shall enter,
And safety shall prevail in the center.
This circle is cast.
Grant it shall last.

Tanya sat up. "I've got to pee."

Ellen sighed as she returned the paper with the words back to the night table and then went back to the couch to sleep. She had just *finally* drifted off when Tanya touched her shoulder and woke her.

"What are you doing out here?" Tanya asked.

"Trying to get some sleep. I'll be okay."

"Are you sure?"

"I'm sure. Good night."

Ellen closed her eyes. As she tried once more to drift off into sleep, she heard Tanya muttering the words to close the circle.

Sometime near dawn, Ellen was awakened by Sue's shout.

"I saw him!" she yelled.

Ellen jumped from the couch and turned on the lights in the room where Tanya and Sue had been sleeping.

"He was standing at the foot of the bed," Sue said, pointing at the end of Tanya's side. "I saw him clear as day. He vanished as soon as I saw him."

"He didn't break the circle, did he?" Ellen asked.

"I don't think so," Sue said.

"Did you see him, Tanya?"

Tanya shook her head and then pulled the covers over her. "I need another hour or two of sleep."

"Try to go back to sleep, Sue," Ellen said. "He hasn't tried to hurt us. Maybe he's just trying to tell us something."

Ellen went back to the couch, but she didn't fall asleep. She kept opening her eyes and scanning the room for signs of the shadow man.

Later in the morning before breakfast, Ellen used her laptop to track down the anthropologist who had helped Don Ross search for the unmarked mass graves back in 1998. She found him listed on the University of Oklahoma website.

"Oh, no," she said to her friends, who were still getting dressed. "It says here that after thirty years with the Oklahoma Archaeological Survey, he's retired."

"Maybe he'd still be willing to work with us," Sue said as she melted her eyeliner with her lighter and finished making up her face.

"It says he's still working part-time as an anthropology professor," Ellen said. "Maybe we can make an appointment to see him at his office on campus."

"OU is in Norman," Sue said. "Email him and ask if we can meet with him on Thursday, since Norman is right by Oklahoma City, where we get on the train."

Ellen found his email and began to compose a message. Then she read it to her friends for approval.

"That sounds good," Tanya said. "Send it and hope for the best."

Ellen didn't hear from Carrie French until late in the afternoon, when Carrie texted to say that they'd all just woke up after a night of research on site and were going back to her place to review the footage, if Ellen and her friends wanted to join them.

Aside from the dowsing rods pointing to the ground north of the building and the sketches created by Miss Myrtle, the most interesting piece of evidence continued to be the appearance of the shadow man beside Tanya. The dark figure moved its arms maniacally whenever Carrie asked questions about the location of the riot victims and their bodies.

Feeling that the property must have the answer to a nearly century-old mystery, Ellen and her friends made the decision that afternoon to move forward with closing on the purchase. All three of their husbands were wary, but the ladies convinced them over the phone to support them.

Paul suggested that they could save themselves another trip by requesting that the closing be moved up. Ellen was pleasantly surprised when Gayle called back with the good news that the agents and title company could accommodate the change. They would meet tomorrow morning—on Wednesday.

With nothing planned for Tuesday night, Sue convinced Ellen and Tanya to use the Ouija Board to try and speak with the shadow man.

"We spent seventeen bucks on it," Sue argued. "We may as well get some use out of it. I say we order room service and hang out here and see if we can find out just who this shadow man really is."

They ordered turkey paninis, and, while they waited for the food to arrive, they crowded around the Ouija Board. As before, Tanya sat crossed-legged (yoga style) on the edge of the king-size bed facing Sue and Ellen, who sat in the armchair and desk chair respectively. The board lay across Tanya's lap, and they each touched their fingertips lightly to the plastic indicator.

As soon as they were ready, Sue said, "We're hoping to speak with the shadow man that followed us from the property near Cain's Ballroom. Shadow man, are you here?"

Without hesitation, the planchette practically flew to *Yes*.

They glanced at one another nervously. Ellen was excited and frightened, but mostly curious.

"What is your name, shadow man?" Sue asked.

Immediately, the planchette spelled out: V-A-N-H-U-R-L-E-Y.

"Vanhurley?" Tanya muttered.

"I think it's a first and last name," Ellen said. "Van Hurley. Why does that name sound familiar?"

Without having addressed the shadow man, Ellen flinched when the indicator began to move again. It spelled out: 1-9-2-1.

"Were you alive in 1921?" Sue asked.

The planchette moved to *Yes*.

Then it circled around and spelled out: T-U-L-S-A-P-O-L-I-C-E.

Ellen's heart started beating very rapidly. "Do you think this means Van Hurley was a member of the Tulsa police force in 1921?"

She'd been addressing her friends, but the planchette moved to *Yes*.

Ellen's eyes widened with astonishment. She glanced at each of her friends, seeing their expressions mirrored her own. They were communicating with a spirit who'd been alive during the race riot.

"Do you have a message for us, Van Hurley?" Sue asked.

Ellen held her breath as the planchette glided across the board beneath her fingertips. It spelled out: P-A-T-T-Y-C-O-L-E.

"Who's Patty Cole?" Sue asked.

Swiftly, the plastic indicator spelled out: G-R-A-N-D-D-A-U-G-H-T-E-R.

"Patty Cole is your granddaughter?" Ellen asked.

The planchette moved to *Yes*.

"Is she still alive?" Sue asked.

The planchette circled around and returned to *Yes*.

"Do you want us to give her a message?" Ellen asked.

The planchette moved to *No*.

"No?" Tanya muttered. "That's odd. Why would he say no?"

The indicator circled around and spelled out: M-Y-P-E-R-S-O-N-A-L-E-F-F-E-C-T-S.

"Your granddaughter has your personal effects?" Sue asked, excitedly.

The indicator moved to *Yes*.

"But why would he tell us this?" Tanya whispered. "Does he want us to look through his personal effects?"

The indicator circled the board and returned to *Yes*.

"Do you know where we can find Patty Cole?" Sue asked.

The planchette circled the board again and returned to *Yes*. Then it spelled out: 1-1-4-E-L-M-T-O-P-E-K-A-K-A-N-S-A-S.

"He wants us to go to Topeka?" Ellen whispered.

The indicator moved to *Yes*.

"Oh, my gawd," Sue said. "There must be something in his personal effects that he wants us to see."

The planchette circled around and returned to *Yes* again and again, so rapidly, that after five revolutions across the board, it flew across the room and landed on the carpet near the balcony.

"I think we should go to Topeka as soon as possible," Tanya said.

Ellen couldn't help but smile back at her friends. A jolt of excitement traveled down her back. This was exactly the kind of adventure she'd been hoping for.

CHAPTER EIGHTEEN

Road Trip

A lthough Sue and Tanya slept on the king-size bed with another circle of protection surrounding them, Ellen got a goodnight's sleep on the sofa sleeper in the front room. Now that she knew Van Hurley was the shadow man and that he'd been a police officer, she was no longer frightened by his presence. In fact, she had a feeling he'd been watching over them, just like Vivian had.

As excited as Ellen was to track down Patty Cole in Topeka, she was first and foremost overjoyed when she opened her email and found a reply from Dr. Robert Brooks, the anthropologist at OU. In his reply, he wrote:

> *Hi, Ellen,*
> *I am, indeed, the anthropologist who led the search for mass graves in Tulsa between 1998 and 2000. I would be happy to meet with you on Thursday. Would 2 p.m. work for you?*
> *Best,*
> *Bob Brooks*

Ellen read the message to her friends.

"Let him know that works for us," Tanya said. "That's actually perfect."

"Then when are we driving up to Topeka to look for Patty Cole?" Sue asked.

"How about today after we close?" Ellen suggested. "According to Google, it's a four-hour drive. We could stay in Topeka tonight and then drive straight to Norman in the morning to visit Bob Brooks."

"What if we drive all the way up there, and then she won't talk to us?" Tanya asked. "Shouldn't we call her first?"

"I don't think so," Sue said. "It would make me pretty suspicious if someone called up asking to see my late grandfather's personal effects."

Ellen hadn't thought this all the way through. "You both make good points. What should we do?"

"I think we're better off showing up and winning her over with our sparkling smiles and impressive personalities," Sue said.

Ellen laughed.

"I'd hate to go all that way only to discover she wasn't at home," Tanya said. "Isn't there some way we can confirm that she'll be there?"

"Maybe Van Hurley can help," Sue said with a twinkle in her eye. "Fetch me that Ouija Board."

They had less than an hour before they needed to meet Gayle at the real estate agency, but they all three sat around the board with their fingertips on the plastic indicator, hoping to speak with Van Hurley.

"Van Hurley, are you there?" Sue asked.

The planchette did not move.

Sue asked three more times, but nothing happened.

"He must not be here," Tanya said.

"So, now what?" Ellen asked.

"We have to take a chance and make that drive," Sue said. "What choice do we have?"

If Ellen had thought the train ride felt long, driving four hours with Sue and Tanya seemed interminable. Tanya had to stop to pee every thirty minutes, and Sue wanted to run through a drive thru at least once every hour for snacks and drinks.

By the time they had pulled up to the curb in front of 114 Elm, they still weren't sure what they were going to say if they got lucky and Patty Cole answered her door.

The house was a two-story craftsman-style bungalow—green with white trim and columns with red brick on the bottom. Three round shrubs lined the front porch, where a white swing hung in the corner. Steps up to the porch led from the driveway. On the side of the house, they could see a window near the ground in what must be a basement. At the end of the driveway was a detached garage.

As they stood at the bottom of the steps, Tanya asked, "So what's the plan?"

"Let's just tell her the truth," Ellen said. "Maybe Van Hurley will help us."

"What if she's not at home?" Tanya pointed out.

"Then we'll find a way inside," Sue said with determination.

Before they'd made it up the stairs to the front door, a very thin woman about their own age with round glasses and white-blonde hair dashed from the door and said, "It's about time! I'm ten minutes late for my dental appointment. I left a check in an envelope on the kitchen bar. Don't forget to lock up when you're finished. I have a hair appointment afterward and probably won't make it back before then."

The woman said all of this as she was hastily skipping down the stairs past them and heading to the keypad on her garage door. Ellen stood on the steps staring blankly at the woman.

"Should we tell her she's mistaken us for someone else?" Tanya mumbled.

"No way," Sue said. "For all we know, Van Hurley went to a lot of trouble to make this happen. Just smile and wave."

As the homeowner drove away in her shiny black Lexus, Sue led the way into the house.

"What if she's not even Patty Cole?" Tanya whispered.

Sue pointed to a stack of mail on a console in the foyer. The envelopes were addressed to *Patricia Cole.*

"And what are we going to do when the real people she's expecting show up?" Tanya asked.

Ellen went through the living room to the kitchen bar, where she found an envelope addressed to *Merry Maids.*

"She thinks we're here to clean her house," Ellen said.

"If the real help shows up," Sue said, "we'll just pretend to be Patty's cousins from out of town. Now come on, you scaredy cats. Help me look for Van Hurley's personal effects."

They combed the first floor—a living room, study, kitchen, and master bedroom—and found nothing that looked like it might have once belonged to Patty's grandfather.

"I wish I knew what we were looking for," Ellen mumbled.

They all three froze when a clicking sound came from the fireplace.

"What the heck was that?" Sue asked.

"Now who's the scaredy cat?" Tanya whispered.

"It's just the wind." Ellen sounded more confident than she felt. "And I have a feeling we should be looking in either the attic or the basement. I bet what we're looking for isn't something you would display in your house, but would store, like in a box."

Sue and Tanya exchanged quizzical looks.

"What?" Ellen asked.

"And what exactly gives you that feeling?" Sue wanted to know.

Ellen shrugged. "It seems *logical* to me."

"It just seems awfully suspicious that we hear a spirit enter through the fireplace and then you get a *feeling* about where to look and what to look for," Sue explained.

Ellen rolled her eyes. "Let's start with the basement."

"Is that the spirit talking?" Tanya teased.

Sue found the basement stairs behind a door near the kitchen. She pulled a chain over them to cast light on the otherwise dark and eerie space below. The stairs moaned beneath their weight as they made their way to the bottom, which was a bare concrete slab full of cracks, where moisture seeped in. The beams, joints, pipes, and electrical wiring were exposed and full of cobwebs. A little light came in through one window, but the basement was mostly dark and musty until Tanya found another light switch.

"That's better," Sue said.

Ellen wasn't so sure she agreed. The light only made more visible the moisture, bugs, cobwebs, and clutter contaminating the room.

"Are you getting anymore feelings, Ellen?" Sue asked.

Ellen sighed as she glanced at the cardboard boxes that were haphazardly discarded on the floor and on an old wooden table. "I wish. Van Hurley's personal effects could be anywhere in these boxes."

"So, we better get looking," Tanya said, opening one of them.

They used the torch app on their phones to help them rifle through the contents of the old, dusty boxes. Ellen found mostly old clothes that should have been donated to Goodwill, in her opinion. Another box contained a bunch of tattered paperbacks. And in another, she found some porcelain figurines and vases wrapped in newspaper. Ellen was beginning to believe that these boxes had at one time been meant to be donated, and Patty never got around to it.

"Here's something interesting," Tanya said. "It's a nice wooden box with a bunch of papers inside."

Sue and Ellen looked over Tanya's shoulder.

"What kind of papers?" Sue asked.

"Old," Tanya whispered. "I think this must be it. It's an affidavit from October 1921."

They all three leaned over the paper.

"It's Van Hurley's testimony," Ellen whispered.

"Oh, my gawd," Sue whispered. "City officials of Tulsa planned and carried out an aerial attack on Greenwood."

"It wasn't a spontaneous riot." Ellen's jaw dropped open.

Tanya's eyes were wide. "It was a planned massacre."

"There must be at least thirty pages here of Van Hurley's sworn testimony," Sue said, skimming through the old, yellowed papers.

"Let's take them and go," Ellen said.

Ellen recalled the moral crisis she'd experienced last Christmas eve, when she'd stolen a can of cranberry sauce from the supermarket. That had been such a soul-searching dilemma, so why was she ready to take these important legal papers without so much as a slight hesitation?

Just then the basement stairs creaked and moaned, and a girl, maybe fifteen or sixteen years of age, shouted, "Who are you, and what are you doing down here?"

With her back to the girl, Sue quickly stuffed the thirty pages of the affidavit into her bra.

"We're the Merry Maids," Ellen said.

"Then who are the ladies upstairs actually cleaning?" the girl asked, full of anger and fear. Her face was red, and her hands were trembling. It made Ellen feel terrible.

"There must have been a mix-up at headquarters," Sue said.

"We were down here looking for cleaning supplies," Tanya added.

"In cardboard boxes?" the girl demanded.

"Okay, look," Ellen said, taking several steps toward the girl. "It's true, we're supposed to be cleaning. We got curious, that's all. We saw these boxes of perfectly good clothes, and we thought of our grandchildren. Do you know if your mom plans on donating these boxes? Because Christmas is going to be lean for us this year."

"So, you're really with Merry Maids?" the girl asked.

Ellen and her friends nodded.

"We'll go check with our boss to find out what happened," Sue said. "There must have been some confusion with the dispatcher."

As Ellen and her friends skirted past the teenager on the stairs, the girl said, "I'll ask my mom about the boxes."

Now Ellen worried she'd draw Patty Cole's suspicion if her daughter mentioned that the maids were interested in the boxes. "No, please don't. I'm actually a little embarrassed now that I said anything to you about wanting them."

The teen seemed to understand as they made their way to the kitchen. The real maids were nowhere in sight, thank goodness, as Ellen and her friends crossed the living room to the front door. They were nearly home free when Sue turned and asked the girl, "Shouldn't you be in school?"

The girl's face turned pale. "I won't tell about your snooping if you don't mention I came home early. Deal?"

Sue nodded and followed Tanya and Ellen out the door.

An hour and a half later, after they'd checked in at a local hotel, they sat in a booth at a nearby diner for an early supper. They were waiting for their food and looking over the papers they'd stolen from Patty Cole's basement.

Was it really stealing if the ghost of the original owner *told* them to do it? Ellen frowned. He hadn't actually *told* them to take the papers—only to look through his personal effects. She doubted they'd have much of a case if Patty Cole ever discovered her grandfather's papers were missing and decided to press charges. Fortunately for Ellen and her friends, Patty Cole didn't know them from Adam and had no way of tracking them down—unless they'd left their fingerprints behind. Ellen's stomach turned a somersault.

"Look here," Tanya said, pointing to the affidavit. "He's naming names."

"Oh my gosh. Hurley says that these officials were also members of the Ku Klux Klan."

Sue read, "Aeroplanes dropped nitroglycerin bombs on buildings and homes in the Greenwood district, setting them on fire."

"The mayor and the police commissioner, along with other city officials, also dropped turpentine balls and bombs into the houses in a conspiracy with other Klan agents to kill colored citizens and drive them from the land," Ellen read.

"This is making me sick," Tanya said. "We should have eaten first. I don't think I can stomach anything now."

"We can ask the waitress to pack it to go for us," Sue said. "Maybe we'll feel more like eating back at the hotel."

"The city officials wanted to clear out Greenwood of its colored citizens to make way for a new railroad depot and industrial district," Tanya read. "And at least one oil baron among them was after the mineral rights."

"We own the mineral rights to our new property, don't we?" Ellen asked.

"I don't recall," Sue said. "I'll text Gayle and ask."

"This is so unbelievable," Tanya said. "Do you think Van Hurley was telling the truth?"

"His ghost wouldn't have led us to this document if he'd made it all up," Sue pointed out.

"I remember reading in that riot book that there was talk of a conspiracy, but nothing was ever proven," Ellen said. "Some black citizens even said they'd received warning notes taped to their doors that said *Leave Tulsa by June 1st*. And a whole lot of lawsuits by black survivors who pressed charges against the city were never brought to trial."

"How could the city officials and the Klan get away with this?" Tanya said. "Do you think we can bring them to justice?"

"They're all dead by now," Ellen said. "But maybe the city can still be made responsible. Maybe this affidavit can help the descendants of the victims get reparations."

"I think it's too far past the statute of limitations," Sue said. "I don't think anything can be done."

"We need to find and identify those bodies," Ellen insisted. "We've got to do whatever it takes to get Bob Brooks to help us."

CHAPTER NINETEEN

Skeleton Hunting

The OU anthropologist wasn't at all what Ellen had expected. He was tall and thin—except for a round pot belly—and had a receding hairline of white tufts and a short white beard. His blue eyes were stunning, as if made from some magical crystal he'd unearthed. But it was his smile that was the most unexpected aspect of him. Ellen had expected a pompous academic only to find a friendly, outgoing, and very relaxed earth digger.

"Come on in," he said, jumping up from behind his desk when Ellen tapped on his opened office door. "Please excuse the mess. I'm Bob." He shook each of their hands as they introduced themselves. "Please make yourselves comfortable." He pointed to three human skulls sitting on the top of a tall file cabinet. "Don't mind my friends. They're meant to cheer up the place, not freak you out."

Ellen and Sue sat on a wrinkled leather loveseat tucked between two overflowing bookshelves. Tanya took a chair in front of the professor's desk. Instead of returning to his seat behind the desk, he pushed a stack of papers aside and sat on the corner of it. "What can I do you ladies for?"

When neither Sue nor Tanya replied, Ellen realized that was her cue to speak. "We're hoping you can tell us about your search for mass graves in Tulsa back in 1998."

He frowned. "Well, there's not much to tell. We found squat. End of story."

"Do you think the mass graves exist?" Sue asked. "Or do you believe those were empty rumors."

"At least one has to exist," he said. "The reports from eyewitnesses were incontrovertible—too many to be based on rumors."

"We think we may have a lead on a possible site," Ellen said.

"What kind of lead?" he asked.

Ellen glanced at Tanya and Sue.

"Bob, do you believe in ghosts?" Sue asked.

"Absolutely," he said. "No one who's seen and heard what *I* have could believe anything else."

Ellen was glad but surprised. Most scientists looked down their noses at any mention of ghosts. Ellen had, too, just over a year ago. The more she got into this paranormal thing, the more she realized how obtuse she'd been.

"We've been investigating an abandoned building in Tulsa," Ellen said.

"With a team of seasoned paranormal investigators," Sue added.

"And we have reason to believe a mass grave of riot victims is on the property," Ellen said.

"Would you be willing to help us?" Tanya asked. "Can you test the ground for signs of the bodies?"

Bob folded his arms across his chest. "Who owns the property?"

"We do," Sue said.

He lifted his brows. "Oh? Good. That's good. That means I don't need to get any special permissions."

"Does that mean you'll help us?" Tanya asked.

"Well, now hold on," he said. "Let's not jump the gun. First tell me more about why you think this is the sweet spot."

Ellen and her friends told the anthropologist about their experiences—about the whispers, "Don't ignore us," and "We are here." They also told him about Vivian, about the butterflies, about Eduardo Mankiller and what happened that night with the Indian woman, the bones, the fire, and the wind. They told him about the dowsing rods, and the spirit that came up from the ground. They told him about the shadow man, who'd identified himself as Van Hurley through the Ouija Board. And they showed him the affidavit they'd recovered from Patty Cole's basement.

As he looked over the yellowed papers, his face lit up with excitement. "Ain't this something, ladies! Ain't this something!"

"So where do we go from here?" Ellen asked.

"We need to get a move on to beat the snow," Bob said. "Once the snow falls, my work gets a million times more difficult."

"We also need to draw up an agreement of some kind," Sue said. "Are you going to need us to pay you for your services?"

"All I want is a paper out of it," he said, "and the credit for finding the grave, if we find it."

"*We* don't need the credit, do we?" Sue asked Ellen and Tanya.

"That doesn't matter to me," Tanya said. "I just want to help the spirits find peace."

"Me, too," Ellen said.

"How soon can you start?" Sue asked him.

"Tomorrow," he said. "My classes are on Tuesdays and Thursdays, so I'll drive up there with my equipment and take some initial readings, working through the weekend. Then we'll go from there."

"Fantastic," Ellen said, beaming.

Sue handed him a scrap of paper. "Here's the address."

"There's a stick in the ground marking the spot the dowsing rods pointed to," Ellen added, handing over a copy of the key. They'd received three at closing. "This will get you through the gate."

"You ladies aren't coming?" Bob asked. "It's pretty exciting stuff."

"We have to head back to San Antonio," Tanya explained.

Ellen frowned. She really didn't want to miss this. "Unless we postpone our trip back home."

That night, the ladies shared a hotel in Norman, where they discussed the possibility of delaying their trip back to San Antonio.

Sue went online and discovered that they could upgrade their train ticket to a ten-ride pass, which would allow them to travel back and forth between Oklahoma City and San Antonio up to ten times over a 40, 60, or 180-day time frame. They wouldn't be able to cancel their existing ride to San Antonio, scheduled for the next day, but by upgrading, they wouldn't lose their money, either.

"We'd still have nine trips after the upgrade," Sue said. "I think this is a better deal, anyway. Don't you?"

"Sure is," Tanya agreed. "I didn't know about the multi-ride option."

"I didn't either," Ellen said. "I wonder if Nolan knows."

"Can you take off another week of work?" Sue asked Tanya.

"I have something I've been meaning to tell you guys," Tanya said.

"What?" Ellen asked, studying her friend's face.

"I've been thinking about this since my mother died, and now that we've decided to make ghost healing a thing for us, well… I'm thinking about putting in my two weeks' notice to the Immigration Office."

"Really?" Sue asked.

"They'd been letting me do a lot of work from home, so I wasn't sure I should quit," Tanya said, "but it's been soul-sucking, you know? I want to have the same freedom as the two of you to travel to different places, to find more ghosts to heal."

"What does Dave think?" Sue asked.

"He wants me to be happy," Tanya said. "As long as we can make money on our projects. Do you think we can?"

"Of course, we can," Sue said. "I mean, yes, there's a risk. But I really think we can do this."

"So, it's settled then?" Ellen asked. "We stay another week?"

"I'm good with that," Sue said. "Tanya?"

"Will you help me draft my letter of resignation?" she asked them with a smile.

Ellen hugged each of her friends. "I know we can do this, ladies! We're strong, independent women who can make our dreams come true."

"I think this calls for a round of margaritas," Sue said.

They decided to put on their shoes and go downstairs to the hotel bar for a quick celebration.

"We should form a limited liability company and call ourselves Ghost Healers," Ellen said after taking a sip of her margarita.

"Ghost Healers, LLC.," Sue said. "That has a nice ring to it."

"We should get shirts made and maybe business cards," Tanya said. "Maybe we could even set up a website where people could post about haunted places they know about."

Ellen clinked her margarita glass against Tanya's. "That's actually a great idea. I could use my graphic art skills to create a killer website."

"I could do our bookkeeping and our taxes," Tanya said.

"And I'll just smile and look pretty," Sue said as she clinked her glass against each of theirs with a laugh.

Friday morning, after breakfast, they returned to Tulsa. The two and a half hours went by quickly as they brainstormed for more business ideas. It was noon when they arrived at their property to find Bob's pickup already there. The anthropologist was pushing something resembling a lawn mower, over the ground where the dowsing rods had crossed. A cold front had blown in, and Ellen was wishing she'd packed a jacket. With all the hot flashes she'd been experiencing, she hadn't anticipated needing one.

Ellen and her friends crossed the dusty yard to where Bob was working. They stood there, watching, not wanting to interrupt his work, when he suddenly noticed them.

"Hello, there," he said, turning off his machine.

He walked up to them and shook each of their hands.

"Having any luck?" Ellen asked.

"Not with finding bodies," he said. "But I do have some good news for you ladies."

"Oh?" Sue asked.

"That spirit you thought came out of the ground, here? That was gas from an oil seep."

"What does that mean?" Tanya asked.

"You ladies are sitting on top of oil right here," he said. "Please tell me you own the mineral rights."

Ellen looked at Sue. "What did Gayle say?"

"I forgot to text her," Sue said, pulling out her phone. "I'll do it right now."

"Oh, my gosh," Tanya said. "I'm so nervous."

As excited as Ellen was about the prospect of striking oil, she was disappointed about the mass grave. "No sign of bodies at all?"

"None here," he said. "That doesn't mean there isn't a grave somewhere on the property. I'll keep looking."

"She says yes," Sue said, jumping from the ground.

Ellen had never seen Sue jump.

"We own the mineral rights!" Sue repeated.

"You need to hire yourselves an oil well service," Bob said. "There's definitely something there."

Their excitement was interrupted by the arrival of a police officer who walked up from the fence to meet them in the middle of the field.

"Hello. I'm Officer Ryan," he said. He was tall, with brown curly hair and green eyes. He was probably in his thirties and was round but solid and a little intimidating to Ellen. "Can I see some identification, please?"

Bob pulled his wallet from his back trouser pocket and handed over his ID, asking, "What seems to be the problem, officer?" as Ellen, Sue, and Tanya dug theirs from their purses.

"I'm just wondering what you folks are up to," he said. "This is city property. Do you mind telling me why you're here?"

"*We* own the property, Officer," Sue said, shooting a thumb toward Ellen and Tanya.

"We just closed on it yesterday," Ellen added.

"You can check with Gayle Boring at the ReMax Office in town," Tanya said.

"Is that right? Very good, very good." The officer returned their ID's. "Just out of curiosity, what are you planning to do with this old building?"

"We hope to make apartments," Sue said.

"Unless we find the mass grave of riot victims," Ellen said. "In that case, maybe we'd do something else with it."

"Like what?" Tanya asked. "We haven't discussed that."

"I don't know," Ellen said. "I'm just saying we should be open to other possibilities."

"What other possibilities?" Sue asked. "You mean like a museum bed and breakfast?"

Tanya bent her brows. "Like the Gold House?"

"Wouldn't it be cool to restore it to the social club that it once was?" Ellen asked. "There's always people next door at Cain's. I think someone might be interested in running an entertainment business here. Think how cool it would be to have the skating rink, bowling alley, ballroom, and dining room operational again. We could preserve the history and create a money-making business for someone."

"Did you say you're looking for a mass grave?" the officer asked.

"That's right," Bob answered.

"That's why he's here," Sue added, shooting a thumb toward Bob. "He's an anthropologist from OU."

The officer frowned. "What prompted you to look here?"

"Oh, just a hunch," Bob said.

"I wouldn't waste your time," Officer Ryan said with a laugh. "You might as well go digging for gold. There's no mass grave."

"Oh, there's a mass grave, all right," Bob insisted. "It might not be here on this property, but I assure you, it's somewhere in Tulsa."

"I thought that can of worms was closed a long time ago," the officer commented.

"Yes, sir," Bob said. "But then these ladies here have gone and opened it again."

The police officer looked them over warily. Then he thanked them for their time and walked away.

When he was no longer within earshot, Ellen said, "He didn't seem too happy with us."

"Get used to it," Bob said. "If you plan to keep looking, you're bound to piss off a whole lot of people in this town."

CHAPTER TWENTY

Stakeout

That night, Ellen and her friends invited Bob to join them at the hotel bar, where Sue said she'd had her best margarita ever, and since she was the authority on the quality of all food and drink, the hotel bar it was. Although they wouldn't know with any certainty if the oil seep would lead to a lucrative well, they'd decided to celebrate, just in case. Bob seemed convinced that the land was on top of a significant reservoir that would make them good money for years to come.

"So maybe Miss Myrtle wasn't blowing us off when she told us we were about to come into some money," Ellen said, clinking her glass against those of her friends.

"Were you serious when you said you wanted to restore the building to its original form?" Tanya asked. "Because I don't think it's a bad idea, actually."

"I've been thinking about that, too," Sue said. "At first, I thought we'd get more if we broke it up into several apartments, but we'd also have to spend a whole lot more to do that."

"That's what I was thinking," Ellen said. "And I like the idea of restoring a historic building back to its original glory."

"Cheers to that," Bob said, clinking his mug of beer against her margarita glass.

She met his smile. There was something very attractive about those stunning blue eyes and openly friendly mouth. If she weren't already married…Blood rushed to her cheeks, and she looked away, down at the wooden table, and wiped up some condensation from her glass with her cocktail napkin. She hadn't had a thought like that in years.

"Is it decided then?" Tanya asked.

"As far as I'm concerned," Sue said. "Ellen?"

"Count me in!" she clinked her glass against theirs once more and laughed—maybe a bit too loudly.

"You know what else I was thinking?" Tanya said. "Wouldn't it be great if we made enough from the oil to, I don't know, give to Green-wood to invest in the black community?"

"That's quite a generous thought," Bob said.

"I like it," Ellen said. "I guess it depends on how much it earns. I still think we should check into the legality of suing for reparations."

"It's too late," Sue said. "But I'd be open to creating a charitable fund for Greenwood. It would help offset the new income taxes we'll be responsible for."

Ellen shook her head. "If only we could find those bodies. Can you imagine what it would mean?"

"I've imagined it a million times," Bob said, once again meeting her eyes with his stunning blue ones. "We'd have indisputable evidence about what really happened. I've never believed it was anything but an organized holocaust."

"Not to mention the peace we'd bring to the ghosts and to any of their living descendants," Ellen said.

Bob squeezed her hand. "You three ladies are the most generous souls I've ever met. I'm glad I got to meet you. And I hope as much as you that we find those bodies."

That night, Ellen had a dream about Bob—a pleasant change from the nightmarish flames. When she woke up, she held onto the dream, re-calling the passion that had surged though her. Then she admonished herself for entertaining the fantasy. She loved her husband, and her at-traction to Bob and the feelings of passion he had awakened in her reminded her further that she needed to reconnect with Paul. He was the father of her children, and a kind, handsome, smart, witty man. At least he used to be. She needed to find the old Paul again. And maybe to do that, she needed to find the old Ellen.

But who *was* she?

She was brought from her reverie when she noticed a text on her cell phone. It was from Bob: *You ladies might want to come to the property today when you have a chance. There's something you need to see.*

"Well, could he have been any more mysterious?" Sue said when Ellen read her text aloud.

"Why don't we get dressed and head over there?" Tanya suggested. "It looks like a nice day for a walk."

"Only if we can stop at the bakery on the way," Sue said. "I can't stop thinking about the croissant I had there the day before yesterday."

When they reached the property, Bob was pushing his lawn-mower-like contraption across the front field, stopping every few feet to observe the small computer screen. He waved when he noticed them.

"How's it going?" Tanya asked.

"Nothing promising yet," he said.

"Oh, really?" Sue frowned. "You got our hopes up with your enigmatic text."

He rubbed his chin. "Sorry about that. No, I'm afraid the vermin are coming out of the woodwork, just as I suspected they would."

"Oh, great," Sue said. "Termites?"

"I suppose we should be prepared for these kinds of expenses," Tanya said. "It *is* an old building."

"Not literal vermin," Bob said. "There was a note taped to the gate when I got here this morning." He pulled a piece of paper from his jacket pocket. "Take a look at this."

Scribbled in blue ink were these words:

Go back to where you came from, or the mass grave will be your own.

Tanya covered her mouth. "Who would say such a thing?"

"And why?" Sue asked. "Who stands to lose if we find the bodies?"

"Well, the city of Tulsa," Bob said, "if you can make a case for reparations. Possibly even the state of Oklahoma or the federal government, since the National Guard was involved."

"Are you saying this note might have been written by a city, state, or federal official?" Ellen asked.

"Wouldn't be surprised." Bob pulled a newspaper clipping from his other jacket pocket. "But I suppose it could have been anyone who didn't like what *this* had to say."

"What is it?" Tanya asked.

"It was in this morning's *Tulsa World*," he said. "I thought you ladies might like to see it."

Ellen took the article and read the headline: *Brooks Resumes Search*

She skimmed the article. "It mentions our names! How did they get our names?"

"Do you think Officer Ryan had anything to do with it?" Sue asked.

"Anyone could have gotten your names from the city's real estate agency," Bob said. "But unless someone else recognized me, he's the only person besides you three that knows I'm here."

"You didn't tell anyone in Oklahoma City?" Ellen asked.

"Just my wife."

"This is scary, guys," Tanya said. "Shouldn't we report this to the police? To someone other than Officer Ryan?"

"Wouldn't do any good," Bob said. "Scott Ellsworth and I, and others doing the work for the Tulsa Riot Commission, got far worse. No one did anything about it. Hell, like I said, the people who should help are probably the ones behind the threats."

"That's a serious accusation," Sue said.

"If the shoe fits..." Bob mumbled.

Ellen tucked the note away in her pocket. "Maybe we should invest in better security."

Sue snapped her fingers. "It might be that old woman we saw the night we came with Eduardo."

"Yeah," Tanya agreed. "Maybe she has nowhere else to go and thinks she can scare us off."

"Maybe," Ellen said.

"Have you heard from the online lab yet?" Bob asked.

Ellen shook her head.

"I wish I'd known you then," he said. "I'd have analyzed the bones for you for free."

"Maybe it was the old woman's child," Sue said. "She couldn't let go of it, so she keeps its skeleton wrapped up in a blanket."

"Creepy," Tanya said. "Especially now that it's missing an arm."

"Maybe she sleeps with it at night," Sue said.

This gave Ellen an idea. "We should look for the old woman and offer to help her find a homeless shelter."

"And how do you plan to do that?" Bob asked.

"We could hide out here tonight and wait for her," Ellen said.

Tanya laughed. "You want to stay here? With all the ghosts?"

"Van and Vivian will protect us," Ellen said.

"How can you be so sure?" Sue asked. "Another *feeling*?"

"As a matter of fact, yes."

"I don't know why we're paying for a hotel if we aren't going to use it," Sue complained later that evening as they walked from their hotel room at dusk back toward the property.

They'd spent the day interviewing contractors, oil well services, and attorneys—though they hadn't made any decisions yet. They'd also checked into having the fence mended and secured with electrical wire and a few surveillance cameras, but the fees were pricey, so they'd decided to hold off until they had a better idea what kind of money the oil would bring in. Now they were going to hide out in the building and keep an eye out for the old Native American woman who had confronted them and had nearly set the place on fire. Bob had already gone ahead of them—also by foot so no vehicles would give away their stakeout. He was planning to stay in the room with the dreamcatchers in case the old woman managed to get past Ellen and her friends. If the woman didn't show up, maybe whoever left the threatening note would. Plus, Ellen wanted to try out the equipment in her ghost hunting kit.

Never one to go to a party emptyhanded, Sue had made her famous dip using ingredients she'd bought from a corner supermarket in the Brady Arts District. Tanya carried a bag with a box of crackers, bottle of wine, and plastic cups from the hotel. Ellen carried a bag with flashlights, bottled water, and, of course, her ghost hunting kit.

The sun hadn't gone down, but it was still a bit dark inside the building as they made their way through the hobo camp and down the long hallway past the bathrooms. Once they reached the ballroom with its big windows and skylights, they no longer needed their flashlights—at least for now.

"So where should we hide out?" Tanya asked.

They all three scanned the room, thinking.

"It'll be dark soon," Ellen said. "We could just have a seat on those risers and wait."

"That doesn't sound very comfortable," Sue said. "I need back support, and we have no idea how long we're going to be here."

"She may not come at all," Ellen pointed out.

"How about the dumbwaiters?" Tanya said from the back wall beneath the catwalk.

Ellen was shocked when Tanya climbed inside, pulled up her knees, and closed the door.

"This is perfect," Tanya said from the inside.

"But can you breathe in there?" Sue asked. "Or see? How would you know when the old woman showed up? Besides, there's no way Ellen or I could fit in one of those."

"Speak for yourself," Ellen said. "I could, too, fit."

When Tanya slid the door open, Ellen helped her out and took her place. "See? No problem."

"I want to see you pull your legs to your chest, like Tanya did, and close the door," Sue challenged.

"No way," Ellen said. "Not because I couldn't, but because I'd be too claustrophobic."

"It *was* pretty gross in there," Tanya said. "But I'm trying to push myself out of my comfort zone."

"Well, good for you," Sue said. "But I like my comfort zone just fine, thank you."

"Let's go upstairs and check on Bob," Ellen suggested.

They crossed the ballroom and headed for the skating rink, to the stairs on the west wing.

Sue struggled to keep up. "Maybe he'd like to have some of this dip."

Before they'd reached the room with the dreamcatchers, Bob opened the door and said, "I could hear you ladies coming a mile away. You might need to work on your stakeout skills."

Ellen laughed. "I think you're right."

"We thought you might like some dip before you hunker down for the night," Sue said, indicating the big plastic bowl she was carrying. "Tanya has the crackers."

Bob shook his head. "That old woman could be coming any minute. You really want to risk giving yourselves away over some dip?"

"You obviously have never tasted this dip," Sue said.

"Why don't you three go back to your hotel and leave this to me?" he suggested.

"Not on your life," Ellen said. "He's right, though. We need to take this stakeout more seriously. Why don't we sit over there, at the end of this catwalk? She won't see us in the dark. Then, when she comes…"

"*If* she comes," Sue said. "And I really don't think she will…"

"If she comes up to her room, then we can block the door and trap her, forcing her to talk to us," Ellen said, feeling good about the plan.

"Sounds good to me," Tanya said. "Should we try it?"

"You want us to sit on the floor?" Sue asked. "Once I go down, I may not come back up."

"You can wait in here with me," Bob said. "The bed's pretty comfortable."

Sue laughed. "Are you hitting on me, Bob?"

Bob's face turned red. "No, I mean, no. I'm a married man. I'll take the chair."

"Oh, there's a chair in there?" Tanya asked. "Maybe she could use it out here, with us."

"I don't like to sit in old chairs," Sue said. "They tend to break easily."

Bob backed away from the door to allow them into the room. From the window, Ellen could see that dusk was fading fast, but a bit of light came in from the highway. In addition to that light, Bob had a lantern on the floor at the foot of the bed, and he'd lit the candle with the Virgin Mary painted on it on the bedside table. He also had laid a sleeping bag on top of the bed, where he'd presumably been lying before they'd come upstairs. She shuddered at the prospect of lice and bedbugs infesting his bedding. Next to the bedside table was an old wooden chair.

Bob sat in it. "It's sturdy. And not too uncomfortable."

He got up and let Sue try.

"I guess this will work," she said.

Sue put the bowl on the table next to the candle and took the box of crackers from Tanya's bag. "But we're not leaving this room until you try this."

She held open the box of crackers and stared him down until he took one and scooped it into the dip.

"Well, hell, that *is* good," he said. "Let me have one more."

He took another and ate it up with a smile. "Now let me carry this chair out there for you, and let's try to keep as quiet as we can from here on out. Okay ladies?"

"You want some wine, or some bottled water?" Ellen asked.

"No thanks, I'm good," he said.

He followed them back out onto the catwalk past the other bedroom door.

"We could hide in there," Tanya said.

"But then we wouldn't see her coming," Sue said. "You'd be better off in the dumbwaiter."

"Ladies, you need to whisper if you want this to work," he said. "Or better yet, try not to talk at all."

Ellen covered her mouth to stifle the laugh gurgling from her throat. He might as well be asking them to fly.

What were they thinking in coming here tonight?

She'd been hoping to use her ghost hunting equipment, but now she realized its blinking lights might give them away.

"Maybe we should go back to the hotel," Ellen suggested. "Maybe this was a mistake."

"We just got here," Sue said. "I'm not ready to walk back again. Let's sit in the dark for a while."

Bob gave them a wave before returning to the room with the dream-catchers. Ellen and Tanya sat on the dirty wooden floor of the catwalk. Sue sat in the chair with the bowl of dip in her lap.

Sue whispered, "We can at least drink a little wine while we're sitting. Crack open that bottle, Tanya."

Ellen was surprised by how many creaks and moans she could hear in the building once they settled down and were silent. Except for the soft munching of crackers and the occasional slurp of wine, they managed to be relatively quiet in the ever-darkening building. Once the sun had completely vanished, they stopped their snacking and sat very still.

The wine was making Ellen sleepy. She closed her eyes for a while, leaning her chin on her bent knees, which she hugged—mainly to show Sue she could. It wasn't the most comfortable position, but her back needed a break.

After at least an hour of sitting there, feeling as though she could easily doze off, a flash of light illuminated the building. It was coming from the north, on the side where the highway was.

Tanya jumped to her feet. "What is that?"

Ellen reached out her hand. "Can you help me up?"

Tanya pulled, and Ellen fumbled to her feet. The three of them met Bob across the catwalk in front of the bedroom with the dreamcatcher.

"Do you ladies see that?" he asked them.

"Yes, but what is it?" Sue replied.

"That's another gas seep," he said. "I'm not sure what caused it to produce a flame, or how long the flame will last, but come here and check it out."

They went to the bedroom window behind the bedside table. A single flame shot from the ground about three or four feet into the air.

"It's like a fountain of fire," Ellen whispered.

"It's beautiful," Tanya said.

"That's more evidence of an oil reservoir beneath your property. We need to get down there and put it out before it spreads. Didn't you say you had water bottles?" Bob asked, rushing toward the stairs.

Ellen went back for her bag, which was at the other end of the catwalk. "I'm right behind you."

"Bring that dip, if there's any left," he said.

Tanya grabbed the bowl and followed.

"I wonder what caused it to combust," Bob said, as he continued to descend. "Usually it's lightning."

"The angry spirits!" a voice called from below.

They all froze in place. Then they came back to life and shined their flashlights on the skating rink floor below.

"Who's there?" Bob called out.

"The fire is a warning!" the voice shouted again. Ellen recognized it as belonging to the old Indian woman. "The spirits don't like white people. Leave while you still can!"

An eerie sound of hisses and moans arose around them.

Bob rushed down the stairs, with Tanya on his heels. Ellen followed while Sue shined her light from above.

By the time they'd reached the floor below, there was no sign of the old woman, but the moans coming through the walls were almost deafening.

"What is that?" Bob asked.

"Angry spirits, I guess," Sue said.

Ellen struggled to catch her breath, but in between panting, asked, "Could the old woman have made the flame?"

"I imagine that's exactly what happened," he said. "And maybe she *is* the one who wrote the note."

"We want to help!" Ellen said out loud, in case the woman was hiding in the shadows. "We can help you find another place to live. A safer place."

They waited for a reply, enduring the hisses and moans, but none came.

"We need to extinguish that fire," Bob said. "Come on."

When they reached the flame, Ellen was relieved to find that it hadn't spread. She handed one of the water bottles to Bob while she quickly unscrewed the lid from another.

"Scoop the dip on top, to smother it," Bob told Tanya when the water did very little to the fire.

Sue was still making her way across the field toward them. When her dip did the job, Ellen thought she'd be happy to know that she'd saved the day.

"That was a close call," Bob said. "The dead grass around here could have easily caught and spread over this entire lot, not to mention the nearby properties.

"Can you imagine if it would have set fire to Cain's?" Tanya said with a hand on her cheek.

It was a Saturday night, and Cain's was alive with people and music.

"There are places around the world that have what are called eternal flames," Bob said. "Usually lightning hits a gas seep, and then they can go on burning forever. They've figured into the mythology of many ancient peoples and are used today by a few notable groups."

When Sue caught up to them, she said, "Thanks a lot for leaving me behind with the weirdo."

"Did she do anything?" Bob asked.

"She yelled at me," Sue said. "Scared the heck out of me, too."

"You should have grabbed her," Bob said.

"She ran off. And my lightning speed failed me." Then Sue noticed the empty bowl. "What happened to all the dip?"

CHAPTER TWENTY-ONE

Miss Margaret Myrtle

Sunday morning, Ellen and her friends slept in, and then, after brunch with Lexi on the other side of town, they parked at the hotel before walking down to the property to check on Bob, who was at it again with his ground-penetrating radar device.

"I found another note," he said, pulling a piece of paper from his jacket pocket. "Have a look at this one."

Ellen took the note. It read:

Be gone by tomorrow. Consider yourself warned.

"This doesn't sound like the words of the old Indian woman," Sue said. "This was written by someone else."

"I agree," Bob said. "You ladies need to be careful."

"I'm not going to let this stop me from doing what's right," Ellen said. "We can't give in to terrorism."

"Just be ready for a fight," he said.

"We're going to see if we can help speed up this process by paying a visit to Carrie French," Ellen said.

"She just returned my text," Sue said. "She's out of town."

"What about Eduardo or Miss Myrtle?" Tanya asked.

Sue tapped on her phone with her thumbs. "I'll text Eduardo first." Then she said, "That was quick. He says he's tied up all day today and tomorrow but could see us on Tuesday."

"Might as well book him before he makes other plans," Tanya suggested.

"Okay, done," Sue said. "Now I'll call Miss Myrtle."

"You ladies carry on," Bob said. "I better get back to the grind."

They waved goodbye as he walked back to his machine and continued to push it along the ground.

"Miss Myrtle?" Sue asked over the phone. "This is Sue Graham. Ellen and Tanya and I were wondering if you had any time to see us today. What? I'm so sorry to hear that. What's that? Of course, we can. We're on our way." Sue hung up the call.

"What's wrong?" Tanya asked.

"Miss Myrtle said she's feeling very sick and uneasy because she senses a terrible catastrophe on the horizon. She wants us to come to her house right away."

Tanya covered her mouth. "That doesn't sound good at all."

As they walked back to the rental car, Ellen's phone rang. It was Paul.

"Hi, honey," she said.

"What's going on, Ellen? Is there something you haven't told me about?"

"I don't know what you mean? Why?"

"I just got a crank call from some guy who said I needed to take better control of my wife. What's he talking about?"

Ellen held her breath, stunned. She stopped in her tracks on the sidewalk.

"Ellen?" Tanya asked. "Everything okay?"

"Oh my gosh," she said into the phone. "How did they get your number?"

"How did who get my number?" Paul asked.

Ellen glanced around at the people walking by her on the street. She lowered her voice and said into the phone, "Honey, I can't talk about this right now, but I promise to call you as soon as I can. I promise I'm not doing anything wrong. But we've received a few threats…"

"What?" Paul hollered, nearly making Ellen deaf in her right ear. "Why am I just now hearing about this?"

"Paul, I'm sorry. Let me call you back when I can talk."

"Don't forget," he said.

"I won't. I promise."

She hung up and told her friends about the call.

"Oh, my gawd," Sue said. "This is getting ridiculous."

"And scary," Tanya added.

They reached the rental car, climbed in, and headed for Miss Myrtle's house in the Greenwood District. While Sue drove, Ellen called Paul back to explain what had been going on, and she listened to him rant about needing to come home right away before she got herself killed. She listened for a few minutes and then said she'd call back later. Tanya called Dave to check in with him. He hadn't received any threatening calls, thank goodness. Once they'd pulled up to the curb in front of Miss Myrtle's house, Sue called Tom. He had nothing to report, either.

Who had gotten Paul's number?

When Miss Myrtle opened her door, Ellen was instantly worried. Margaret's usual smile was gone. She wasn't wearing makeup or jewelry. Her usually pretty nails were speckled with chipped polish. Worst of all, she had dark rings around her eyes, as though she hadn't been getting enough sleep.

"Miss Myrtle, are you okay?" Ellen asked.

"Come inside, friends," she said. "Come sit down."

Ellen and Sue squeezed against Tanya on the white sofa in the front room. Miss Myrtle closed the door behind them, moving more slowly than usual, and moaned as she fell into the chair across from them near the front window.

"Do you want us to take you to the hospital?" Sue asked.

"No. I'll be alright," she said. "But I can't shake this feeling that something really bad is about to happen, and I think it has something to do with you three. I was gonna call you, but you beat me to it."

"If you change your mind, let us know," Tanya said. "You don't look so good."

"Now tell me why *you* called *me*," Miss Myrtle said.

"We were hoping you would come back to the site and help us look for the bodies," Ellen said. "We've got that anthropologist from OU looking with his machine, but he's come up with nothing so far."

"Why do you care so much about finding those bodies, anyway?" Miss Myrtle asked, her mood changed. "You just gonna turn that old place into apartments for a bunch of young white people to take over? You afraid the black folk will haunt them and ruin your chances of making money?"

Ellen felt the blood leave her face.

"Not at all," Sue said. "You got us all wrong."

"Oh, yeah?" she challenged.

"We're planning to restore it to its original state," Ellen explained. "Back into the social club it once was."

Miss Myrtle scrutinized them for a minute. "You know who built that place, don't you?"

"Um, someone by the name of Monroe?" Tanya said. "Why?"

"You read about George Monroe, didn't you?" Miss Myrtle asked.

"He was the one whose hand was stepped on by the white invaders on the night of the riot as he hid with his siblings beneath a bed," Ellen said. "Right?"

"He was only five years old when they burned down his place," Miss Myrtle said.

"Was he related to the Monroe who built our social club?" Tanya asked.

"Yes, he was," Miss Myrtle said. "His father built it and managed it right up until after the riot. George used to talk about how much he loved playing in that place when he was a little boy, especially at the skating rink, because he was the youngest kid out there, and he could do all kind o' tricks."

"But I thought the area was segregated," Ellen said.

"That came later," she said. "At first, black and white businesses thrived alongside one another. But then the blacks were driven back, little by little. We weren't *relocated*, like the Jews were in Europe, but it was nearly the same thing. And it's still happening today. What do you think 'urban renewal' means? It means get the colored out the way and make room for white prosperous businesses."

"And you think we're part of that?" Sue asked. "You think we're part of the efforts to take over Greenwood?"

"You tell me," she said.

Ellen leaned forward, scooting to the edge of the couch cushion. "The opposite is true, Miss Myrtle. We want to help build the community—the white *and* the black. Wouldn't it be something if some day Monroe's and Cain's were full every night with both white folk and black folk having fun together, at both places? That's our vision. Integration. Opportunity for both races to heal from the past and live in harmony together."

At that moment, a loud crash rang through the room, and broken glass flew onto Miss Myrtle, whose back was to the front window. A ball of fire struck the floor and alighted the carpet. Ellen screamed and jumped up, stomping on the fire with her feeble shoes. She was in too much shock to know if her skin was burning.

Sue and Tanya plucked the pieces of glass that had lodged in Miss Myrtle's back and arms and then helped her away from the front room. Once Ellen had the fire out, she called 9-1-1.

Then they waited in the back of the house for the police and the ambulance to arrive.

"This must be the catastrophe you sensed coming," Sue said as she pressed a towel against Miss Myrtle's wounds to stop the bleeding. "I'm so sorry if we brought this on you."

"This ain't your fault," Miss Myrtle said. "This ain't your fight, either. It's been going on for decades, and I doubt it'll ever go away."

CHAPTER TWENTY-TWO

The Hunt

After having been treated for first degree burns on her left foot and having stayed up all night with Miss Myrtle at the hospital, Ellen slept long and hard Monday morning. Bob had come by to check on them, but Ellen had slept though it and wouldn't see him again until he returned to Tulsa from Norman on Friday morning.

Sometime after noon, she finally got up and got dressed. She'd been feeling defeated after what had happened to Miss Myrtle, but after a hard sleep, she was ready to fight back again.

"We can't let them win," she said to herself in the bathroom mirror.

During lunch, she and her friends made a decision about which contractor to use, and, afterward, they met him at the building to discuss their plans and to give him a key. He said he hoped to get his cleanup crew started on Wednesday. From there, they drove to a copy place, where they made two copies of Van Hurley's affidavit before their appointment with their attorney, which Tanya had made that morning. To be on the safe side, they'd chosen a black lawyer, a woman maybe ten years younger than they. Jillian Bridges was excited about the document and said a suit against the city would make her career. Then right before dinner, they returned to the site to meet the oil well guy. He conducted a preliminary investigation of the place and said he'd start the rig assembly on Thursday, if there were no complications getting the permit from the city. Ellen gave him a key to the gate so he could come and go to take soil and rock samples as needed. Then they went by a floral shop and got flowers for Miss Myrtle and took them to her in the hospital. They'd convinced the doctors to let her stay a couple of days while the police investigated the vandalism to her house.

To celebrate their productive day, they then treated themselves to a very expensive steak dinner at what they'd been told by the hotel staff was the best restaurant in town.

Now, they were heading back to the site to conduct their very first, very own, paranormal investigation.

In addition to the ghost hunting equipment, they brought along the Ouija Board, the electric lantern they'd borrowed from Bob, and some croissants from the corner bakery for later—though after that big steak dinner, Ellen couldn't imagine getting hungry again. Maybe she'd leave hers for the Indian woman.

By the time they'd arrived, night had fallen, even though it wasn't yet eight o'clock, but Bob's lantern really lit up the place. Tanya went through the skating rink and upstairs to get the one chair for Sue, and they placed it next to the wooden risers in the back of the ballroom. Sue had packed a few towels from the hotel, so they wouldn't have to sit on anything dirty. Ellen made herself comfortable on one of the lower risers and opened the ghost hunting kit to check out the equipment.

Ellen picked up one of the devices and said, "This is the EMF detector. It measures the electromagnetic fields, and if…"

"Ellen, we've seen *Supernatural*," Sue said. "We already know about all this stuff. You don't have to tell us."

"Well, don't get all snippy about it," Ellen said. "How do I know what you *know* and what you *don't* know? And what's *Supernatural?*"

"Oh, gawd." Sue rolled her eyes. "You've never seen *Supernatural?* You really are a newbie."

"It's one of my favorite shows," Tanya said. "I'm kind of obsessed with Dean."

"Sam's my favorite," Sue said with a gleam in her eye.

Tanya lifted her hands in the air. "He's just a baby."

"So is Dean compared to you, sugar pie," Sue pointed out.

Ellen put her face in her hands. "Can we please get back to our investigation?"

"This really is more of an art than a science, Ellen," Sue said. "You of all people should know that."

Ellen's mouth dropped open. "What is that supposed to mean? You don't want to investigate?"

"Of course, I do," Sue replied. "But you need to chill, woman."

Ellen stood from the riser with the EMF detector and the infrared thermometer and walked around the room, looking back and forth between the needle on the EMF meter and the digital reading on the thermometer.

"Shouldn't we be recording this?" Tanya asked.

"Good idea," Sue said. She took out her phone and pointed it at Ellen. "Here we are on Monday, November 7th, 2016. While the rest of the nation is at the height of one of history's most exhausting election seasons, we are here making some history of our own."

"Wait. Did you hear that?" Tanya asked.

"What?" Ellen hadn't heard anything.

Sue pointed the camera at Tanya. "Tell us what you heard."

"It sounded like a thud. Like something fell on the ground."

"Upstairs?" Ellen asked.

Tanya shook her head. "Outside."

Ellen went to the front windows but couldn't see past the shrubs and dead vines. "I'll run upstairs and let you know if I can see anything."

She took her EMF meter and thermometer along, checking them as she neared the second floor. Still nothing unusual. When she reached the second floor, she went inside the back bedroom—the east wing's mirror to the dreamcatcher room—and looked down. Her breath caught. Down below, a crowd had gathered.

"Oh my gosh!" she cried to her friends. "Something's happening outside. I can't tell what."

"Should we go out there and see?" Tanya called up to her.

Ellen slipped the EMF meter and thermometer into the pockets of her trousers and used her flashlight to guide her down the steps.

"I think we should get out of here," Ellen said. "I don't know what's going on, but there's a crowd of trespassers out there, and that can't be good."

"Didn't we lock the gate behind us?" Tanya asked.

"Yes," Ellen said. "I'm sure of it."

"Maybe it's just a group from Cain's out for some fresh air," Sue said. "Maybe they don't realize someone owns this place now."

"Some of them are wearing black hoods," Ellen said. "Maybe it's the Ku Klux Klan."

"Are you sure they weren't *hoodies*?" Sue asked. "It *has* gotten chilly out there."

Just then, they heard footsteps and the sound of men's voices in the room where the hobo camp was. It sounded like at least three, maybe four, people coming toward them. Ellen moved close to her friends, shut off her flashlight, and whispered, "Turn off your lights."

She killed the lantern and put a hand on Sue's shoulder, where she was sitting in the wooden chair in the darkness. Tanya stood on the other side of Sue. Ellen could hear them both breathing rapidly. She couldn't control her trembling hands or her suddenly very weak and shaky knees. Sue took out her phone, and Ellen's heart stopped. She worried the light from it would give them away. She watched anxiously as Sue dialed 9-1-1.

"Turn it off," Ellen whispered as she turned off her own, worried Paul would call and get them all killed.

Maybe she was letting her imagination get the best of her. Why would these people want to kill them?

Sue put the phone on mute and tucked it into her purse, leaving the call to 9-1-1 connected. Then she reached further into her purse and pulled out her gun.

Beams of lights flashed all over the room.

One of the men shouted, "The bitches are in here somewhere. I saw them go in."

Ellen's mouth fell open. She and her friends were being hunted.

She held her breath as a beam of light came dangerously close to falling on them. She involuntarily squeezed Sue's shoulder to prevent a cry from escaping her throat. She prayed to Vivian, to Van Hurley, and to any other benevolent beings that existed to please protect them from harm as the men searched the room and continued onto the next.

She may have even peed a little.

One of the lights went out.

"What's wrong with this damn thing?" someone said as he walked from the ballroom into the skating rink.

Her heart stopped again—or at least seemed to—when she heard Sue whisper, "Tanya, go into the dumbwaiter and call 9-1-1."

Ellen wanted to object, to say they should stick together, to say Tanya might be heard, but she was too afraid to speak. When it was evident that the men had moved onto the next room, Tanya peeled away from Sue and crept to the dumbwaiter. A wooden floorboard creaked beneath her, and Ellen thought their goose was cooked. She couldn't see whether Tanya had made it inside, but she heard the scrape of the metal door as Tanya pulled it closed. If the men hadn't heard them before, they had to have heard that. Ellen froze, waiting for her fate, sure that tonight was the night she would die.

One of the men rushed back into the ballroom. "I'll check upstairs on this side."

A flash of light streaked across her body as someone ran over the wooden floor toward the stairs. Ellen prayed with all her might that he hadn't noticed her.

Please don't see us. Please don't see us. Please don't see us.

Suddenly she thought of the spirits from the mass grave who had been praying out for decades:

Don't ignore us. Don't ignore us. Don't ignore us.

She stood there, trembling and unable to breathe, wondering why she and Sue hadn't at least attempted to hide behind the risers, as the man climbed the stairs and searched the second and third story bedrooms of the east wing.

Another man came into the ballroom from the skating rink and hollered, "Find anything?"

The guy upstairs came out onto the third-floor catwalk and flashed his light down on the ballroom below. "Not yet, but I know they're here." Then in an eerie voice, he said, "Come out, come out, wherever you are."

His light went out. Ellen heard him say, "What the devil? I just put new batteries in this thing."

Ellen silently thanked whatever spirit had caused that.

"Come on down." The guy downstairs continued to flash his light around the ballroom. He started at the front, along the wall opposite them.

As he searched, he said to his buddy coming down the stairs, "Do you think there could be any truth to there being a mass grave?"

"Nah. It's all lies spread by Blacks to make Whites look bad."

"But the people conducting the search are white."

"Nigger lovers."

"Yeah," the man downstairs agreed.

"Don't those dames know that Blacks just want money without having to work for it?" the guy coming downstairs said. "You hear that, bitches? I know you can hear me."

Ellen wanted to lash out at the man's ignorance and stupidity, to tell him how wrong he was. She was so angry, that if she had been the one holding the gun, she might have shot him.

"We work hard for our money, and those lazy asses just want to leech off us," the man coming downstairs continued. "Reparations my ass. It's more like free money. We'll we ain't gonna let that happen."

"Besides, why should we be held responsible for something our great-grandparents may or may not have done?" the guy already downstairs added.

Ellen wanted to shout that the city, as an entity, was responsible—not individual people. The city allowed, and possibly caused, the atrocious events of 1921, and its victims, or the descendants of its victims, who got a worse start in life as a direct result of their parents and grandparents losing everything, deserved compensation. It was about justice.

Someone else came in through the east entrance and shouted, "What's the hold up? James is ready for the cross-lighting ceremony, and we think we hear sirens coming our way."

"Shit!" the man downstairs shouted. "The bitches must have called for help. I'm gonna kill them when we find them."

Ellen's knees nearly gave out. She clung to Sue, propping herself up.

But her shift in weight made the floorboards creak, and suddenly two lights were on her like flies on dung.

"There they are," one of them said. "Been here the whole time."

Ellen screamed as Sue started blindly firing off her gun. Unsure whether to run for her life or stay by Sue's side, Ellen was paralyzed as several men swarmed them, pulling them away from one another.

"Give me that gun!" a man shouted. "This dame almost shot me!"

"Stop this!" Ellen shouted. "This is crazy!"

"You're the crazy ones!" the one pinning her arms to her side said. "Now tell me where your friend is."

"She's not here," Sue said.

"Liar!" another man shouted as he struck Sue across the face. "I saw her with my own eyes."

"Tell us or we'll kill this one," the man said to Sue.

The one pinning Ellen's arms down whispered, "Are you ready to die?"

The door to the dumbwaiter scraped open. "I'm right here. And you better get out of here because the police are on their way."

"That dumb bitch."

"Stuff her back in there, and tie the lid shut," the one holding Ellen said. "I'll do the same with this one. I saw another one of those elevators in the other room."

"What about this one?" the guy holding Sue asked.

"Did she see your face?"

"I don't think so."

"Bring her."

"Please!" Ellen pleaded. "Let us go."

She heard Tanya pounding on the dumbwaiter door, begging to be released as Ellen and Sue were dragged into the skating rink. Ellen was stuffed into the other dumbwaiter, the door slammed shut. She fell in at an odd angle, nearly on her back, with her knees crammed up to her face. She fumbled for her cell phone, hoping to call 9-1-1, but the phone was dead.

She screamed and kicked and pulled at the door, until her throat burned, and her body ached, but it did no good. She was trapped.

CHAPTER TWENTY-THREE

Catastrophe

A red light began blinking in the darkness of the dumbwaiter, where Ellen had been kicking and screaming for her life. She stopped and watched the soft red glow go on, off, on, off, in rapid succession.

"What is that?" she whispered.

The clack of a gunshot brought her from her reverie.

Sue moaned.

"That's what you get for shooting at me, bitch!" Ellen heard someone shout.

"Sue?" Ellen screamed. "Sue, are you okay?"

No one answered her.

Tears fell from Ellen's eyes, and she sobbed and hugged her knees. Poor Sue! Please, God, let her be alive!

What had she gotten them into? Ellen was the one who'd said they needed to help ghosts find peace. She should have listened to Paul. They should have quit when things got serious. They were three middle-aged women—hell, senior citizens—with no real skills. What could *they* do, especially when the living were more evil than the dead?

She should be home preparing her nest for grandchildren, not traipsing around the country solving old mysteries.

Don't ignore us.

The whisper was loud and close to her ear. Ellen froze, suddenly realizing where the blinking red light was coming from. It was coming from her pocket. The EMF meter was picking up on a high electromagnetic field. Paranormal investigators believed it was an indication of the presence of a spirit.

We are here.

"Help me!" Ellen whispered back to the spirits. "Help me get out of here!"

She leaned all the way down on her back and lifted her legs over her head, kicking at the top of the elevator. She felt it budge, so she kicked some more until it cracked open and dust fell in her face.

She spat and gagged and rubbed her eyes, all the while trying to maneuver back to a sitting position. It had gotten frigidly cold, and her breath was making little puffs of smoke in the soft red blinking glow of the EMF detector.

"Tanya! Can you hear me?" she shouted as she pulled at the top of the elevator to get her feet beneath her. "Tanya?"

Even colder air rushed into the dumbwaiter from above her. She grabbed onto the sides of the broken elevator and pulled up to a standing position. It was too dark to see anything, so she fiddled for her flashlight in her trouser pocket.

"Dang it!" It was dead.

She brought the EMF meter up and shined it into the space between the walls, looking for a way out.

"Tanya?" she cried again.

"Ellen?"

It was Tanya! Relief swept through her.

"Are you okay?" Ellen shouted.

"I can't get out! I'm stuck! What about you?" Tanya shouted back.

"I'm looking for a way out!"

"What about Sue? Was that a gunshot?" Tanya called back.

"I don't know!" Tears welled in her eyes again at the thought of her friend lying in a heap on the dirty floor, dead. "I don't know, Tanya!"

The distant sound of sirens was becoming louder and louder. Help must be on the way.

Ellen looked up, hoping for a window. Seeing none, she looked down. Something below caught her eye. She waited for the red light to blink several more times as she tried to make out what she was seeing.

A human skeleton stared back at her.

She flinched, as a chill ran down her back.

She looked again. Beneath the skeleton, was another, and another, and another.

"Oh, my God," she murmured.

She'd found the mass grave.

The bodies had been *inside the wall.*

Before she could share the news with Tanya, she heard a loud pop, like a bomb exploding, from somewhere on the other side of the wall, outside toward the highway. Then she heard an eruption of screams and wails. The screams weren't like the moaning and hissing she'd heard from the spirits in the building. They sounded like the living. Something had happened to the group outside.

Were the police shooting at them?

No, because then she would have heard a series of gunshots, not a single loud explosion.

Had the police bombed the group?

That seemed unlikely, too.

Then a chill crept down her spine as she suddenly realized what had probably happened. The cross-burning ceremony must have caused an explosion over the gas seep. Ellen covered her mouth as she continued to hear the cries of men outside. Then the light from the flames illuminated the space where she was trapped—from where the light came, she wasn't sure. Down below, the skeletons lay piled on top of one another. Why weren't they hissing and moaning from the fire, like they had in the past? Was it possible that *they* had caused the explosion? Had they gotten their revenge?

No, Ellen thought. Those dummies outside had done it to themselves.

Had they deserved it? Ellen decided it wasn't her place to judge, but she couldn't help but feel a little satisfaction from it.

The loud sound of sirens now overshadowed the wails of fire victims. Along with the soft red glow of the EMF detector and the dancing light from the fire was an even bolder blinking of blue and red, probably from police cars and hopefully a firetruck and ambulance. Now that she'd figured out what was happening outside, a new fear paralyzed her.

Would the building catch fire while she was trapped inside? Was it her fate to join the victims of the 1921 riot below?

She longed for her husband and children. She had to live to see them again. This couldn't be the end. It couldn't!

Tears stung her eyes as she cried, "Help! Help!" over and over, kicking at the dumbwaiter door.

"Tanya? Are you still there?" Ellen shouted.

"I'm still here! Still stuck! Can you hear what's going on out there? It sounded like an explosion. I think I see fire, and I smell smoke. What if this building catches fire with us in it?"

"Don't think that way!" Ellen shouted back, though she had just been thinking the exact same thoughts.

And now she, too, could smell smoke coming into the walls.

Like a frenzied animal, she kicked and screamed and pounded her heart out.

Suddenly the scraping of the elevator door caught her attention, and she stood paralyzed by fear and hope. As the door slid open, Ellen stooped to her trembling knees and crouched down to see either her persecutor or her savoir. The person staring back at her was the old Native American woman.

"Come," she said, offering Ellen her hand.

Ellen took the old woman's hand. "Thank you."

Then Ellen fumbled on her sore and trembling legs through the skating rink to the ballroom, where the other dumbwaiter door was tied to the risers with a length of rope.

"Tanya! I'm out. I'm getting you out now, too."

The old woman helped her with the knot, and then the two of them pulled open the metal door. Tanya practically fell into Ellen's arms.

"Where's Sue?" Tanya asked.

Ellen looked at the old woman, who shrugged.

Tanya and Ellen rushed around the building like chickens with their heads cut off calling out for Sue.

Ellen stumbled through the skating rink toward the old bowling alley. It was darker in here, without the light from the windows, and her flashlight and phone were both dead.

"Sue? Sue, are you in here?" Ellen called out.

"Over here," came her barely audible voice.

"Tanya!" Ellen shouted, full of excitement. "I've found her, and she's alive!"

"Barely," Sue whimpered.

Ellen fumbled in the dark toward the sound of Sue's voice. Tanya soon followed, shining her flashlight.

"There she is," Ellen said, rushing to Sue's side.

She lay splayed out on the bowling lane on her back, with her arms above her head and her legs out, one knee slightly bent.

"What happened?" Tanya asked, shining her light all over Sue.

That's when they saw the blood.

"Oh, my God!" Ellen cried. "She's been shot!"

The Native American woman appeared beside them with a handful of dry dirt. "Put this on the wound. It will stop the bleeding."

"It's my foot," Sue said. "The bastard shot me in the foot."

Ellen gently removed Sue's shoe.

"Leave the sock," the old woman advised. "It will help, too."

"But it's soaked," Ellen said.

As the old woman packed the dirt over the top of Sue's foot, Tanya asked, "Did you see what happened outside?"

The old woman nodded. "I told you. The spirits don't like white people. They're all dead."

They heard footsteps coming toward them from the roller rink, and the Native American woman disappeared in the shadows.

"Anyone in here?" came a voice. "I'm a police officer, here to help."

Tanya shined her light on Sue. "Over here! My friend's been shot!"

The officer made his way to Sue's side and assessed her wound. "Do you think you can walk?"

"No way. I could barely walk before my foot got shot. No way I'm doing it now."

Suddenly Ellen recognized the police officer. "Officer Ryan?"

"Yes?"

A chill snaked down Ellen's spine. This may be the very man that instigated the hate crimes against them. Was he here to finish the job?

"Aren't you the one who told the papers about us?" Sue managed to mumble.

"What? I didn't talk to no paper. What are you talking about?"

"I think Sue needs a stretcher," Ellen said. "And she might be delirious from the loss of blood."

"You ladies wait right here," the officer said. "The fire's been contained. You're safe in here. I'll go get the paramedics."

Ellen hoped he was telling the truth and not leaving them in there to die.

Within a half hour, the paramedics had come and taken Sue to one of the ambulances waiting on the curb. For the first time, Ellen and Tanya saw the massive destruction all around them. Charred bodies lay all over the ground on the north side of the building. Huge billowing black smoke rose from the ground into the dark sky. Ellen coughed as some of it filled her lungs. First responders rushed around them, looking for survivors and finding none. The feeling of satisfaction over their misfortune, which Ellen had felt while trapped in the dumbwaiter, was replaced by profound sorrow and grief.

No one deserved this fate.

CHAPTER TWENTY-FOUR

Stairwell to Nowhere

The next day, while the rest of the nation was focused on the election, Ellen and Tanya were visiting Sue in the hospital. Lexi was at her mother's side, waiting on her hand and foot. *Sue's* foot, which had been shattered by the bullet, was in a cast, and Sue was recovering from the loss of blood with an IV and antibiotics to prevent infection. The doctor hoped to release her later that day.

The first thing Ellen had done the night before, after leaving Sue in the hospital and returning to the hotel with Tanya, had been to call Bob Brooks and share the news about the bodies. He'd been nonplussed about the events and the devastation but ecstatic about the discovery, as she'd expected. He'd said he would begin assembling a team of anthropologists to help him recover the bodies, relocate them to a lab, and begin the arduous process of identifying remains and looking for their causes of death. He'd said the work would take months, and he couldn't wait to get started.

While they were at the hospital, Officer Ryan and another officer came to see them in Sue's room to question them about the events of the night before.

Sue introduced the officers to her daughter, Lexi.

"Nice to meet you," the younger officer said.

Officer Ryan was all business. "Tell me what happened that night, from the moment you entered the building."

Sue told most of the story. Ellen told about being trapped in the dumbwaiters and being saved by a homeless Native American woman.

"Did you get an ID on any of your attackers?" Officer Ryan asked after he'd listened to their story.

"It was too dark," Sue said.

Ellen and Tanya agreed.

"Do you think you could recognize their voices if we brought them in for a lineup and had them speak?" the other officer asked.

Ellen shrugged. "I don't think so."

"There wasn't really anything distinctive about any of their voices," Tanya said. "They sounded like everybody else from this part of the country."

The officers nodded. The younger one took notes.

"Were there any survivors?" Sue asked.

"We're not sure," Officer Ryan admitted. "The death count was eighteen, but we have no idea how many were gathered there before the fire broke out. We didn't come upon any survivors, anyway. Unless we count the three of you."

"Eighteen," Ellen repeated beneath her breath, unable to believe, though she'd seen more than that gathered outside the building before the fire. "That's horrible."

"As part of routine procedure, we have to ask this," Officer Ryan continued. "Did you have anything to do with the fire? Had you added any kind of flame propellant—such as propane, gasoline, or lighter fluid—to the area around the building?"

"Gosh, no," Tanya said.

"Absolutely not," Ellen said.

"Why would we?" Sue asked. "We'd just bought the place, and it isn't even insured yet."

"Just answer the question, please," the other officer said to Sue.

"No. We had nothing to do with the fire," Sue said.

"You should speak with Bob Brooks, the anthropologist from OU," Tanya suggested. "He can tell you that there's a gas seep on the property. That's what probably caused the explosion and rapid spread of fire."

"We'll look into that," the other officer said.

"Hey, Charlie," Officer Ryan said. "Would you mind grabbing us each a coffee for the ride home? I just want to ask a few more questions of these ladies, and then I'll meet you down in the lobby."

The younger officer nodded and left the room.

Ellen wondered what was going on. Should they feel threatened? She noticed Sue had pushed the "call nurse" button.

Once they were alone with him, Officer Ryan said, "You asked me something about talking to the papers last night."

Ellen frowned. She noticed Tanya biting her lip.

"There was an article about us in the paper the day after you carded us on our property," Sue explained.

"I didn't talk to the papers, but I did talk to someone else on the force about it—not this young man with me today. Someone else. He pushed me for more information and seemed pretty riled up about it."

"He wasn't killed in the fire, was he?" Ellen asked.

"No. He was on duty last night. But a mutual friend on the force was."

"Why are you telling us this?" Tanya asked.

Officer Ryan stared each of them down, his face serious. "I'm concerned for your safety. I think you're better off leaving this town, for your own good."

"Are you threatening us?" Sue asked. She reached for Lexi's hand.

"No, ma'am," he said. "Just warning you. You've upset a lot of people in this town by looking for those graves. I'd put the building back up for sale and leave, if I were you."

"Well, you aren't us," Sue said.

Ellen cleared her throat. "Thanks for your concern, Officer. But we aren't backing down."

He nodded. "I understand. Then let me advise you ladies to take extra precautions as you move forward. Don't go to the building alone at night. Hell, you might even have others with you there during the day. This is serious. I don't like it any more than you do. I'm not a racist. I don't agree with the Klan. I may be against looking for a grave and doling out reparations. And maybe I'm sick of this whole business about the riot. But I'd never try to threaten or kill anyone over it. I'll do my best to protect you, but you need to be careful. You understand?"

Ellen glanced at Tanya and Sue. They nodded.

"Maybe you could keep a low profile for a while," he continued. "Put some time between what happened last night and breaking ground on your renovations, perhaps."

"Thank you," Ellen said. "We'll think about it."

As the officer was leaving, Eduardo Mankiller entered with a beautiful bouquet of flowers. The intense energy was immediately gone, and Ellen could finally breathe again.

A nurse came in behind him to answer Sue's call.

"Could I get another Coke?" Sue asked her.

"Yes ma'am," the nurse replied before leaving the room again.

"And who is this adorable person?" Eduardo asked of Lexi.

Lexi turned bright pink.

"This is my daughter. Lexi, this is Eduardo, a local psychic."

"Nice to meet you," Lexi said, offering Eduardo her stool.

Eduardo sat and listened as they relayed the events of the night before for a second time.

"As terrible as I'm sure it was," he said, "I'm glad you found the bodies."

"We don't know for sure that they're the riot victims," Ellen said, "but I have a feeling they are."

"There's no way three hundred of them are inside those walls, though," Tanya said. "Don't you think?"

"The Brady Theater," Sue said. "The rest of them are inside the walls of The Brady Theater."

"How do you know that?" Eduardo asked.

They told him about the feeling they'd each experienced—the same suffocating feeling they felt when they'd entered the old social club.

Eduardo agreed to go with Ellen and Tanya on their way to pick up Greek food from the place across from The Tavern for Sue for lunch. Apparently, the hospital food wasn't good enough.

Ellen drove the rental car with Tanya in the passenger seat; Eduardo followed in his Volkswagen bug. As they passed the old social club, Ellen first noticed the burnt lot and the odor of smoke still lingering in the air. But then large words spray painted in white on the brick façade made her jaw drop open:

We will avenge our dead.

Ellen's throat went dry, and a knot formed in her stomach.

"Oh, no!" Tanya cried. "Do you think that's meant for us, from the Klan?"

"Why would they blame us for what happened? How could it be our fault?"

"I don't know." Tears sprang to Tanya's eyes.

"Maybe we should take Officer Ryan's advice and keep a low profile for a while," Ellen said, as she continued past the building toward The Brady Theater.

They parked and met Eduardo at the front door. The stifling feeling overcame her again, and she could tell by Tanya's face that she was feeling it, too.

"What do you think?" Ellen asked Eduardo.

"I see what you mean," he said.

"Have you never felt it before?" Tanya asked.

"Carrie has done some work here, but that was before I joined her team. This is my first time to visit this place. Let's go inside and check it out."

He opened the door to an art deco lobby that led to a box office. A young black man with short hair and a goatee beard was seated behind the window.

"Can I help you?" he asked.

Eduardo approached the box. "Would it be possible for us to tour the facility?"

The young man hesitated. "The theater is being cleaned. I don't think…"

"Please?" Eduardo asked. "We don't care about the cleaning. And we won't take much of your time. In fact, I'd love to buy you a drink sometime as a thank you."

Ellen was mesmerized by Eduardo's skills of persuasion. His good looks, deep voice, and charming smile were impossible to deny.

The young man put a sign in the window indicating that he'd return in 15 mins. Then he came from the box into the lobby and said, "Okay. But let's be quick."

Ellen and Tanya followed the two men from the lobby into a magnificent medium-sized theater, with coliseum-style seating facing a stage and orchestra pit on one end of the oval. The art deco style was prominent, and the historical charm made up for the chipped paint and worn carpet.

"How many people does this place hold?" Tanya asked.

"Twenty-eight hundred," the young attendant replied.

"Who's performing tonight?" Eduardo asked as they walked further into the theater.

"A magician and comedian named Michael Carbonaro."

"Oh, I love him!" Ellen said. "And he's one of Sue's favorites! How long will he be here?"

"Just tonight. We have a few tickets left, if you're interested."

Ellen turned to Tanya. "Should we go for it?"

"I'll text Sue and see what she says. I don't know if she'll be feeling up to it."

"It would definitely cheer her up," Ellen pointed out. "And you and I could use a few laughs, too."

After they'd walked down the aisle toward the stage, Eduardo turned to the attendant. "Isn't there a basement?"

"Yes, but it's not really open to patrons. It's used for storage and for servicing the building."

"Would you mind taking us down, just for a second?" Eduardo asked in his charming voice.

"I don't know, man. I could get in trouble."

"Is your manager here?" Eduardo asked.

The young man shook his head.

"We won't tell if you won't," Eduardo said.

"Do you mind telling me why you want to see it?" the young man asked.

Eduardo glanced at Ellen and Tanya.

Ellen took a deep breath. "We're picking up on some paranormal vibes in this building."

"This place is definitely haunted," the attendant said. "You don't need to see the basement to know *that*."

"We're looking for bodies," Eduardo said. "Victims of the Tulsa Race Riot."

The young man's eyes widened. "You think they're here?"

"In the walls or under floorboards," Ellen said.

"My great grand-father disappeared in the riot," the attendant admitted. "I've heard rumors about mass graves, but nothing was ever found."

"How would you feel about going to the basement with us and seeing if we can make contact with any spirits haunting the place?" Eduardo asked.

"Are you for real?"

Eduardo nodded.

"I guess that sounds pretty interesting," the attendant said. "Okay. Follow me."

He led them from the auditorium to a service elevator that took them to the basement.

Ellen was surprised to find it swept clean. Exposed brick and pipes were well-lit by fluorescent bulbs overhead. The ceiling was high, so it didn't feel creepy at all. Nothing seemed out of the ordinary: two water heaters, pipes, wires, and tall pallets storing boxes and equipment. As she crossed the massive room, however, she saw a strange-looking tunnel. She stopped and looked down it as far as she could, not really sensing anything peculiar about it—just pipes along the walls. She continued past a huge boiler, as big as a house, and on the other side of it, she began to feel something pushing against her chest.

"This way," she said to the others.

Her knees began to weaken as she walked past the boiler to the other side of the large room. She could barely breathe as the pressure in her chest became greater and greater.

"I feel sick," Tanya said from behind her.

They came to a wooden door.

"I sense something behind that," Eduardo said. "What's it lead to?"

The young man shrugged. "I've never opened it before."

Ellen swallowed hard as she grabbed the rusty handle and pulled the door open. It was dark inside, so she took out her phone and shined her torch app.

She stared for a moment, as sweat broke out all over her body.

Stuck. Stuck. Stuck.

It took a moment for Ellen to understand the nearly indistinct sounds. At first, she thought she was hearing the f-word, but by the third repeat, she caught the *st* sound.

Stuck.

"Did you hear that?" she whispered to the others.

"I thought I heard something," Tanya said. "But I'm not sure what."

"I couldn't make it out, either," Eduardo said.

"I think it said *stuck*," Ellen said.

"What do these concrete steps lead to?" Tanya asked.

"I can't tell," Ellen replied.

Ellen led the way up the steps. A few feet away, she shined her light on the most suspicious thing she'd ever seen: the stairs led to a concrete wall the size of a doorway.

Why would anyone seal a doorway with concrete?

"They have to be there," Ellen said. "I just know it."

"I sense them, too," Eduardo said. "At least a hundred angry spirits."

"How do we find out for sure?" Tanya asked. "Or how do we prove it?"

"Who owns this building?" Ellen asked the attendant.

"Mr. Mayo. Pete Mayo."

"I wonder how open he'd be to allowing us to drill a peep hole through this wall and insert a camera probe inside, like they do on HGTV with those wireless inspection probes." Ellen was thinking out loud.

"To be honest," the attendant said. "I think most people around here are tired of talking about the riot. They think anyone who brings it up is moaning and complaining about nothing. They say you don't hear the Native Americans complaining about what happened to them, and they were here first, so why we going on and on about those two days."

"You think Mr. Mayo feels that way?" Tanya asked him.

"No, but he cares about what the city of Tulsa thinks. He cares about how people perceive this establishment. You feelin' me?"

Eduardo nodded. "I feel you, man. Hey, thanks for showing us this place. Those tunnels we passed are interesting, too. Are they connected to the other underground tunnels of Tulsa?"

"They just utility tunnels, for servicing the building, as far as I know."

They returned to the lobby where Ellen bought four tickets—one for each of her friends, including Eduardo.

"Will you be working tonight's show?" Ellen asked the attendant.

"Yes, m'am."

"See you tonight," Eduardo said to him, waving goodbye.

As they exited the theater, Ellen said, "After we take Sue her Greek food, we need to head to Home Depot." Then she added, "And after that, Charming Charlie's. I'm going to need a bigger purse."

CHAPTER TWENTY-FIVE

Operation Old Lady on Brady

Sue was happy to have a motorized wheelchair, supplied by her insurance company, but it meant Ellen had to exchange the rental car for something bigger—a handicap accessible van.

"This is just like the model they give you at Disney World," Sue said of her chair. "I could get used to this."

It also meant they had to sit in handicap seating up in the balcony of The Brady Theater, a.k.a. The Old Lady on Brady, that evening. Jared—the attendant who'd sold them the tickets and who'd let them into the basement earlier—escorted them to what he said were some of the best seats in the house, even if the ramp leading up to them was a bit steep and hard to climb. Although he noticed Ellen's exceptionally large purse, he made no comment except, "Enjoy the show," as he returned to the lobby.

Ellen didn't want to waste any time getting started, especially because she hoped to return before the end of the opening act so she wouldn't miss Michael Carbonaro. She'd watched *The Carbonaro Effect* with Paul dozens of times—it was one of the few shows they enjoyed watching together—and she hoped she wouldn't miss his performance tonight.

As the opening act was announced, Ellen led the way down the ramp, past the bar and the men's room, to the service elevator. It was Tanya's job to remain in the elevator and text them the code "9-1-1" if she saw anyone else coming down to the basement. It was Sue's job to hang out on the basement level to distract anyone, like a security guard, who might come looking around. Ellen and Eduardo had the job of drilling the hole with a three-quarter-inch masonry bit and inserting a wireless inspection camera probe that would video record whatever it saw behind the wall.

Eduardo pulled the rusty handle of the wooden door that opened to the stairwell leading to nowhere. It was dark inside. Ellen closed the door behind them and turned on a flashlight. Once they reached the top of the concrete steps, Ellen took the new cordless drill from her purse, attached the masonry bit, and then handed it over to Eduardo.

"Use your muscles," she said.

As soon as he'd started drilling, a shrill scream of metal grinding into concrete exploded in the stairwell. Eduardo stopped and looked at Ellen. It was a lot louder than either of them had expected it would be. They probably should have worn ear protection because the noise was painfully loud. Ellen even stuck a finger in each of her ears to make sure they weren't bleeding.

"We're going to get caught," Eduardo said.

"Let's just do this," Ellen said. "As quickly as we can. If you're having second thoughts, give it to me and go."

Eduardo took a deep breath and continued to drill.

Ellen held the flashlight for him, wincing at the painful explosion of sound reverberating in the passageway. She kept an eye on her phone, in case either Tanya or Sue alerted her to trouble.

Then her phone went dead.

In another minute, Eduardo had the drill bit all the way through the wall. She took the drill from him and told him to watch his phone, in case Sue texted him. He could barely hear her, and vice versa. Their ears were ringing with the reverberation, almost as if the drilling hadn't stopped.

Ellen quickly attached the tiny mirror to the camera probe and the probe to the video recorder. Then she stuffed the wire through the three-quarter-inch opening and turned the machine on. The probe used full spectrum lighting, so it would capture images in the dark. Ellen watched the monitor as she pushed the probe forward and backward.

"Can you see anything?" Eduardo asked in a loud voice.

"Not yet."

She pushed the wire in as far as it would go, so that it hung down on the other side, and that's when she got her shock.

"Oh, my God!" she muttered.

"Is that what I think it is?"

First, she saw a rib cage, then a skull twisted at an odd angle to the rest of the body. Then another skull. Then another.

Ellen nodded, feeling victorious. "We were right. They're there, on the other side of this wall."

They packed their tools into Ellen's purse and carefully made their way down the concrete steps to the wooden door. Ellen opened it just a crack, to be sure the room outside was clear.

Sue was no longer waiting for them in front of the boiler. Where had she gone? Could someone have abducted her?

Goosebumps raised up and down Ellen's arms as she made her way to the service elevator. When it opened, Tanya wasn't inside, where she was supposed to be.

"What happened to them?" Eduardo said.

"Maybe they returned to their seats."

Eduardo bought cocktails for each of them at the bar by the men's room, so they'd blend in better, and then they climbed up the ramp to their seats on the balcony. Tanya and Sue weren't there.

"Can you try to text Sue?" she asked Eduardo.

Her heart was beating so hard in her chest that, combined with the ringing in her ears, she couldn't hear anything Michael Carbonaro was saying, even though their seats put them close to the stage.

As soon as Eduardo took out his phone and began to text, an attendant—not Jared—asked him to put it away.

"Sorry, sir. No cell phone use in the theater, please," he whispered.

Eduardo apologized. Then he descended the ramp and left the theater proper to contact Sue, leaving Ellen alone to wonder what was going on.

Ellen wasn't sure how much time had passed—maybe twenty or thirty minutes—when the three of them returned to the balcony carrying bar drinks.

"Where were you?" Ellen asked.

"I'll explain later," Sue said.

Ellen tried to relax and enjoy the rest of the show, but there were too many emotions swarming around inside of her. On the one hand, she was elated to have discovered the bodies in both the old social club and in the basement of Brady Theater. She was also excited for Bob Brooks to begin the work of recovering and identifying the remains and for the contractors to begin the work of clearing out the garbage to prepare for the restoration of the social club. The oil crew would be coming on Thursday, and the anticipation of how much money the oil would bring had her feeling downright giddy.

Mixed with these positive feelings were others. She felt devastated for the families of the eighteen victims that lost their lives in the fire. She also felt guilty, because if she and her friends hadn't bought the building, the Klan wouldn't have been there protesting, and the fire would not have happened. And then there was the anger. What gave the Klan members the right to stuff her and Tanya into the dumbwaiters and shoot Sue's foot? What gave them the right to try to drive Ellen and her friends from Tulsa?

But greater than the elation and the excitement and the anticipation; greater than the devastation and the guilt and the anger; greater than any other emotion was the fear.

How far would the Klan members go to stop Ellen and her friends?

After the show, they drove around the corner to a place on Main called The Chimera Café for coffee and dessert with Eduardo, who rode with them. Having a handicap vehicle made parking a cinch. During the ride, Sue and Tanya explained why they had disappeared during Operation Old Lady on Brady.

"One of the attendants came down to the basement," Sue said.

"Not by way of the service elevator," Tanya added.

"Either she'd already been down there, or there's another way down," Sue said. "And I could tell she was trying to figure out where the noise was coming from."

"Oh, God," Ellen said.

"Anyway, she asked me what I was doing," Sue continued.

"Oh no," Ellen said. "What did you say?"

"I said I was lost. I told her someone told me the handicap restroom was on the lowest level, and I'd assumed that meant the basement."

"Smart thinking," Eduardo said.

"So, the attendant took me to the service elevator, where we met Tanya," Sue said. "Tanya pretended to be looking for me."

"And then the attendant escorted us to the ladies' room," Tanya said. "I sent you a text."

"My phone died," Ellen said as she unbuckled her safety belt and then went to the back of the van to help Sue out in her chair.

The bistro was more crowded than they'd expected on a Tuesday night. They asked the hostess for a corner table for some privacy.

"So, you said you got something," Sue said, once the waitress had left with their order. "Show us what it is."

Just then, Sue's phone rang.

"Hello? Yes. Thank you. That's great news."

Sue ended the call and said, "That was Jillian Bridges. She's got a court hearing with the city of Tulsa set for December first at eight a.m. She's going after reparations for Greenwood."

Ellen stood up and did a little dance around the table. A couple at the bar raised their glasses to her. She laughed and returned to her seat.

"Show a little more excitement, why don't you?" Sue said. "This is a big moment."

"Congratulations, ladies," Eduardo said. "And, honey, you've got some good moves," he said to Ellen.

"Now show us what you got in the basement," Tanya insisted.

Ellen pulled the wireless inspection probe from her big purse and turned on the video. Then she passed it around the table. She watched with amusement at the reactions on each of their faces as they studied the recording. Predictably, each one of them went from confused to disgusted to elated.

"That's incredible," Tanya said. "Way to go, coming up with this idea, Ellen."

"I saw the Property Brothers do it once on HGTV," she said as the waitress arrived with their coffee and desserts.

"You should text Bob the news," Sue said. "I can't wait to see what he thinks about what we did tonight."

"Now we need to decide our next move. I think we should go see our attorney." Ellen took a bite of her chocolate muffin.

"You mean Jillian Bridges?" Tanya asked.

Ellen nodded, swallowing down her bite. "I think we should tell her what we did and ask her to advise us on how to proceed."

"Any evidence obtained illegally can't be used in a court of law," Eduardo said. "I watch a lot of *Law and Order*," he added with a smile.

The ladies laughed.

"I think you're right," Tanya said. "Maybe we shouldn't admit to Jillian how we got this."

"Maybe we should take it to Pete Mayo and see if we can get him to cooperate with us," Ellen said.

"We need a bargaining chip," Sue said. "Very few people do things out of the kindness of their hearts. He's going to want to know what's in it for him."

"Well, the place could use some freshening up, don't you think?" Ellen said. "Depending on how much oil our well produces, we could make him an offer."

"That's not a bad idea, if we can afford it," Sue said. "This means we should wait and see how the well does before we do anything with this evidence."

"Agreed," Tanya said.

Ellen clinked her coffee cup against the others. "Agreed."

"Wait a minute," Tanya said. "We got Van Hurley's affidavit illegally, too. Does that mean it won't hold up in court?"

Ellen felt the blood leave her face. "You're right. What do we do?"

"We're going to have to put the original back," Sue said. "Or, better yet, you two are, because there's no way I'm sneaking into the house in my wheelchair."

"But how will you explain where you got your copies?" Eduardo asked.

"There's no way I'm lying under oath," Ellen said.

"I think we need to give this more thought," Tanya said.

Just then, their waitress arrived with three drinks.

"We didn't order those," Sue said.

"I know," the waitress said as she tossed three cocktail napkins onto the table and set down the drinks. "They're from the gentleman over there at the bar."

Ellen scoured the crowded bar stools. "Which one?"

The waitress glanced back. "He's wearing…oh, wait. I don't see him anymore."

"What kind of drinks are these?" Tanya asked.

The waitress smiled. "Bitch Slappers. They're made with vodka, orange juice, and a twist of lemon."

Ellen's brows shot up. The men who attacked them before the fire had called them bitches. Had at least one of them survived the fire?

"Are you sure you don't see him?" Eduardo asked the waitress.

"I'll go see if he's still there," she said before leaving the table.

Tanya pushed her drink away from her, toward the center of the table. "This is scary."

"Do you think it's one of the men who trapped us in the dumbwaiters and shot you?" Ellen asked Sue.

"I don't know. It could be."

"Do you think you're being followed?" Eduardo asked.

"It would seem so." Sue took a sip of the drink. "It's delicious, though. May as well not waste it."

The waitress returned. "I think he left. Sorry."

"Can you describe what he looked like?" Tanya asked.

"Older gentleman with green eyes and curly hair."

"Was he a police officer?" Ellen asked, the blood leaving her face. If Officer Ryan was behind this, she was going to be sick. All his talk about wanting to protect them must have been empty air.

The waitress shrugged. "He wasn't wearing a uniform."

"Did he by chance pay with a credit card?" Sue asked.

"I think so. I don't know. I have so many customers. It's hard to remember."

"Does the last name Ryan ring a bell?" Ellen asked.

"It does, actually. Maybe that was him. Can I get you all anything else?"

"We're ready for our check," Sue said.

Once the waitress had left their table, Tanya asked, "Do you think it was Officer Ryan?"

"The only way to know for sure is to ask him," Ellen said, anger filling her heart and, for a moment, overcoming the fear. "In the morning, I think we need to pay the Tulsa Police Department a visit."

CHAPTER TWENTY-SIX

Guilt

That night, Ellen and her friends moved into a handicap accessible room—a free upgrade, since it was the only available one in the hotel. It was spacious, with an enormous shower, a sitting room with a sleeper sofa and television, a kitchenette, a set of twin bunkbeds built into a niche that could be closed off with accordion-style doors, and two queen beds in a second room with another flat-screen television.

The hotel even offered to pack up their things and move them into the new room, again at no extra charge.

"I think I'm going to like being handicapped," Sue said, once their movers had left.

"Oh, stop," Tanya said. "It's just temporary, so don't get used to it."

"You never know," Sue said. "I could break my other foot—or a toe. It might be worth it."

Ellen shook her head as she plugged her phone into its charger. That's when she noticed five missed calls from Paul. "Uh-oh. Paul's been trying to get ahold of me."

She moved the charger to the back bedroom and closed the door for some privacy before returning his call.

"Where are you?" Paul asked.

"I'm at the hotel in Tulsa. Why?"

"I've been worried as hell. There was something about a fire there and eighteen dead. It sounded like it was close to where you're staying."

With all that had been going on since last night, Ellen hadn't had a chance to call him to tell him what had happened. And, honestly, she'd been dreading it, because she knew exactly what he was going to say.

"It *was* close," she said. "In fact, there's something I need to tell you."

She told him everything that had happened the night of the fire. She also told him about Officer Ryan's advice at the hospital and the Bitch Slappers they think he sent them at the Chimera Café. The only bit of information she withheld was the drilling and probing she'd done at The Brady Theater. She would eventually tell him, but she knew, when she did, he would go nuts, condemning her for breaking the law and launching into his typical, pessimistic speech about all the ails that would befall them, as a result. So, to spare herself, she omitted it for now.

"Are you taking the train home tomorrow?" he asked.

"We're heading back Friday."

"Ellen, for God's sake. Your lives have been threatened. Don't you think you're being selfish? Don't you care about how your children will feel if, God forbid, something happens to you?"

She was speechless for a moment, letting his words sink in. Was she being selfish? That hadn't crossed her mind. She'd thought she was being brave, but now that he'd brought it up, she supposed it was true.

"Ellen, are you still there?"

"I'm here."

"You need to come home as soon as possible. Okay?"

"Honey, I'll think about it. We have so much to do tomorrow, so we can't leave by then, but maybe we can come home on Thursday."

"Let me know what you decide."

"I will."

"I love you, Ellen."

Her breath caught. She hadn't heard those words in such a long time—since last Christmas. Tears welled in her eyes.

"I love you, too, Honey. Good night."

The guilt she felt was unbearable.

In the morning, they drove by their property on the way to breakfast and saw their contractor's crew—at least eight men of various ages, sizes, and ethnicities—already busy at work hauling garbage and junk into the four large dumpsters parked on the lot. Ellen couldn't wait to stop by later and check on their progress, already imagining how much more incredible the place would look free of trash.

They ate at the Chimera Café again because Sue was obsessed with a pastry that she'd eaten there the night before. Afterward, they drove across town to the Tulsa Police Department.

When the officer at the front desk—a woman in her late twenties with short, auburn hair and intense brown eyes—asked them how she could help them, Sue asked for Officer Ryan.

"Which one?" the officer asked.

"He's got green eyes and curly hair," Ellen said.

The officer's severe face transformed into a smile. "They both do. Do you want Big Joe or Little Joe?"

"You better not let Junior hear you call him that," another officer said as he brought a stack of papers to the front desk. "You'll be dead meat."

The second officer laughed at his own joke and then returned to wherever he had come from.

"So, which Ryan are you looking for?" the officer repeated.

"They both have curly brown hair that just barely covers their ears?" Ellen asked.

"Big Joe's is mostly gray."

"How old is Little Joe?" Sue asked.

"Mid-thirties, I believe," the officer replied.

"Then that's the one," Tanya said, glancing at Ellen and Sue. "Don't you think?"

"Definitely," Ellen agreed.

"Alrighty," the officer said. "I'll ring him up and let him know you're here. May I tell him the reason for your visit?"

Ellen wasn't sure what to say to that. She couldn't very well tell the officer they wanted to confront him about the Bitch Slappers.

"I want to know if my gun was ever found after it was taken Monday night at the scene of the fire on Main next to Cain's."

Thank God for Sue, Ellen thought.

"Yes, ma'am," the officer said as she picked up the phone. "You can wait over there." She indicated a row of empty chairs next to the front window. "I'll let him know you're here."

A few minutes later, Officer Ryan entered the front office and met them in the receiving area. "Morning, ladies. No sign of the gun. I'm sorry. To be honest, I think you're probably safer without it. How's your foot?"

"You're entitled to your opinion," Sue said. "Will you call me if it's ever found?"

"Yes, ma'am," he said. "I told you I would. Is there anything else I can help you with, or did you come all the way down here just for that?"

"We also wanted to thank you for the drinks last night," Ellen said bravely.

"They were delicious," Sue added. "I'd never had a Bitch Slapper before."

The officer's face turned red. "I don't know what you're talking about."

"Our waitress at the Chimera Café brought us drinks, courtesy of a gentleman whose name she believed was Ryan," Sue said. "We assumed she meant you."

"Are you saying it wasn't?" Tanya, who was not usually one for confrontations, asked.

"That's exactly what I'm saying. It wasn't me. But if I do happen to see you at a bar in the future, I'll be sure to send one over, for each of you."

As they returned to the van, Tanya asked, "Do you think he was lying to us?"

"I don't know," Sue said.

"Did you see how red his face turned?" Ellen said. "He had to be lying, that jerk."

From the police department, Ellen drove the rental van over to the Greenwood District to check on Miss Myrtle. They were nonplussed when she wouldn't let them in.

"I'm not taking any visitors right now," she said from behind the front door. "I hope you understand."

"Are you feeling okay?" Ellen asked.

"I'm fine."

"Did you hear about the fire?" Tanya asked her. "The eighteen people who died?"

"Yes, I did."

"Did you know that we were there?" Sue asked from the sidewalk, since there was no ramp to the front porch. "Did you know that I got shot?"

"No, I didn't. I'm sorry to hear that."

"For some reason, they left us out of the papers," Sue added.

"I'm glad you're okay. Now please excuse me." Miss Myrtle closed and locked her door.

As they returned to the van, Tanya said, "That poor woman is scared out of her mind."

"Do you blame her?" Ellen asked as she unlocked the back and helped Sue in. "Her grandmother was murdered, and then she was attacked in her own home. It's no wonder she won't see us."

"Do you think she blames us for what happened to her?" Tanya asked. "I feel so guilty, like we somehow caused it."

"Let's go grab some lunch," Sue said. "I'm hungry for Mexican food."

Ellen drove them to the Mexican Border Café on Brady Street, caddy-corner to The Brady Theater. Half-way through their very delicious meal, Sue lowered her voice and said, "I think we're being watched."

She lifted her chin toward a table by the entrance where a single man was looking down at his phone.

He was an older man, probably early sixties, wearing a flannel shirt, blue jeans, and a baseball cap.

"He came in not long after us, and he hasn't ordered anything but a drink," Sue whispered.

"So?" Tanya said. "Don't be paranoid, Sue."

"That's fresh," Sue said with a laugh. "*Tanya* telling *me* not to be paranoid."

Ellen had to laugh, too. Sue was right.

After they'd paid their check and left, they waited in the van to see if the man followed. Sure enough, he left the building only minutes after they had.

"Let's see what vehicle he gets into," Sue said from the back of the van.

"He's walking down Brady toward Main," Tanya said. "Should we follow him?"

"Not yet," Ellen said. "We don't want to be obvious. Let's watch him as far as we can see him."

"He's getting into a Jeep Cherokee," Tanya said. "Do you see that?"

"Where?" Sue asked. "What color is it?"

"Black," Tanya said. "A half a block away. Let's see if he pulls out."

They waited for a few minutes, when Ellen said, "He's going to know we're on to him if we wait too much longer. Let's drive past him and see if he follows."

"I'll try to get a photo of the vehicle," Sue said.

Ellen drove the van down Brady past Main for a few more blocks before she circled around and headed to their property next to Cain's.

"Did you get a photo?" Tanya asked.

"Yes, but maybe I *was* being paranoid," Sue said. "He doesn't seem to be following us."

Ellen pulled up to the curb, where they could see the crew still busy hauling junk from the building.

"Why don't you stay here, Sue?" Ellen said. "Tanya and I'll be right back. We're just going to check on their progress."

"Don't leave me out here alone," Sue said. "There may be a killer after us."

"You just said he wasn't following us," Tanya pointed out.

"But we don't know for sure. Besides, I want to see the progress, too."

"The terrain isn't very handicap-friendly," Ellen said. "We'll take pictures. Just lock the van. You'll be alright. Call 9-1-1 if anything happens."

The brush around the front entrance had been cleared away and the boards over the doors removed. Ellen and Tanya took the concrete steps up and entered the massive ballroom, which was clear of everything. The old risers, the trash, and the blankets that had been left behind by transients were gone and the wooden floor had been swept clean.

"This is incredible," Tanya said before snapping a photo with her phone.

Ellen couldn't agree more. "Amazing. I'm so excited!"

They walked through to the old skating rink. The stable remnants, risers, hay, and trash were all gone. It too had been swept clean.

"These rooms are massive," Ellen said.

She and Tanya both took a few photos before they made their way to the west wing, toward the bowling alley. Everything had been cleared out except for the bowling pins, which had been stacked against one wall. The four lanes looked like all they needed was a good refinishing. Ellen and Tanya took more pictures and then headed back toward the roller rink. Ellen glanced into the restrooms. The toilets and sinks had been stripped out and covers had been placed on the floor on each of the sewage pipes.

"It doesn't smell so bad anymore, at least," Tanya said.

"We need to decide if we want to salvage or demo the tile," Ellen said, moving on.

"Let's check out the upstairs," Tanya said. "You think they've gotten to it yet?"

"I saw bed frames in one of the dumpsters. Let's go see."

Ellen followed Tanya up to the second floor, to the room with the dreamcatchers—only now, the dreamcatchers were gone. Everything was.

"We should have saved her things for her," Tanya said.

"I didn't think about it," Ellen said. "But you're right."

The closet door opened, and the old woman showed herself. She was trembling and pale-faced and clinging to the candle holder with the Virgin Mary on it. "This was my home for forty years."

"I'm sorry," Ellen said. "I really am. Why don't you come with us? We'll put you up in a hotel for the night and help you find another place to live."

"I don't want another place. I want this place."

"We bought this property and the building on it," Tanya said. "It belongs to us now. It never really belonged to you. You were living here illegally."

"Let us buy you a meal," Ellen said. "Come with us. I'm Ellen, by the way. And this is Tanya."

"Will that make you feel better?" the old woman asked. "If you buy me a meal and a hotel room for one night, then you will feel no shame? No guilt?"

"We have no reason to feel that way," Tanya said. "We aren't the ones breaking the law. You are."

"Laws made by white people."

"Tomorrow, the abatement crew is coming to remove the asbestos," Ellen said. "You can't be here. It'll be too dangerous."

The old woman sighed.

"What's your name?" Ellen asked.

"Simol."

"Why does that sound familiar?" Tanya asked.

"It was painted on the front door," Ellen said. "Simol was here, like in 1975 or something like that."

"Seventy-seven," the old woman said. "I didn't think I would stay back then."

"Why did you?" Tanya asked.

"I had no place else to go, and this room was comfortable. Other people came and tried to stay here, but I soon learned how to use the spirits to scare them off."

Ellen pointed through the window toward the oil seep. "The fire?"

Simol nodded.

"Were you born in Tulsa?" Tanya asked.

"Kansas."

Tanya folded her arms. "What brought you here?"

"My husband beat me, even when I was pregnant. I ran away and went from town to town until I found this place."

Ellen was feeling guilty as hell. She glanced at Tanya, whose face had turned pink.

"Please let us help you," Ellen said. "Not just for a night. We'll help you find a permanent solution. We promise."

The old woman sighed again. "Fine. You can get me a hotel and buy me dinner." Then she added. "They threw out my clothes. They weren't much, but now all I have is what you see."

"They're probably still in the dumpster," Tanya said. "We can dig them out."

"We'll take you shopping," Ellen said. "Okay?"

The old woman shrugged.

"Thank you for helping us the other night," Ellen said as she followed Tanya down the stairs with Simol behind her. She wanted to ask about the child skeleton, but she didn't want to upset the woman. "You may have saved our lives."

Tanya led them through the roller rink to the east wing, so they could check out what was once the old dining hall on their way out. It too had been cleared of all mattresses, garbage, and boxes and had been swept clean. Now that all the junk was gone, they could see it had an industrial-sized kitchen in the back of the room. The appliances were shot, but the layout was good.

"I still can't get over how amazing this place looks," Ellen said.

"Oh, no," Tanya said. "Sue just texted me 9-1-1."

"Let's go!"

Ellen and Tanya hurried from the building with Simol on their heels. The van was still parked on the curb. Nothing seemed out of the ordinary. Tanya ran ahead to the van and peered inside.

"She's still in there," Tanya said. "Sue, let me in."

When Ellen and Simol caught up to them, Sue said, "The black Jeep Cherokee just drove by. I saw the driver glare at me."

CHAPTER TWENTY-SEVEN

Simol

With the deposits required for the contractor and the asbestos abatement company, Ellen was cash-strapped and relying on credit cards. If Bob Brooks was wrong and there was no oil, she was going to be in major financial trouble until they sold the social club—*if* they sold it.

What if they never found a buyer?

She could already hear what Paul would say.

She tried not to worry about money right now as she waited in her hotel room for Simol to finish showering. Tanya had loaned the old woman a pair of sweats and a hoodie to wear shopping. The pants would be too long, but anything of Ellen or Sue's would drown the petite Native American.

As they waited, Ellen touched up her makeup using the mirror over the sink at the kitchenette. "We should let her stay here, in our room. There are plenty of beds."

"No way," Tanya said, from where she sat on the sofa flipping through the channels on the television with the remote control. "I don't trust her."

"She did save our lives," Sue, who was brewing coffee at the desk and scanning through the photos Ellen and Tanya had sent her of the building, pointed out.

Tanya stood up and paced the room. "What if she steals all our cash and credit cards in the middle of the night? We don't know anything about this chick. She could slit our throats now that she knows we're taking her home away—the only home she's known for forty years. There's no way I'm sleeping in the same room with her. If you want her to stay, fine. I'll get my *own* room."

"Calm down, Tanya," Ellen said. "We'll get Simol her own room."

Just then, Ellen got a call from Bob Brooks. He'd just arrived in Tulsa and had been to the property.

"It sure looks different," he said. "That building is a beauty."

"Yes, it is," Ellen agreed.

"I was hoping to meet you ladies for dinner to run something by you. Oklahoma Joe's BBQ is right next door to Cain's. Want to meet there at seven?"

"Hold on." Ellen turned to the others. "Oklahoma Joe's BBQ tonight with Bob?"

"Sounds good," Sue said.

Tanya nodded. "You might warn him about Simol."

"What *about* me?" Simol asked as she came out of the shower in Tanya's sweats.

Into the phone, Ellen said, "We'll see you there" and hung up.

"That shower is amazing," Simol said. "I usually bathe in the river—except this time of year. When it gets cold, I'm limited to sponge baths in the sink where I work."

"Where do you work?" Sue asked.

"I'm the dishwasher at Oklahoma Joe's BBQ."

"Uh-oh," Ellen said. "We better choose a different restaurant."

"That's where we were going to take you tonight," Sue explained to Simol. "Maybe we should let you pick the place."

"I'm not picky," Simol said.

"But surely you don't want Oklahoma Joe's, do you?" Tanya asked.

Simol shrugged. "Food is food."

"We'll go there for dinner," Sue said, "but tomorrow we'll take you somewhere else."

"It'll have to be lunch," Ellen said. "We're heading to Oklahoma City in the evening, aren't we?"

"I work tomorrow," Simol said. "From ten to six."

"Then we'll take you to breakfast," Tanya said.

Simol shrugged and said, "Whatever."

Simol proved to be as indifferent to clothing as she was to food. After visiting a string of shops in a mall across town, they'd settled on five tops, three pairs of blue jeans, underclothes, socks, a new pair of sneakers, and a puffer coat that tied at the waist.

By the time they'd reached Oklahoma Joe's BBQ, it was fifteen after seven.

"You brought friends with you tonight, I see," the hostess said to Simol at the door.

Simol glanced over them but said nothing.

"We're meeting someone," Sue said. "His name is Bob, and he's got white hair and gorgeous blue eyes."

"Would you like to check if he's here?" the hostess asked.

"I'll do it," Ellen said.

She found him at a corner booth for four, which was fine, because Sue could sit in her wheelchair on the end. Ellen waved the others to follow her.

"Sorry we're late," Ellen said as she scooted in next to Bob. "And we brought a friend."

Tanya slid in across from Bob, and Simol sat next to her. Sue's wheelchair sort of trapped everyone in their seats, but hopefully no one would need to get up and use the restroom anytime soon.

Sue asked Simol what she would recommend, but the old woman shrugged. "It's all good. Food is food."

As they waited for the waitress to come back for their order, Ellen pulled out the inspection camera from her new purse and showed Bob the video she'd taken during Operation Old Lady on Brady.

"Where did you get this?" he asked.

Ellen told him the story, keeping her voice down, so as to not be overheard. The waitress came in the middle of it to take their order, and after she disappeared, Ellen continued.

"We aren't going to approach the owner until we have some kind of bargaining chip," Sue explained. "We're hoping to be able to make him an offer."

"What kind of offer?" Bob asked.

"We'll pay to freshen up the old place if he'll allow us to open up that wall," Ellen said.

"I can't tell you how thrilled I am. It makes perfect sense that a mass grave would exist at that location."

"Can you believe a concrete wall?" Sue asked. "It's a literal stairway to nowhere."

"Speaking of opening up walls," Bob said. "I asked you here because I want to be there tomorrow during the asbestos abatement."

The waitress brought their drinks, after which, Bob continued.

"They may need to go inside those walls," he said. "And if they do, I want to make sure the remains aren't badly disturbed."

"You'll have to wear protective gear, won't you?" Tanya asked.

"Yes," he said. "They'll give me what I need. I've done this before. I just need you to tell them to allow me to participate."

"I'll text the contractor now," Sue said, tapping the screen on her phone.

"As soon as they're done with the asbestos removal, I'd like to bring in my crew to recover the bodies before you go any further with your renovations."

"Of course," Ellen said. "How long do you think that will take?"

"A day, maybe two. Getting them out's the easy part. Identifying them—well that could take us a very long time."

"Where did they come from?" Simol asked.

Bob told Simol about what he called the Tulsa Race War of 1921. The waitress brought their food just as Bob was finishing his story.

"No wonder they don't like fire," she said. "Or white people."

"They saved us from you," Sue pointed out. "That night you lit the place on fire."

"I didn't light the place on fire," Simol said. "It was my home for forty years. Why would I do that?"

"Then what happened?" Tanya asked.

Simol waited for the server to finish handing over the plates of food. She asked if she could bring them anything else. Sue asked for Tabasco sauce, and the woman left to get it.

Meanwhile, everyone began to dig in. The meat melted in Ellen's mouth.

Sue purred, "This is delicious. Definitely better than that other place we went to."

After the waitress had delivered the Tabasco sauce, Tanya nudged Simol. "Will you tell us what happened that night?"

"I held up the flame, to make the spirits hiss and scream, to frighten you away. Something pushed my lighter from my hand. I didn't drop it by accident. I don't know what pushed me."

"The spirits stopped the fire from spreading and saved our lives," Ellen said. "After Sue asked them for help."

"That's right," Sue said.

"The skeleton you left behind," Bob said. "Do you know where it came from and where it is now?"

Ellen held her breath. She'd been dying to ask the question but had been too afraid of losing the woman's trust.

"I found it not long after I moved there," the old woman said. "It was inside one of the bedroom closets wrapped in a blanket in a box on a high shelf. I was lonely, so I started talking to it, and I felt like it protected me from the bad spirits. I noticed that whenever I was holding the child, I could control the fire. I could make the fire appear and disappear. I believe she was helping me—I imagine the bones belonging to a little girl. I call her 'Achak,' which means 'spirit.'"

"Where is she now?" Bob asked.

"I buried her behind the building so the workers wouldn't take her away."

"I'm sorry I took her arm," Ellen said. "One day, I'll get it back, and I'll bury it with the rest of her, if you show me where you put her."

Simol nodded.

"You still haven't heard from the lab?" Bob asked Ellen.

Ellen shook her head.

Bob turned back to Simol. "Can you tell us a little about your life? Have you always lived in Tulsa?"

"I grew up on a small reservation in Kansas. I stupidly married the best-looking boy in my tribe. He was a brute, but I didn't mind it, until I became pregnant. When my baby was born blue and cold, I decided to leave. I was so angry. I hated everyone. I didn't want to have anything to do with my family. They betrayed me by telling me I should stay with my husband. And I didn't want to have anything to do with other people. They seem to betray one another at every opportunity."

"Where did you go?" Tanya prompted before taking another bite of her chicken.

"First, I went to Kansas City, but I could find no work there. I went from town to town. I hitched a ride with a trucker. He stopped here in Tulsa. I decided to stay. When I found that place that I call home, there was no one there. I didn't plan to stay, but I liked it. I took a job cleaning bathrooms at Cain's. When this place opened, I moved here. This has been a good place for me. I get one free meal a day, and they let me wash up in the restroom before and after business hours. I don't have far to walk from home. I make enough money to buy the few things I need—mostly food and clothes and wine." Then she added, "But I guess that's all in the past. I'll have to find a new home."

Tears filled the old woman's eyes.

"We'll help you," Ellen insisted.

Simol made no reply.

CHAPTER TWENTY-EIGHT

Home Again

Thursday morning, Ellen and her friends woke up early and met Simol in the lobby before taking her to breakfast at the Gypsy Coffee House, a couple of blocks east of Cain's.

"Did you sleep okay?" Ellen asked her during the ride over.

Simol merely shrugged.

"Well, we paid for the room through the month," Sue said.

"It's easy walking distance to Oklahoma Joe's," Tanya added.

Ellen pulled into a parking spot. "We're coming back on December first for a court hearing, and after that, we'll help you find a more permanent place."

Simol said nothing.

While they were waiting for their food, Ellen received a call from Bob.

"I have bad news," he said over the phone.

"Spit it out," Ellen said, her stomach clenching into a knot.

"Are you sitting down?"

"Yes."

"What's wrong?" Tanya whispered.

Ellen held up a hand. "Spit it out, Bob."

"The building was trashed."

"What do you mean, trashed?"

"I mean someone broke in last night or early this morning, spray-painted vulgar threats all over the walls and floors, broke most of the windows, and busted all the bowling pins. Pieces of them are lying all over the place."

"Oh, my God," Ellen whispered, finding it hard to speak. Would they ever get a break?

"Ellen what happened?" Sue demanded.

"We'll be there as soon as we can," Ellen managed to say into the phone before hanging up.

"Is everything okay?" Tanya asked.

Ellen could find no words. It was all becoming too much for her. She covered her face with both hands and burst into tears.

When their food arrived, they asked the waitress to pack theirs to go, and they sat with Simol while she ate. The old woman told them to go on without her, that she could walk, but they didn't feel right leaving her. They were all upset over Bob's news, including Simol. They dropped her off at Oklahoma Joe's before pulling up to the curb of their own lot. The gates were wide open, and a huge truck was parked next to the building. A crew of four men in white hooded jumpers and gas masks were taping yellow caution tape around the entire perimeter, and they had already sealed off the windows and doors with plastic.

One of them waved and said, "You can't go in there. We're removing asbestos."

"We're the owners," Sue said as she held on to Tanya and Ellen for support. She wanted to see the damage, too.

"Have you actually started the removal yet?" Ellen asked.

"No. I guess it's okay for you to enter. But we'll be starting soon."

"We just want to take some photos of the vandalism, so we can report it," Tanya explained.

"Okay," the man said. "Let me know as soon as you're done."

Ellen and Tanya hobbled with Sue between them through the east entrance, at the dining hall. The floors were swept clean, but yellow spray paint defaced the floors and walls. When they reached the ballroom, they found glass all over the floors along with some of the broken bowling pins. Threats were painted across the brick walls:

Leave Tulsa.

Get out.

Signed, the Bitch Slappers

They found more of the same in the roller rink. Bob was there. He was wearing a white jumper and hood, like the other men.

He removed his mask and said, "I'm sorry, ladies. This is terrible, I know."

"We're not going to let this stop us," Ellen said with resolve.

"But we need to seriously consider beefing up our security," Sue said. "I think we need to call that company back and let them install the electric fence, coded gate, and security cameras."

"I agree," Tanya said. "We've already invested quite a lot of money. I don't want to lose it to vandals."

Ellen wasn't sure where she was going to come up with more money. "Let's hope the oil well pays off."

"Speaking of which," Bob said. "Did you see them back there?"

The ladies shook their heads.

"They're already back there, behind the building. They were here when I arrived, assembling the rig. I spoke with the owner of the company. Nice guy."

"When will we know if there's an oil reserve there?" Ellen asked.

"We already know it," Bob said.

"I think what Ellen means is, when will we know how lucrative it is?" Sue clarified.

"It'll take a few days to assemble the rig," Bob said. "Then I believe they have to pass an inspection before they can move forward. They'll have to install casing pipe and wait for the cement to dry. Once they get down there, they can take measurements that will give you a fairly accurate prediction. I don't know, maybe a few weeks?"

Ellen bit her lip. Meanwhile, the expenses kept adding up. Maybe Paul had been right. This was a money pit. Now she had to go home and face him.

After scheduling the company to come out and secure their property the following week, Ellen and her friends drove to Oklahoma City Thursday night (Nolan was unavailable) and caught the train back to San Antonio Friday morning. Sue enjoyed the special treatment she received as a handicapped passenger. Ellen would have been embarrassed to drive a wheelchair onto a lift and be stared at by everyone in line waiting to board the train. But not Sue. She thoroughly enjoyed being the center of attention.

They had a layover in Fort Worth, where they grabbed Subway sandwiches. Tanya's husband Dave met them at the station in San Antonio at midnight to take them home.

Paul was already sound asleep when Ellen arrived. She could hear the buzz-saw sound of his snoring. Even though she had slept like a dog during most of the train ride, she still felt unrested. So, without waking her husband, she crept to her son's old bedroom, changed into a nightgown from her suitcase, and crawled into bed. For the first time since they'd received their first threat in Tulsa, Ellen felt safe.

But she had a hard time falling asleep. She hated that she didn't have better news for Paul and for other friends and family members who would be asking about her project. Most of them had been naysayers, like Paul, warning her of a money pit. Now she would have to say that she and Sue and Tanya were still waiting on this, still waiting on that. Ellen didn't know if the bodies she discovered in the walls were riot victims. She didn't know if Jillian Bridges would be able to use Van Hurley's affidavit in the reparations suit, since it had been stolen from Patty

Cole's basement. Ellen didn't know if she would be able to convince Pete Mayo to let them recover the bodies that she'd found in The Brady Theater. She didn't know if they would strike enough oil to pay for the rig and the drilling, much less the massive restoration. She didn't know how much asbestos was in the building, or how much the removal would cost. She wasn't even sure how bad the final cost would be for the added security—at least a hundred thousand dollars, she'd been told. She didn't know how much the restoration would be, since the contractor was working with too many unknown variables when he bid on the work. And she didn't know if, once the place was finally restored—if it was ever restored—they would find a buyer.

And then there were the threats and the fear.

On top of all of this was the extreme guilt she felt over displacing Simol.

White people's rules.

Ellen tossed and turned but could not fall asleep.

Sometime after the morning light had filtered in through her son's curtains, Ellen heard Paul moving around. She held her breath as he walked down the hall toward Nolan's room. Not ready to face him, she closed her eyes and pretended to be sleeping. He opened the door.

When she didn't hear the door close again, she wondered if he had left it ajar, or if he was still standing there. She didn't have to wait long for the answer, as she heard him shuffle across the floor to her bedside. Was he planning to wake her? Was there no postponing the inevitable?

Still holding her breath, she was shocked when she felt him lean over and gently kiss her cheek.

Had someone broken into her house?

She blinked several times and met his tender gaze.

"Good morning," he said.

"Good morning."

"Want some breakfast? Eggs? I could make waffles?"

She let out the breath she'd been holding. "You don't have to do that."

"I know. I want to. I'll go get the coffee started."

He turned to go, but she grabbed his hand. "Wait, Paul."

"What's wrong?"

"I think you were right—about that building being a money pit." Tears filled her eyes. "I'm so sorry I didn't listen to you."

"Let's not talk about it now," he said. "I'm just so God-damn glad you made it home alive."

The tears spilled down her eyes, and, in that moment, she remembered the old Paul and the old Ellen. She remembered why they'd married and who they were. She remembered that she loved him and that he loved her. And she wondered how on earth it had come to her sleeping in a different room, speaking in code, and feeling unable to simply reach across the room for him as she was doing now.

"Paul," she whispered.

He took her in his arms, and she found that old, familiar place she'd been longing for.

CHAPTER TWENTY-NINE

Calling Van Hurley

Over the next several days, Ellen got back into the swing of being home. She went to the grocery store and planned meals for each day of the week. She dusted, swept, mopped, and cleaned the bathrooms. She reorganized the Tupperware and the canned goods in the kitchen and cleaned out the microwave, the oven, and the refrigerator. She washed all the bedding and all the other laundry. She caught up on two of her favorite shows. She read a new mystery novel. She called each of the kids and had long conversations with them, inviting them all to come up for Thanksgiving the following week. She also called her brother, Jody, and invited him and his family to join them.

And She watched television with Paul, and, some nights, even shared his bed.

Their bed.

Tonight, they were watching *The Carbonaro Effect.*

"Did I tell you I saw him perform in Tulsa?" she asked Paul.

"No. Was he in a shopping center or something?"

"On stage at The Brady Theater."

"How was he?"

"Amazing."

She realized as she watched the magician on television that she'd been hiding lately. Yes, she'd been very productive and had gotten everything done in preparation for Thanksgiving, but she was throwing herself into those tasks to avoid solving the problems in Tulsa.

She continued to distract herself until the Saturday before Thanksgiving, when a box arrived addressed to her from the online lab. She carried it to the kitchen table. Paul had gone to play golf, so she was alone in the house. Her hands trembled as she cut the box open and pulled out the letter lying on top of a sealed plastic bag.

The letter read:

Dear Ellen Mohr:

After several studies, we at Forensic Anthropology Labs, Inc. believe the specimen you sent to us to be the humerus, elbow, radius, ulna, wrist, and phalanges of a human female child who died in the range of eighty to one hundred years ago.

We believe the specimen to be human due to the circular and oblong patterns of trabeculae in the spongy bone of the shafts. This is usually more dense or granular and often homogenous in animal bones, without the pattern seen in human bones. Additionally, your sample lacks a sharp line or border between the spongy midshaft and the internal aspect of the bone. That is almost always present in animal specimens.

Please note the rate of correct species identification using this method to be between 82-87%.

Our belief that the sample is from a female child is based on measurements taken of the bones and used in a time-proven formula trusted by forensic pathologists for nearly a century. Two formulas were used on your specimens. First, we measured the length of each bone and divided it by the diameters of both their midshafts and the rounded ends. Second, we took the diameter of the midshafts and divided them by the diameters of the rounded ends. Using both formulas, and applied to all skeletal pieces, we concluded them to be from a female who was in the range of three to five years of age at the time of death.

Please note the rate of correct adult/child identification using these methods to be in the order of 88-90%, and the rate of correct gender identification to be 76%.

Our belief that the postmortem age of the sample ranges from eighty to one hundred years is based on our observations of the condition of the bones, using a bone-weathering grid, used by forensic pathologists for over sixty years, and including the following: The lack of grease, soft tissue, and marrow suggests the specimens are older than one year. The severe longitudinal cracking places the specimens in the 50-100-year range. The severe flaking of the outer surface of each bone puts the specimens in the 40-80-year range. The coarse, rough, and fibrous texture of the surface of each bone, along with the presence of splintering on each specimen, places them in the 70-100-year range. One such splinter completely detached during our observation, causing a crack to the inner cavity, which suggests a 80-100-old specimen. The presence of heavy fragmentation, exfoliating powder residues, and open cracks suggest the specimens to be at least eighty years old (postmortem) but no more than one hundred.

Please note that postmortem time range estimates are usually large, encompassing twenty to fifty years, and so the correct time range estimate consequently has a higher success rate, usually in the order of 96-98%.

We hope our services have been helpful to you. Please contact us if you have any questions or if you need further assistance. We have enclosed our bill and an envelope for your convenience, along with your bone specimen, wrapped per our specifications.

Cordially,

Carl Fromme, Senior Forensic Anthropologist

Ellen reread the letter, her heart in a flurry of erratic beats. She couldn't wait to share this news with Bob, because the postmortem time estimate suggested that the child was also a victim of the 1921 race riot.

Why had a child been killed and hidden away in a closet for Simol to find years later?

The arrival of the box spurred Ellen to action, reminding her that she was on an important mission.

First, Patty Cole needed to be convinced that her grandfather had led Ellen and her friends to his personal effects in the basement.

On the Monday before Thanksgiving, she called Sue to suggest that they needed to have a séance and use the Ouija Board to communicate with Van Hurley.

"We need to get information from him that will persuade Patty that he spoke to us—something only she would know about her grandfather," Ellen said.

"When we spoke to him before," Sue said, "*he* came to *us*. He initiated contact. If we're going to *summon* him, we're going to need something of his, something we can burn."

"What if we tear off a corner of one of the pages from his original affidavit?" Ellen suggested.

"Good idea. That just might work."

"We could do it here, at my place. Paul always stays in the den."

"Tom's not going to be home tonight," Sue said. "He's driving up to Stillwater to pick up his mom, so she can be here with us for Thanksgiving, since Tom's brother had to go to Europe for his job. We could do it at my house after dinner. Sound Good?"

"Why can't Lexi and Stephen bring Tom's mother down?"

"They've chosen to spend their first Thanksgiving with *Stephen's* family."

Ellen could imagine how hurt Sue must be, especially since Lexi and Stephen lived in the same town as his parents and could see them whenever they wanted. "I'm sorry to hear that. I bet you're disappointed."

"Believe me, my feelings would have been terribly hurt if we weren't going up to Tulsa the week after. Lexi and I will spend some time together then."

"What time should we be there tonight?"

"Let's shoot for eight."

"I'll call Tanya and let her know."

That evening, Ellen made lasagna for her and Paul, and then after they had eaten, she put the dirty dishes into the sink to soak and took a pan of brownies down the street to Sue's. Tanya was already there, setting up the three candles on Sue's kitchen table.

"Want a margarita?" Sue asked. She was wearing a boot on her foot and using a cane to help her get around.

"Sure."

They each had a drink as they caught up on what they'd been doing since they'd returned from Tulsa. Like Ellen, her friends had been busy getting ready to have family over for Thanksgiving, just a few days away.

"Even if we succeed in contacting Van Hurley," Ellen finally said, "and even if he gives us the information we need to convince Patty that we're sincere, how will we approach Patty about this? Do we call her up and say, 'Hey, we've been talking to your dead grandpa'?"

"We don't want to frighten her," Tanya said.

It seemed like an impossible task to Ellen, but they'd already gone this far—too far to give up now.

"We'll send her a handwritten letter," Sue said. "That way, she'll have time to process everything and not feel caught off guard, like she would with a phone call. Then, when we go up after Thanksgiving to prepare for the hearing, we'll ask her if we can meet with her."

"We should meet someplace neutral, like a coffee shop," Tanya said.

"Okay," Ellen said. "I'll write the letter."

"Ready to begin?" Sue asked.

Tanya and Ellen nodded. Sue turned out all the lights in the house so that the candles could better attract the spirit. They set food and drink on the table with the candles, put the Ouija Board and planchette in the center, and then Ellen and her friends sat around the table.

"How can we use the Ouija Board *and* create a circle by holding hands?" Ellen asked as she passed Sue the corner of the paper she'd torn from Hurley's original affidavit. "It's impossible."

"True," Sue said. "Thanks for reminding me. I need to create a circle of protection with salt, so nothing evil will come and pretend to be Van Hurley."

"But will Van Hurley's spirit be able to cross into the circle?" Ellen asked.

"Only the spirit we summon by name may enter," Tanya explained.

Sue got up and hobbled over to her spice cabinet, pulling out a carton of salt. Then she poured a line of it on the hardwood floor around the table. "If I would have remembered about the salt, I wouldn't have offered to have it here. Now I'm going to have to sweep again."

"Poor thing," Tanya teased.

Sue sat back down and picked up her phone. "Let me find the words."

"I memorized them," Ellen said.

"Good for you!" Tanya laughed. "Go ahead then. Close the circle, Ellen."

Ellen held out her finger, like a wand. "Clockwise, right?"

"It doesn't matter," Sue said. "As long as you do the opposite when you want to open it again."

Ellen took a deep breath, and as she waved her finger along the line of salt, said:

Guardians of the North, South, East, and West,
Elements of Earth, Air, Fire, and Water,
Bless this circle and protect those within,
Whether father, mother, son, or daughter.
No unwanted entities shall enter,
And safety shall prevail in the center.
This circle is cast.
Grant it shall last.

Ellen returned to her seat as Sue took the torn corner from Hurley's affidavit and held it to one of the candle flames.

"Van Hurley, we summon your spirit, if you are willing," Sue said as the paper burned. "We've gathered here tonight to ask your help in contacting your granddaughter for permission to use the affidavit you signed in October 1921, which you led us to find among your personal effects. Please join us in our circle of protection, Van Hurley, and guide us to better serve you."

Once the corner of paper had turned to ash, Sue placed her fingers lightly on the planchette. Tanya and Ellen followed suit.

Then Sue said, "Van Hurley, are you here with us?"

The indicator did not move.

Sue repeated her previous speech, calling to Van Hurley. She ended with, "If you're here with us, please move the planchette to *Yes.*"

Again, nothing happened.

"Van Hurley, my name is Sue Graham. I am here with Ellen Mohr and Tanya Sanchez. You made contact with us in Tulsa and directed us to find your personal effects at your granddaughter's house in Topeka. Please visit us now here at my house in San Antonio and give us information that will help us convince Patty Cole to cooperate. We want to help you bring justice to the Tulsa riot victims. Please help us help you." Sue took a deep breath. "Van Hurley? Are you here? Please move the planchette to *Yes.*"

Nothing.

"Do you think the circle of protection is keeping him out?" Tanya whispered.

"It shouldn't," Sue said.

"Why don't we open it, just in case?" Ellen suggested.

"It wouldn't be the smart thing to do," Sue said, "but I guess desperate times call for desperate measures. Go ahead and open it."

Ellen stood up and moved her hand above the line of salt in two circles, counterclockwise.

"I might as well sweep that up now, before it goes everywhere." Sue fetched her broom from her pantry closet and handed Tanya the dustpan. "It's easier for *you* to bend over than it is for me."

"I didn't realize you'd invited me over to do housework," Tanya teased.

216 | EVA POHLER

Once the floor was clean, Sue and Tanya returned to their seats and lightly touched their fingers to the plastic indicator. Ellen joined them, and Sue began again.

"Van Hurley, we summon you to join us at our table. Please follow the light of the candles and the scent of the food. We seek your help in convincing your granddaughter to cooperate with us. Van Hurley, are you here? If so, please move the planchette to *Yes*."

Quickly, and without hesitation, the indicator moved to *Yes*.

Ellen sat up, full of renewed energy and hope. She smiled at her friends, who appeared equally as excited to have finally made contact.

"Is this the Van Hurley who lived through the 1921 Tulsa Race Riot?" Sue asked.

The planchette circled around and moved back to *Yes*.

"Thank you for coming, Mr. Hurley," Sue said. "We need your help. We found the affidavit in your personal effects, but we took it without telling your granddaughter. It was a mistake, and we're sorry, and we're hoping you can help us rectify the situation. Are you willing to help us?"

The planchette circled around and returned to *Yes*.

"Thank you, Mr. Hurley," Sue said. "Can you tell us something personal that only your granddaughter would know? Something we could use to get her to trust us? If so, please spell it out for us by moving the planchette."

The planchette did not move.

"Van Hurley?" Sue asked. "Please tell us something only your granddaughter would know, like the name of her favorite pet or of her favorite toy when she was a little girl."

The planchette began to move: T-H-I-S-I-S-N-O-T-V-A-N-H-U-R-L-E-Y.

Sue bent her brows. "Then who is this? Is this Vivian?"

The planchette moved to *No*.

"Please tell us your name," Sue said.

The planchette circled around and returned to *No*.

"Blow out the candles!" Sue cried as she jumped from the table and turned on the lights.

Ellen and Tanya blew out the flames and exchanged looks of confusion.

"What's happening?" Ellen asked.

"I knew we shouldn't have broken the circle," Sue said. "Why did I let you talk me into it?"

"You think that was an evil spirit?" Tanya asked.

"That's exactly what I think. How am I supposed to sleep tonight with Tom out of town?"

"You can spend the night with me," Ellen offered.

"I may have to take you up on that."

"We should do a sage smudge stick ceremony, just to be safe," Tanya said. "What if it attaches to me and follows me home?"

"Good point," Sue said. "Can you call Jeanine for an emergency session?"

"Yes," Tanya said, turning on her phone.

Jeanine was too busy to perform the ritual herself—she'd been busy packing and finishing up some last-minute things before she needed to leave to visit her family in Wisconsin for Thanksgiving—but she offered to drop a sage smudge stick and abalone shell off at Sue's on her way out of town that night.

Ellen and her friends were so grateful, that they sent the half-empty pan of brownies with her to eat during the drive.

Once Jeanine had left, it was up to them to cleanse Sue's house of the bad spirit.

They began by lighting the sage.

"Lord, please don't let me burn my house down," Sue prayed.

Then they blew out the flame so that only embers burned at the end of the stick. Sue held the stick in one hand and Tanya held the shell bowl beneath it, to catch the ashes.

"You have to protect us with the smoke," Tanya said. "So the spirit doesn't try to enter any of our bodies."

"Aren't we supposed to open all the windows first?" Ellen asked.

"First bathe, then open," Sue said.

Ellen caught at the smoke with her hands and washed it all over her, laughing inside about how ridiculous it had seemed to her just last year, when Jeanine had performed the ritual in the Gold House. She recalled Miguel, the locksmith, and the way he had followed Jeanine's directions with fervent conviction.

Next, Ellen and Tanya opened all the windows, both upstairs and down.

"Start downstairs," Tanya said, after she'd gotten the last window upstairs to open. "That's what Jeanine does, because smoke rises."

Tanya and Ellen returned downstairs, where Tanya said, "Now tell all the impure spirits to leave, fly away, never to return."

"I know what to do, Tanya—unless you'd rather take over."

"No," Tanya said, getting the message. "You go ahead. I'll shut up."

"I cleanse this house of all impurities, negativity, and evil," Sue said in a loud voice as she hobbled on her cane and waved the smoke around the bottom floor with Tanya right behind her holding the bowl. "Leave, bad spirits! Fly away, never to return!"

Ellen followed them from room to room. When it was time to go upstairs, Sue said, "Can y'all go on without me? It's hard for me to go upstairs."

"No worries," Ellen said, taking the sage smudge stick. "Come on, Tanya."

Tanya took over the talking. "I cleanse this house of all impurities. Fly away, evil spirits. Fly away, negativity. Fly away, never to return!"

They were cleaning the last room in the house when they heard Sue shouting downstairs.

"Hurry, guys! Come quick! Come quick!"

Ellen followed Tanya through the hall and down the stairs, to where Sue was sitting at the table with her phone.

"What happened?" Ellen asked, out of breath. And the smoke from the sage wasn't helping her to breathe.

"You won't believe this," Sue said. "I just got a text from someone saying she's Patty Cole, Van Hurley's granddaughter."

Ellen's mouth dropped open. "What does the text say?"

Sue read:

Hi, Sue Graham. If you think I'm crazy, I won't blame you for not returning this message, but I had to try. My grandfather gave me your name and number. The crazy part is...he's been dead for over forty years. If you want to know what he told me, please call me at your earliest convenience.

Regards,

Patty Cole

"I'm calling her, guys." Sue said.

Ellen and Tanya sat at the table to listen to the conversation. The sage smudge stick continued to spill smoke into the air around them.

"Hello, Patty?" Sue said.

"Put her on speaker," Tanya whispered.

Sue nodded and put the phone on the table.

"Yes?" they heard Patty say.

"This is Sue Graham, and I don't think you're crazy."

"Seriously? Because I'm not so sure," she said with a laugh.

"Will you tell me what happened?" Sue asked.

"Well. Just a little while ago, I had fallen asleep in front of the television, and I had a dream about my grandpa," Patty said over the phone. "In the dream, he very clearly told me I needed to contact Sue Graham, and he said your phone number. He repeated it over and over and told me to listen to what you had to say, that I could trust you. Well, when I woke up, I thought it had just been a crazy dream, right?"

"That's what I would have thought," Sue said.

"But then I noticed I'd written your name and number down on a notepad on my coffee table—or I guess it was me who wrote it. I don't remember doing it, but it looks like my handwriting. So, I decided to text you and see if a Sue Graham replied. And you did. And now I'm officially freaked out."

"Don't freak out, Patty," Sue said. "I can explain, but this is going to be hard to believe."

"After this, I think I can believe almost anything."

"Two of my friends and I are restoring an old building in Tulsa."

"But this isn't a Tulsa zip code," Patty said.

"You're right. We live in San Antonio," Sue explained. "And while we were up there, we conducted a paranormal investigation of the building we bought, and long story short, your grandfather made contact with us."

"That's incredible! How? What did he say?"

"He asked us to look through his personal effects, and he told us we could find them at 114 Elm in Topeka, Kansas."

"That's my address."

"I know." Sue glanced up at Ellen and Tanya, who nodded their encouragement.

"You're doing good," Tanya whispered.

"The thing is," Sue began, "we thought you would think we were crazy if we knocked on your door and asked to see your grandfather's personal effects because he asked us to."

"Yes, you're right. I *would* have thought you were looney."

"Well, we did come to your house, Patty."

Ellen held her breath.

"You did?"

"You assumed we were the Merry Maids."

"Oh, that's right! I remember you now!"

"We found your grandfather's personal effects in your basement."

"You went through my house?"

"Only because Van Hurley asked us to. I'm so sorry."

"I don't know how I feel about that."

"And, Patty, we found a very important document among his things. Were you aware that he had signed an affidavit in October 1921 regarding the Tulsa Race Riot?"

"No. I've never really looked through any of those old papers."

"We'd like to use that document in a court hearing in Tulsa on December first, and we were hoping we could have your support."

Patty was quiet on the other end of the phone.

"Patty, are you still there?" Sue asked.

"Yes, I'm here. But in what way would you need my support?"

"Could you come to the hearing and testify that the affidavit did belong to Van Hurley and that it's been in your basement for x amount of years?"

"Did you say December first?"

"Yes. At eight o'clock in the morning. We'd be happy to put you up in a hotel room if you want to come the night before."

"I guess I can do that. I guess this was important to my grandfather, or he wouldn't have gone to all this trouble."

Ellen and her friends broke out into relieved smiles.

"Thank you, Patty!" Sue said. "Thank you so much! I'll make your reservation now and text you the details."

"Okay, Sue. I'll talk to you later."

They hung up and had another margarita to celebrate their good fortune.

CHAPTER THIRTY

An Unexpected Turn

Ellen couldn't have asked for a better Thanksgiving with her family. Since Ellen and Jody still hadn't decided what to do with their mother's house (Ellen couldn't believe it had already been sitting there, vacant, for a year), he and his family slept at their childhood home across town. They came to Ellen's and spent all day at her house on Thursday, Friday, and Saturday before they got on the road and headed back to Kentucky. Nolan drove down from Oklahoma City on Wednesday and stayed Thursday night; but, he had to return on Friday morning. Lane and Alison drove down together from Austin on Tuesday and stayed though Sunday.

Even the news from the asbestos abatement company that their final bill came to $175,000 for the removal of all plumbing, insulation, and ceiling tiles—all found to contain asbestos—didn't ruin her holiday, as long as she didn't think about it.

She and her family members went shopping, played board games, watched movies, and sat together and visited, enjoying one another's company. Although Ellen was anxious to get to the hearing in Tulsa and to check on the status of the building and the oil rig, she wasn't ready for the holiday to end. She was never ready for her children to leave.

Monday came early.

Paul dropped Ellen and her friends off at the train station at six-thirty in the morning. Sue traveled in her motorized wheelchair and enjoyed another trip with special treatment from the staff. They spent the night in Oklahoma City and drove to Norman for a meeting with Bob at IHOP in the morning.

They made small talk until the waitress took their order and delivered coffee to their table. With the jolt of caffeine, Ellen was ready for business.

"Can we have a progress report, Bob?" she asked.

"My team of forensic anthropologists has been able to establish that one hundred and twelve individual bodies were recovered from the walls of your building," he said before taking a sip of his coffee.

"I wonder how many more are behind that concrete door at The Brady Theater," Sue said.

"From Ellen's video footage, I would suspect more," Bob said. "At least two hundred."

"Were you able to identify any of the bodies?" Tanya asked.

Bob laughed. "Let's not get ahead of ourselves. That's going to take quite a bit of time. And we are very unlikely to be successful without medical records for comparisons. What we have been able to accomplish, however, is a biological profile on each of the individual skeletons—most of which we had to piece together, by the way. They were nowhere near perfectly preserved inside that wall."

The waitress arrived with their food.

"Sounds like a lot of painstaking work," Tanya admitted.

"That's an understatement," Bob said. "Anyhow, we've been able to show that all but two of the subjects are of African ancestry. One is Native American and the other is Caucasian."

"That supports our theory that they're victims of the riot," Sue stated.

Bob nodded. "And we've placed the postmortem age of the bones to between eighty and one hundred years, which also supports our theory."

"That's awesome," Tanya said. "Great work, Bob!"

Bob's statement reminded Ellen about the forensic report she'd received from the lab. Although she'd called Bob to tell him about it, she now handed over a copy of the report for his records and for Thursday's court hearing.

"I brought the skeleton arm back with me," she said. "When I see Simol tonight, I'll ask her to show me where she buried the rest of Achak."

After their meeting with Bob, Ellen drove to Tulsa, heading straight to their property. They didn't even check into their hotel first. They were dying to see the progress.

Ellen pulled up to the curb. The new driveway leading through their coded gate was blocked with the trucks of the workers—both those working on the building and those working on the oil rig. Ellen was anxious to get updates from them, but first she had to see the inside of the old social club.

Sue hobbled across the field with her cane behind Ellen and Tanya. The front entrance now looked stately with the wooden doors refinished. And the porch was more visible with the dead vines, weeds, and brush cleared away. The property would need quite a bit of landscaping eventually, but for now, it looked much improved.

When they entered the ballroom, the sight of the massive room with its refinished wooden floors, new windows and skylights, and streams of natural light beaming throughout took Ellen's breath away. Tears formed in her eyes, and when she blinked, they fell onto her cheeks.

"It's incredible," Tanya murmured as she wiped away tears.

"Now don't break down just yet," Sue said. "We still have more to see."

The skating rink was equally stunning, as was the bowling alley—the four lines waxed to perfection. It lacked pins and bowling balls, but the infrastructure was there and waiting to be properly fitted out.

Even the dining hall had been completely refurbished, the new appliances already installed. One of the workers greeted them and showed them that the water was on. The sinks and toilets were fully functional—even though the bathrooms were still incomplete. The tile work, stalls, mirrors, lighting, and fixtures still needed to be installed.

Most of the lighting throughout the building still needed to be installed, but the electrical work had been completed and the power had been turned on.

"I know it will ultimately be up to the buyer," Ellen said as they stood in the dining hall. "But I think we should call this place Monroe's Social Club—maybe even have a sign made."

"I like that," Tanya said.

"It's definitely something to consider," Sue agreed.

As they made their way from the eastern exit (it was strange to Ellen that only a month ago, they'd referred to it as the hobo camp), Ellen was surprised by how many workers were behind the building at the oil rig. She hadn't realized such a large crew was required. At least a dozen men and one woman gathered around the machines and equipment. Ellen wondered what was going on.

One of them noticed Ellen and her friends watching, and he walked over to them and introduced himself.

"Hello, I'm Gregory Clive of Best Well Services," he said shaking each of their hands. "I believe I've spoken on the phone with at least two of you."

"That would be me," Ellen said.

"And me," Sue said.

"Well, I thought you ladies might like to know that we got the okay to begin pumping, and in the last two days, we've consistently produced an equivalent of a net gain of twenty-thousand dollars—per day."

Ellen felt her stomach flop. "What does that mean?"

"That means that your well is making you twenty thousand dollars a day," he said. "That's net. After I take my cut."

Ellen's knees started shaking and her heart was pumping out of control.

"How long do you expect the well to produce at that rate?" Sue asked.

"We can't give you a precise time frame, but based on our findings, you have at least a good five years' worth of steady production here. The reservoir is one of the deepest we've seen in Tulsa."

"Unbelievable," Sue whispered.

Tanya had covered her face with both hands, as though she couldn't bear the sunlight.

Twenty-thousand dollars a day for five years? Ellen couldn't think, couldn't speak. She couldn't calculate what that amounted to. Even divided by three, it was an enormous sum. She felt like she was going to faint.

"I need to sit down," she finally said.

Gregory Clive laughed. "I felt the same way when I realized what we had here. I'm grateful you hired my company for the job. Things have been slow in my industry lately. This find is like a shot of java straight to my veins."

They had barely had a moment to recover after they'd made their way back to the van when Sue, who was looking at her phone, suddenly cried, "Oh, no!"

"What's wrong?" Tanya asked.

"I just got a horrible text! Oh, my gawd! I need to call Lexi!"

Sue tapped on the screen of her phone and put it on speaker.

"It was a threat!" Sue said as the phone rang. "The text said that if I wanted to see my daughter again, I would make sure Thursday's court hearing is a failure."

"I can't believe that!" Ellen said. "Should I head toward her apartment?"

"Yes! And Tanya, I need you to call 9-1-1 and give them Lexi's address."

"What is it?" Tanya asked.

"Hello?" Lexi's voice came over the phone.

"Oh, thank gawd," Sue said in between heavy breaths. "Lexi, where are you?"

"I'm at home. Why?"

"Is Stephen with you?"

"No. Mom, what's the matter?"

"Where is he? At work?" Sue asked as she took a pen and paper and wrote down Lexi's address for Tanya.

"He stayed home today, but he went to the store a while ago. We're out of everything, and I've been under the weather."

"I'm on my way to your apartment now," Sue said. "But I want you to stay on the phone with me until we get there. Tanya is on the phone right now with the police."

Tanya was speaking over Sue, delivering the address to the 9-1-1 dispatcher on the phone. "That's right. A threatening text." Tanya summarized the message.

Meanwhile, Lexi asked, "What? The police? Why?"

"I'm not trying to scare you, Lexi, but I just received a threatening text. It said that if I wanted to see my daughter again, I'd make sure Thursday's court hearing was a failure."

"If you're not trying to scare me, you're not doing a very good job of it."

"Listen to me, Lexi. Make sure your doors and windows are locked. Close all your blinds and curtains. Can you do that?"

"I'm doing it right now."

"Have you noticed anything unusual lately?"

"Not really. Well, there was one thing, but I thought I was imagining it. But now…"

"What, Lexi. Tell me."

"For the past few weeks, I've felt like someone was following me. Maybe we just go to all the same places. I don't know."

"Could you tell what the person looked like or what kind of vehicle it was?" Sue asked.

"I never saw the guy good enough to see what he looked like, but he drove a black Jeep."

"Oh, gawd," Sue moaned. "Can you drive any faster, Ellen?"

Ellen sped up. "You're going to have to tell me what exit to take."

"Mom, Stephen's calling me on the other line. I'm going to put you on hold."

"No, Lexi. Stay with me."

"Just hold on. I'll be right back."

Tanya continued to talk to the 9-1-1 dispatcher. "Lexi just put her mother on hold to take another call."

"Exit in one mile," Sue said to Ellen. "Creek Turnpike. Go right, er, south."

"Mom?" Lexi's voice was shaking.

"I'm here. What's wrong?"

"They've got Stephen downstairs in the parking lot," she said breathlessly. "They said if I don't come out, they're going to kill him. What should I do? I don't know what to do! Oh, God!"

"Oh, lord help us!" Sue cried. "Lexi, listen to me! Do NOT go outside. You've got to find a way to stall them until the police arrive."

Tanya relayed to the 9-1-1 dispatcher what Lexi had just told them.

"No, Mom. They gave me five minutes, or they're going to shoot Stephen in the head."

"She said they were giving her five minutes," Tanya said into her phone. "Or they would shoot her husband." Then she turned to Sue. "Tell Lexi that they won't kill him, because he's the only leverage they have."

"They're bluffing!" Sue shouted into the phone. "Don't listen to them. They want *you*, not *him*. If they kill him, they won't be able to get you to cooperate."

"Mom, I'm sorry. I can't take the chance. I'm going down there."

"No, Lexi. Please." Then she said to Ellen, "Exit here. In three miles, take the 31st Street exit."

"I love you, Mom," Lexi said through sobs. "I'm unlocking the door and going out into the hall. So far, I'm alone."

"Please go back inside," Sue begged. "The police are on their way."

"I can't," Lexi cried, her voice cracking. "I'm so sorry."

"I'm the one who's sorry," Sue said, as she broke down into heaving, desperate sobs.

Ellen was so flustered that she could barely think. She nearly missed her exit.

"I'm so sorry that I got you into this mess, my darling," Sue cried.

"I see them," Lexi said.

"The police?" Sue asked.

"No, Stephen and the man who's holding him at gunpoint. I can't believe this is happening in broad daylight. Where is everyone?"

"Stay where you are, Lexi. Have they seen you? It's not too late to turn back."

"I hear the police coming. Mom, I'm so scared. I've never been so scared."

"I am, too, darling. That's why I want you to wait. Wait for the police. I'm almost there. We're turning onto your street now."

"They're in the parking lot right in front of my building. Be careful, Mom. Oh."

"What? Lexi?"

"They see me."

"Turn here," Sue said, "This is her apartment complex."

Ellen saw a cop car up ahead parked behind the dumpster with its lights off. She realized then that it was hiding. The officer was crouched behind the dumpster with his gun pulled. Ellen followed the line of the officer's gun and lost her breath when she saw an older man with a gun trained on Stephen's temple.

The man was tall and round and muscular with gray curly hair that just covered his ears. In fact, he looked a lot like the officer that was hiding behind the dumpster.

They were the two Ryans—father and son. Was the son there to help *Lexi* or *his father?*

Ellen stepped out of the van, her heart pounding in her ears.

"Where are you going?" Sue called to her.

But Ellen could barely hear her. She could only wonder where the other police officers were. Hadn't Lexi said she'd heard them coming?

As she walked toward the younger Officer Ryan crouched behind the dumpster, she noticed Lexi step out from a line of parked cars to stand in front of Stephen and his abductor.

"Here I am," Lexi said. "You said you wouldn't hurt him if I came."

The gunman shoved Stephen to the side and trained his weapon on Lexi. "Come with me!"

The younger Ryan darted from his position behind the dumpster and pointed his weapon at the gunman.

"Drop it!" the younger Officer Ryan commanded.

The older man looked at the officer, startled. Then he smiled and said, "You wouldn't shoot your own father."

"Drop it, or I'll shoot!" the younger officer insisted.

The older Ryan trained his gun on Stephen, who'd been slowly backing away.

As a weapon fired, Lexi screamed, and, for a moment, Ellen wasn't sure who had shot whom. But then she saw the older Ryan down on the ground, on his back, bleeding from the chest, and gasping for air.

Lexi and Stephen ran into each other's arms.

The younger Ryan hurried to his father's side, all the while screaming into his phone, "Officer down! I need an ambulance right away!"

Ellen was speechless and unable to move, until she saw Sue driving her motorized wheelchair across the parking lot toward Lexi. For some reason, the sight of that made her laugh, and once she'd started, she couldn't stop.

CHAPTER THIRTY-ONE

Reparations

Things did not go as planned in court.

Ellen was caught off guard when the city's defense attorney questioned her on the stand, focusing on how she came to be in the possession of a document which the prosecution claimed had been signed in October 1921, by Tulsa Police Officer Van Hurley. Ellen told the truth (without mentioning the Ouija Board), but the defense attorney—a dark-haired woman with a thin nose, brown, beady eyes, and straight white teeth—undermined everything Ellen said by bringing up Patty Cole's testimony about her grandfather's ghost.

"Are you asking the court to believe that the spirit of Van Hurley led you to this document, and that it is an authentic affidavit from 1921?"

"Yes," Ellen said. "I think how I found the document is less important than the fact that it exists."

"No, Mrs. Mohr," the defense attorney said. "How you found it completely discredits you as a witness and this document as evidence."

"Objection, your honor," Jillian Bridges said.

"Sustained. Miss Carson, do you have further questions for this witness?"

"No, your honor, I do not."

Ellen wasn't allowed to be present in the court while the other witnesses provided their testimony, so she sat in the courthouse lobby, waiting. When Sue had finished, she joined her. Eventually, Tanya, too, came out. With lowered voices, they told each other about their experiences, none of which were good.

"I really thought we had this in the bag," Sue said.

It wasn't until Bob came to join them in the lobby after having given his testimony that their spirits were lifted.

"The judge seemed impressed with my findings," he said. "I think it's enough to take the lawsuit to trial."

On Friday, Ellen and her friends had a lunch date with Pete Mayo, the owner of The Brady Theater. They met him at the Greek restaurant across from The Tavern at Main and Brady. After they ordered, they began with small talk—about how much they had enjoyed seeing Michael Carbonaro perform and how much they appreciated the historical integrity of the building.

"It could use a little freshening up, though," Sue said. "And that's why we wanted to meet with you today."

"I don't understand," Pete Mayo said as the water delivered their drinks. "While I do plan to repaint the ceiling tiles this year and replace some of the seats the next, it will be some years before I can manage extensive renovations. Are you here representing a firm? If so, this meeting is a waste of time."

"No, sir," Ellen said. "We aren't a firm. We aren't trying to sell you our services. We want to donate a half a million dollars to you in exchange for a small favor."

Mr. Mayo's brows lifted. "You aren't with the mafia, are you?" He laughed nervously.

Sue also laughed. "Nothing like that."

Ellen brought out the wireless inspection camera and video monitor and showed him the recording. "Can you see those skeletons piled on top of one another?"

"Oh, yes. Yes, I can see them. Where was this video taken?"

Ellen and her friends exchanged nervous glances. There was a long pause as their waiter brought them their plates.

Finally, Ellen said, "In the basement of your theater."

"In my theater?" he took a bite of his pork.

"Those bodies are behind the concrete wall at the end of the stairwell to nowhere," Ellen explained.

"I don't understand," Pete Mayo said. "How? I was told the concrete was put there to keep some old asbestos materials from contaminating the rest of the building."

"In the interest of history and justice, we hope you won't press charges, especially since we want to give you a half a million dollars," Sue said. "Ellen? Tell him what we did."

While Sue dug into her gyro, Ellen told Mr. Mayo all about Operation Old Lady on Brady.

When Ellen had finished, his only reply was, "I'll need to give this some thought and confer with my attorney."

"Of course," Ellen said.

They finished their meal in relative silence.

That night, they took Simol to eat at the Mexican Border Café and offered her a deal. Tanya had been the one to think of it, and they'd discussed it on the train ride from San Antonio—along with other plans they had for the Monroe Social Club. They offered Simol a place to live in the building she'd called home for forty years.

"While it's being renovated, you can keep an eye on the place for us," Tanya said.

"And when we sell it," Ellen added, "we'll try to negotiate for the next owner to keep you on as the caretaker of the property."

"Would you like that?" Sue asked, as she dipped a chip into a bowl of salsa. "We don't want you to feel like you have to say yes. We're only offering this to you if you want it."

Tears gathered in Simol's eyes, and although the expression on her face was answer enough, she said, "I would like that very much."

As they ate their meal, Ellen told Simol about what she'd learned from the online lab.

"We can give Achak a proper burial, if you'd like that," Ellen added.

Again, Simol said, "I would like that very much."

Over the weekend, they still heard no word from Jillian Bridges about the judge's decision. Sue spent Saturday with Lexi, and Tanya and Ellen went to a movie. They also stopped by Monroe's to check on the progress. Some of the lighting had been installed, and stalls had been assembled around all the commodes.

Saturday night, Ellen received a text from Pete Mayo accepting their offer. As soon as half a million was transferred into his account, he would allow the concrete wall in his basement to be opened up—on the condition that any asbestos threats were contained, and the expense of the wall's demolition and restoration were not taken from the half-million-dollar renovation budget.

Ellen replied with their agreement. Pete Mayo texted that his attorney would draw up a legal, binding contract, which he'd have ready for all parties to sign on Monday.

Sunday afternoon, Ellen, Sue, and Tanya sat around the desk in their hotel and sketched out a vision for their property. They would hide the oil rig with a decorative tower made of a taupe-colored limestone that would complement the red brick on the building. They drew a flower garden around it, which was trimmed with a red brick border and capped with the taupe limestone—to form seating along the perimeter of the tower. They drew walkways from the east and west wings that converged and circled around the tower. At the northern most point, the walkway continued toward the highway, to the very back of the property. There, they envisioned a memorial wall listing all the names of the riot victims identified among the remains of the two mass graves—

both the one at Monroe's and the one at The Brady Theater. After talking to Bob, they realized he might not be able to provide them with names, but they were willing to give him as much time as he needed, and they would continue to hope for the best. Unless the descendants of any known victims requested something different for their ancestors, it was also the hope of Ellen and her friends that the bodies of the victims would be laid to rest beneath the memorial wall, where a beautiful water feature would be erected, so the spirits would never fear fire again. Perhaps the act of conferring them to the ground would be enough to bring them peace.

Ellen and her friends also decided to create a charitable fund for The Greenwood Cultural Center, to be used as the center determined. They would ask Jillian Bridges to help them set up an account to which ten percent of their net well earnings would go every month. This would give the community an opportunity to continue to grow and thrive, even if the city was never required to provide fiscal reparations.

On Monday, Jillian finally called Ellen and told her that the judge had decided to take their suit against the city to trial. There was no guarantee that the Citizens of Tulsa versus the City of Tulsa would lead to reparations, but at least it was a possibility. More importantly, the city was being forced to face its demons once again, and instead of sweeping them under the rug, as they did in 2000, when they decided to stop searching for the mass graves, the city of Tulsa now had the chance to heal from its wounded past.

THE END

Thank you for reading my story. I hope you enjoyed it! If you did, please consider leaving a review. Reviews help other readers to discover my books, which helps me.

Please enjoy the first chapter of the next book in the series, *French Quarter Clues.*

CHAPTER ONE

Return to Tulsa

L ike *this*?" Tanya asked, from where her long, thin form lay horizontally across the hotel bed in Oklahoma City. Her blonde hair draped over the edge of the bed.

"Hang your head over a bit more," Sue instructed, as she moved her short, round body closer to Tanya, blocking Ellen's view. "And keep it turned at a forty-five-degree angle."

"What's this called again?" Ellen asked from where she sat on the other double bed.

Sue kept her eye on the timer on her iPhone. "The Epley Maneuver."

Nolan, Ellen's son, who was in medical school, had suggested it at dinner earlier, explaining that the airplane ride that morning had likely dislodged a crystal in Tanya's inner ear, causing the vertigo.

"I really hope this helps," Tanya said.

Ellen hoped so, too. She'd been looking forward to this trip for months. They planned to drive a rental up to Tulsa the next day to lunch with Sue's daughter, Lexi. Jan, Sue's mother and the caretaker of the Gold House in San Antonio, had sent an anniversary gift with them for Lexi, and they were all dying to see what was in the box that Sue had had to lug around two airports, two planes, and a taxi. Jan had said it was a surprise and wouldn't budge, not even with a hint.

"A few more seconds," Sue said as she pushed her dark bangs from her eyes.

After their lunch with Lexi, Ellen and her friends were to attend a scholarship awards ceremony at the Greenwood Cultural Center, which was the main reason for their trip. Afterward, they planned to tour the Monroe Social Club in the Brady Arts District with Simol, the resident manager. They hadn't seen the place since they'd sold it to the new owner over six months ago, within weeks of completing their renovations. Bob Brooks, the anthropologist who'd helped them with the search for the 1921 Riot victims, was still in the painstaking process of identifying the nearly three hundred bodies they'd recovered. He'd given them an update over lunch earlier that day.

From Tulsa, they were going to drive up to Pawhuska, to lunch at the Pioneer Woman's Mercantile and to tour the lodge where her cooking show was recorded.

"Now what?" Tanya asked.

"Turn your head to the other side," Sue said. "For another forty seconds or so."

Ellen stood to look at Tanya over Sue's shoulder. "I thought her eyes were supposed to be fluttering back and forth." That's what Nolan had said, anyway.

"They aren't?" Tanya asked.

Ellen bent over and looked more closely. "No."

"Let's just finish the maneuver and see if it helps," Sue suggested. "Now roll over on your side and hold that position for another forty seconds."

"If it doesn't help, y'all go on without me," Tanya said as she rolled over. "I don't think I can make it in the car for the two hours to Tulsa if this thing doesn't work."

"Let's not get ahead of ourselves just yet," Sue said.

Ellen had been anxious to see the fruits of their hard work, especially after the wonderful article that had appeared in the Tulsa newspaper after The Monroe Social Club's grand opening four months earlier. She was also looking forward to meeting their very first scholarship recipients, awarded with the oil money. And Pete Mayo, the owner of the Brady Theater, had given the Old Lady on Brady the first of three major facelifts with the money they'd given him. All of this had brought them back to Oklahoma, not to mention Ellen's recent obsession with *The Pioneer Woman*. But Ellen didn't want to leave Tanya behind in Oklahoma City.

She sent a little prayer out into the universe, asking for Tanya's healing.

"Okay, now sit up," Sue said, and she and Ellen helped Tanya to a sitting position.

"How do you feel?" Ellen asked.

"I don't know yet," Tanya said. "I think it may have helped. I'm not sure."

"Do you think you can make it through a movie?" Sue asked.

The theater had reclining seats, so Ellen added, "It won't make much difference whether you lay down here or in the theater, will it?"

"I guess you're right," Tanya said, though she didn't seem convinced. "Let's go."

Sue grabbed her purse. "As often as the two of you had to pee during the flight over from San Antonio, I think we may have to hook you each up to a catheter, anyway."

"Speaking of that, I need to go again," Tanya said as she disappeared behind the bathroom door.

Ellen laughed and turned to Sue. "Why don't you ever have to go? What's your secret?"

Sue opened the hotel door and stepped into the hall. "I guess, unlike the two of you, I don't have a bladder the size of a thimble."

Ellen laughed again, but, when Tanya rejoined them in the hallway, her friend seemed quiet. Ellen hoped she and Sue weren't pushing Tanya too hard by taking her to the movie. The Epley Maneuver hadn't seemed to be the miracle cure they'd been hoping for.

Once inside the darkened movie theater, where Sue had smuggled in a can of Cherry Coke and a chocolate muffin, Sue made them move twice. Although Ellen had preferred their original seats in back, she had to admit that she, too, had noticed the horrible smell that had prompted Sue to want to move. But, even now, as they settled into their seats closer to the screen, the odor lingered.

"Did you step in something, Tanya?" Sue, who preferred the aisle seat, even though she had the better bladder, whispered to Tanya.

Tanya, in the middle seat, checked the bottom of her shoes. "I don't think so. Do I smell bad?"

Ellen didn't reply, because she'd come to suspect that Tanya had been the cause of the odor all along. Maybe she had a sour stomach and bad gas.

"They say your nose adjusts eventually," Sue commented as she cracked open her Cherry Coke.

"Is it really that bad?" Tanya asked, her cheeks turning red. "I don't smell anything."

"Evidently, your nose has already adjusted," Sue added. "You must have the superior nose."

"It's fine," Ellen lied.

She took a whiff of her buttered popcorn to combat the other odor.

That night, Ellen was awakened in the hotel room by a shriek. Tanya, sleeping in the bed opposite her, was crying out. Ellen flipped on the bedside lamp and sat up.

"Tanya?"

Tanya turned onto her side toward Ellen. "Huh?" She blinked several times.

Ellen was shocked by the very dark rings beneath her friend's eyes and by her pale, pasty complexion.

"Are you feeling okay?" Ellen asked.

"Just tired," Tanya said as she closed her eyes. "Bad dream."

But Ellen was worried. She wished Sue had stayed in the same room with them, so she could get her opinion. Ellen felt like Tanya might need medical attention.

Ellen crawled out of bed and inspected Tanya's face beneath the light of the lamp. Deciding not to waken Tanya, Ellen climbed back beneath the covers and flipped off the lamp. She lay there, worrying, for many hours.

Tanya slept in the passenger seat for most of the trip to Tulsa, as Ellen drove, and Sue navigated from the back seat. Ellen had hoped her friends would trade places, so she and Sue could visit and make the drive go by faster, but they were afraid Tanya would get carsick in the back. Plus, Sue preferred the back seat because she didn't have to wear a safety harness.

When they were still a good half hour away from Tulsa, Sue leaned toward the front seat, and said, "Tanya? You awake?"

Tanya continued to snore.

Then, to Ellen, Sue said, "I've been Googling her symptoms."

"You don't think it's her inner ear?" Ellen asked.

"If it was, the Epley Maneuver would have worked."

"Maybe we didn't do it right."

Sue frowned. "I followed the video perfectly."

"What does Dr. Google say then?" Ellen asked, secretly wishing Sue would sit back in her seat and wear her seatbelt.

"Well, we know she's not diabetic," Sue said. "Her doctor would have caught that last month when she had her annual checkup."

"True."

"And we know it's not her thyroid, because she just had that checked when they removed that tumor from her parathyroid a few months ago, right?"

"But it could be related to that, couldn't it?"

Sue lowered her voice. "Ellen, brace yourself."

Ellen glanced at Sue's reflection in the rearview mirror.

Sue whispered, "I think it's a demon attachment."

Ellen narrowed her eyes at Sue's reflection. "Seriously? What makes you think that?"

"You didn't think something was strange about the nightmare she had last night?"

At breakfast, Tanya had told her and Sue about a horrible dream in which Tanya had murdered them in their sleep and had gorged on their blood. Tanya hadn't been able to eat breakfast because she had still felt nauseated from the experience, which she'd said had felt disturbingly real.

"It was just a bad dream," Ellen insisted.

"Check this out," Sue said. "Here are some of the symptoms of demon attachment: Severe nightmares or night terrors, strange lingering odors, depression, fatigue, personality changes, blackouts in memory, and abusive behavior."

Ellen laughed. "Tanya is the last person on earth who'd be abusive. And those symptoms apply to at least a dozen health issues I can think of right off the top of my head."

"Maybe, but I think we should be on the lookout, just in case. I've been sensing something unusual lately. It went away when I was in my own hotel room, but it came back when we met for breakfast this morning."

Ellen had learned not to assume that every claim Sue made about her "gift" was based purely on her imagination. While Ellen tended to be a skeptic first and foremost, she'd seen enough to be a believer, too.

She glanced at their friend snoring in the passenger's seat beside her. Tanya's pale complexion and the dark circles beneath her eyes continued to worry Ellen.

"You have to admit we've been a little careless with our use of the Ouija Board and other occult practices," Sue added. "We may have invited something in."

Just then, Tanya opened her eyes and met Ellen's gaze.

"What's wrong?" Tanya asked. "Why are you looking at me like that?"

Ellen frowned, suddenly nervous. "I was just checking on you. How do you feel?"

"Does it really matter?" Tanya snapped, as she closed her eyes and turned to face the window.

Ellen glanced at Sue in the rearview mirror.

"That wasn't like Tanya, to be so rude," Sue whispered.

After Ellen had parked the rental in front of the La Quinta in Tulsa, Tanya lifted her head and looked around.

"Are we here?" Tanya asked sleepily.

Ellen turned to her friend. "What did you mean when you asked if it really mattered how you felt? We care about your feelings and don't want to push you, if you can't handle the trip."

"What are you talking about?" Tanya asked.

Sue leaned forward. "I'm sure she didn't mean it, Ellen."

"Mean what?" Tanya asked.

"Ellen asked how you felt, and you said, 'Does it really matter?'"

"I didn't say that," Tanya insisted. "I would never say that."

"We both heard you, Tanya," Ellen pointed out.

Tanya's cheeks turned pink. "I must have been talking in my sleep."

Later, Ellen and Sue met Lexi for lunch at the Greek restaurant across from the Old Lady on Brady. Tanya had decided to stay behind at the hotel and rest.

As they waited for their food, Lexi opened her present from Jan.

"It's Grandma's cuckoo clock," Lexi said.

"Oh, how nice!" Sue's face lit up. "She must have had it repaired. It's been in the family for decades, you know. I always wished she'd give it to me, but I'm glad she's given it to you."

"It's beautiful," Ellen said, admiring the intricate details. "It's no wonder she didn't want to ship it. It's so delicate."

"It cost a fortune to fix, I'm sure," Sue added. To Lexi, she said, "Be sure to write Grandma a thank you note."

"Mom," Lexi complained. "I'm not a kid anymore. I know I'm supposed to write thank you notes."

"Well, your lunch is on me," Ellen said, "and I'm expecting a thank you note, too." Ellen gave Lexi a wink, to show she was only teasing and didn't expect a note.

Sue laughed. "I'm still waiting on my thank you from Nolan for his high school graduation gift from, what, eight years ago?"

Ellen shook her head. "I have a feeling you'll be waiting a lot longer for that one."

"Do you have time to come see what we've done to our new house?" Lexi asked them.

Sue had bought Lexi and Stephen a new house with some of the oil money. It was the only extravagant thing any of them had done. They were hesitant to spend too much of the money while they still weren't sure how long the well would produce. Plus, all three of them had agreed that Greenwood deserved more than ten percent of the oil money, since the ghosts of their past had been responsible for helping them to find it.

"I'm afraid not," Sue said. "We're worried about Tanya. Maybe next time."

After lunch, Ellen and Sue said goodbye to Lexi and then walked across the street to the Brady Theater to check out its recent renovations. Jared was working the box office and seemed glad to see them again as he showed them the new flooring, seating, and repairs to some of the interior architecture. Ellen took pictures with her phone to share with Tanya, but when they returned to the hotel, Ellen and Sue were shocked with what they found: Tanya was completely naked, her legs stretched up over the headboard, her hips on pillows, and her head hanging over the side of the bed, her eyes closed and ringed with black circles.

"Tanya!" Ellen cried as she rushed to her friend's side.

"Don't touch her," Sue warned. "You don't want the demon on your back, too."

Tanya opened her eyes and blinked several times before she swung her legs from the headboard and tried to sit up.

"Tanya?" Ellen said gently.

"What's wrong?" Tanya asked before recognizing that she was without clothes. She pulled the sheet over her. "I got hot. Isn't it hot in here?"

"We need to take you to a hospital," Ellen said. "Something's not right."

The scholarship ceremony at the Greenwood Cultural Center that evening had been rewarding, but Ellen hadn't been able to enjoy herself, because she'd been worried about Tanya. Ellen could tell Sue was feeling the same way as they left the reception to return to the hospital.

Hooked up to an IV, Tanya was awake and watching television in a private room when they arrived. Her complexion was no longer pale, the dark circles were significantly reduced, and she was even smiling.

"I was dehydrated," Tanya explained. "They couldn't find anything else wrong with me."

"And you feel better?" Ellen asked.

"You look better," Sue commented.

"I feel fine," Tanya said. "They're keeping me overnight for observation, but I should be ready to leave tomorrow. How was the scholarship ceremony?"

Ellen and Sue recounted how impressed they'd been with the six recipients. One would be attending Harvard, two Yale, and three OSU. Although Ellen and her friends had lost their case against the state of Oklahoma and against the city of Tulsa for reparations owed to the descendants of the 1921 Race Riot victims, the oil money was being put to good use in helping repair the damages done to Greenwood. The Greenwood Cultural Center had been put in charge of deciding where to use the funds. Homeowners had been given grants to repair their homes and refresh their landscaping, business owners had been given grants and interest-free loans, and the entire area was prospering as a result. Even Mount Zion Baptist Church had been granted reparations to expand the size of its sanctuary.

"Will you be up to touring the social club tomorrow, do you think?" Sue asked Tanya.

"Definitely," Tanya said. "I feel fine."

Ellen exchanged a worried glance with Sue, doubting their friend was out of the woods yet. If a demon *had* attached itself to Tanya, saline through an IV wouldn't be enough to get rid of it.

Eva Pohler is a *USA Today* bestselling author of over thirty novels in multiple genres, including mysteries, thrillers, and young adult paranormal romance based on Greek mythology. Her books have been described as "addictive" and "sure to thrill"—*Kirkus Reviews*.

To learn more about Eva and her books, and to sign up to hear about new releases, and sales, please visit her website at www.evapohler.com.

Milton Keynes UK
Ingram Content Group UK Ltd.
UKHW022202221223
434840UK00015B/711